MURDER ON THE TRACKS

STORIES OF MAYHEM AND MURDER ON THE RAILWAYS

British Library Cataloguing-in-Publication Data
A catalogue record for this book is available from the
British Library

CONTENTS

CRIME ON THE FOOTPLATE

FREEMAN WILLS CROFTS

The August day was stifling as the 11.55 a.m. express
from Leeds beat heavily up the grade towards the summit
in the foothills of the Pennines. From there the run down
to Carlisle would be easy and rapid. The train was on time
and travelling at the full thirty miles an hour customary at
the place.

On the footplate Driver Deane sat watching the line
ahead and occasionally casting an eye over the faceplate,
with its maze of dials and gauges and handles. For Fireman
Grover, on the other hand, this was the busy time of the run.
With a heavy train on a grade like this, firing was practically
continuous.

The engine, while a splendid machine, was of one of the
older types. The cab was more open than is now usual, having
no side windows, an advantage on this day when the heat of
the sun vied with that pouring from the steel endplate of the
boiler. It was fitted with small doors at each side between

engine and tender, and was driven from the right side of the cab.

All seemed well with the train, yet all was not well. On this footplate, as in the great world beyond, human passions were aflame. For many weeks evil had been festering in Fireman Grover's heart. He had not expelled it while he could, and now he was held in its grip. On this very run and before they had gone a dozen miles further he intended to murder his driver, William Deane.

The story of the madness which had overtaken him was commonplace enough. Some three months earlier he had visited his driver's Leeds home on some railway business. There he had met the driver's wife and immediately had fallen for her. He contrived to meet her again and found out that his feeling was returned.

Rosie Deane was a well-meaning young woman who had made an unwise marriage. She had an unhappy home and accepted Deane, who was many years her senior, as a means of escape. But she had not deceived him. Admitting the truth, she had added that while she liked and respected him, she did not love him, though she would do her best to make him happy. Deane had not hesitated and the marriage had taken place.

For several years she had kept her word. But during this time Deane had suffered an increasing disappointment. He had believed that his wife would gradually come to love him, and when he found that, instead of this, the very opposite was taking place he grew bitter. He became sharp-tongued and suspicious. Rosie resented it and her feeling came out in her manner. Relations between the two went from bad to worse.

It was then that Grover had appeared. His love gave him insight and he soon guessed Rosie's unhappiness. Hatred of his driver grew fanatical when he realised that he was at once the cause of her misery and the bar to its alleviation. The thought of murder had not at first entered his mind, but as he brooded the idea became more and more insistent. He began to consider methods, and when he found one which would infallibly guarantee his own safety, Deane's fate was sealed.

One of Grover's friends was a male nurse in a mental home and the two had frequently discussed inmates and work in such places. Among other things Grover had learned that a certain harmless drug was used to calm patients if they became over-excited. His friend had told him about a dose of this being given to the wrong man, with the result that for some time he had become moody, depressed and ill-tempered. Grover had not forgotten the name of the drug.

During a spare hour in London when they were on the St Pancras link, he had changed into his ordinary clothes, which he had taken up in a parcel, and had purchased a small quantity of the drug at a busy chemist's. No interest had been aroused. Thus his first hurdle was taken.

The second depended on the fact that Deane wore a short beard. The man had been a good deal ragged about it, but Grover had learnt that it was to cover a deep scar on his chin. After getting the drug, Grover had gone on to a theatrical supplies shop and bought a false beard of the correct colour 'to amuse the children'. In the security of his room he trimmed it to the shape of Deane's, and practised putting it on till he could do it quickly and without the aid of a mirror.

His third and last essential was to choose a suitable run for the deed. It must be through sparsely populated country, where observation of what took place on the engine would be unlikely. Also as much time as possible was desirable between block posts. This climb up the bleak Pennine foothills exactly met the conditions.

Grover began operations by doctoring the driver's tea. Before taking their engine out Deane went round it, oiling moving parts and looking out for defects. During this time Grover was alone on the footplate, working at the fire. To slip a daily drop or two of the drug into the other's can was simplicity itself.

When by experiment he had learnt the right amount to

use, he was overjoyed with the result. Deane reacted perfectly, growing more bitter and morose, while his temper became a byword among the men.

Some six weeks later Grover decided to strike, and now this was the run which was to free Rosie and open a new door of happiness for himself. On the previous day he had given Deane a specially large dose of the drug, and the effect had been clear to all.

They were approaching what might be called the last outpost of civilisation, the little town of Sleet, for here the railway left the green, well-cultivated valley and entered on the open moor. As they laboured through the small station, the powerful beat echoing from the buildings, Grover began firing. By the time this was finished they had passed the signal cabin and sidings. That all was well on the footplate would have been noted by the signalman. Now they were out into the open. On these bare slopes figures stood out clearly. Grover glanced carefully around. There were none.

He laid down his shovel and picked up a heavy spanner which he had secreted in the coal. Stepping over to Driver Deane, he bent down. 'I think I hear a blowing gasket,' he shouted, for the noise was considerable.

Deane sat still, obviously listening. Grover immediately brought his spanner down with force on the man's head. Deane made no sound. He remained for a moment motionless, then pitched slowly forward. He fell on his knees against the end of the boiler, rolled partially back, and lay with head and arms hunched up in the corner of the cab.

Grover was breathless and trembling, but he forced himself to stoop and examine him. That the man was dead there could be no doubt, for the top of the head was driven down, though owing to the cap the skin was not broken. Moreover, the body's position was admirable. It had to be well forward, so as to be screened by the cab from the next signal cabin, and also to leave space on the congested footplate for the act by which Grover intended to secure his safety.

Haste was now the prime essential, for before they reached the next station, Ottershaw, already less than two miles distant, he must be ready to put on his act. Quickly he adjusted the false beard, checking its position in a mirror from his pocket. Then he twisted up his cap to the angle Deane affected and glanced ahead through the cab window.

They were just passing the Ottershaw distant signal, off as it always was. As they approached the platform and signal cabin Grover began dancing, waving his arms and singing drunkenly. While he did so he kept a keen eye on the cabin, some twenty yards away across the sidings. What happened thrilled him. His plan was working out.

He saw the signalman stare at the engine, then swing round and pick something up, slide open his window, lean out, and begin frantically waving a red flag.

For Grover it was a moment of sickening anxiety. If the guard saw the flag and applied the brakes, only the most speedy and skilful action could save him. He danced on lest someone else should see him, but in a cold sweat of fear.

The advanced starting signal had gone to danger in front of him, but he took no notice. It was only another attempt of the signalman to attract the guard's attention. As they left it behind without an application of the brakes, Grover experienced a relief so intense that he feared his nerve would crack. Then he rallied himself fiercely. Though the worst was over, the job was not finished. The least weakness and he was as good as hanged.

Haste again was the ruling factor. He tore off the beard and threw it into the firebox, making sure with his mirror that no traces remained. Then came a horrible part of the affair. With the flat of the spanner he struck a heavy blow on his own left shoulder. It hurt so much that he feared he had done damage. So much the better, he told himself grimly. He dropped the spanner and threw himself forcibly down against the tender. Then taking off his cap, he knocked his head back against the steel plating, again and again till he could endure no more.

Struggling unsteadily to his feet, he glanced once more through the cab window. In a little over a mile they would reach Grammond block post, a signal cabin without any station. At this he was sure they would be checked, as the Ottershaw signalman would certainly have wired on 'Stop and examine train'. This, and the fact that the post was approached by a wide left-hand curve from which cabin and signals could be seen for nearly a mile across the bend of the valley, were features of his plan.

A few seconds later they entered on the curve. Yes, there were the signals, all at danger. Things certainly were going as he had hoped. He had only to carry out one remaining essential and the whole ghastly affair would be done.

Once again he glanced carefully round. Here also no spectator was in sight. He now stooped and pulled off Deane's cap, then seizing the body beneath the armpits, dragged it painfully back to the rear of the footplate. The doors between engine and tender were shut, and using all his strength, he laid the body over the left door, with the head and trunk hanging down outside and the legs within.

He was just in time, for the body was scarcely in position when they passed the Grammond distant signal. Now was the moment! He heaved up the legs and the body shot out, crashed on its head on the ground and rolled on partly down the embankment. The cap he dropped at the same moment. Then, gasping, he staggered back to the faceplate.

By this time they were approaching the home signal and

cabin. Grover passed the former without action, intending that his efforts to stop should be seen by the signalman. But just before they reached the cabin the vacuum disappeared on his gauge and the brakes went on. The guard this time had noticed the adverse signal and used his emergency handle. Grover therefore shut off steam, a little earlier than he had intended. Automatically he closed the firebox door and damper and put on the injector, then sank down, shaken and trembling, on one of the cab seats.

The train ground to a standstill, having overshot the home signal by some quarter of a mile. Grover remained seated where he was. No acting was needed to give the impression he desired, for the shock of what he had done added to the blow on his head had left him really weak and dazed. He sat on till a flustered guard climbed on to the footplate. Others followed. To them Grover outlined the story he had prepared. Everyone was sympathetic. His head was bandaged and he was sent home by the first available train.

Next day the police called for a fuller statement. They began by warning him. 'We have to do it, you know,' they told him. 'Matter of form mostly.'

Grover nodded. He had heard that this was their custom. Then he repeated his story: again and again he had polished its every detail. 'Deane had been a bit queer for a few weeks,' he explained. 'Seemed to have something on his mind and was getting worse. You couldn't hardly speak to him about anything: he'd snap the head off you.'

It was a good beginning. To the police the statement had already been attested by many witnesses.

'On this trip he was worse than ever,' went on Grover. 'I was beginning to wonder if I could get a shift to another driver. I signed to him shortly after we left Leeds that the Riglett distant signal was on, and he went off the deep end good and proper: wanted to know if I thought he was blind and that. It never occurred to me his mind was touched, but it settled mine for me. I decided I'd ask for the change.'

The police made encouraging sounds.

'After a while he quieted down. Just sat there and looked ahead same as usual. Then when we got to Sleet the thing happened. I was firing going through the station, but just after we passed it he turned round and threw up his hands and began laughing fit to burst his sides. It was sort of uncanny, him roaring with laughter, but it didn't seem funny to me. At first I didn't interfere, then I asked him what the joke was. That about put the lid on: he jumped up and yelled at me. He looked sort of wild. I knew then that he was mad and I don't deny I was scared stiff. Suddenly he let fly at my head. I twisted and got it on my shoulder. It knocked me back and I hit my head against the tender. Then he went off his rocker altogether. He began to sing and shout and dance about the footplate while I lay there half stunned.'

Grover's belief that the police would have had confirmation of this statement from the Ottershaw signalman was not misplaced. They begged him to continue, and he did so with increasing confidence.

'I can tell you, gentlemen, I was in a proper fix. We're not often checked by signals on this run, but you have to be prepared for it. If we got a check he wouldn't stop and I couldn't.

'Then, easing up on my elbow, I got a peep over the cab door. We were on the big curve coming into Grammond and you can see the signals a mile away across country. They were against us. Well, I had the train to think of as well as my own life, and I hadn't much time to do it in. I don't know whether I was right or wrong, but I gripped a spanner out of the box, and when Deane turned his back, I nipped up and hit him over the head. I only meant to knock him out, but he staggered forward against the door and overbalanced. Before I could catch him he was out over it.'

For this also there was a reasonable amount of corroboration. The signals *could* be seen as described, and they *were* against the train. The place where the body was found worked in with the time element of the story, and Grover bore the bruises which it demanded. Yes, it was a good tale and had confirmation on nearly every point.

Grover's self-satisfaction became impressive when the police thanked him politely and withdrew.

He got his first shock, a terrible numbing shock, when the inquest was adjourned. Then for several days nothing happened. But one night the police returned. They were curt and businesslike. Stunned and incredulous, he heard the inconceivable words, 'Arrest . . . charge with murder . . . anything you say . . .'

Though the exact nature of his mistake did not in a way matter, Grover raged against himself in speechless fury when he learned what it was. His scheme was good, indeed masterly, and it would have worked perfectly but for one quite trivial oversight. He had not examined with sufficient care the position into which Deane had fallen. The driver's shoulders and arms were clear of the boiler, but Grover had been in such a hurry that he had looked no further. On the dead man's leg was a huge scorched wound. Some ghastly experiments showed that at least six minutes' contact with the hot steel plate would have been necessary to produce it.

This gave the police something to think about. When the train was passing Sleet, Deane was alive and well: the signalman had seen that conditions on the footplate were normal. Therefore the man could not at that time have received this crippling injury. Some eight minutes later his body fell from the engine near Grammond. For six of those eight minutes, therefore, he must have been lying with his leg against the boiler: and during that time a bearded man was dancing on the footplate. Only impersonation by Grover could explain it.

At the trial the doctor testified to the finding of a debilitating drug in the remains, though the prisoner's responsibility for this could not be proved. But the whole story of Grover's friendship with Rosie Deane came out, together with the purchase of the false beard. The prisoner's failure to account for the latter on legitimate grounds was the factor which finally swayed the jury.

CHEESE

ETHEL LINA WHITE

This story begins with a murder. It ends with a mouse-trap.

The murder can be disposed of in a paragraph. An attractive girl, carefully reared and educated for a future which held only a twisted throat. At the end of seven months, an unsolved mystery and a reward of £500.

It is a long way from a murder to a mouse-trap – and one with no finger-posts; but the police knew every inch of the way. In spite of a prestige punctured by the press and public, they had solved the identity of the killer. There remained the problem of tracking this wary and treacherous rodent from his unknown sewer in the underworld into their trap.

They failed repeatedly for lack of the right bait.

And unexpectedly, one spring evening, the bait turned up in the person of a young girl.

Cheese.

Inspector Angus Duncan was alone in his office when her message was brought up. He was a red-haired Scot, handsome in a dour fashion, with the chin of a prize-fighter and keen blue eyes.

He nodded.

'I'll see her.'

It was between the lights. River, government offices and factories were all deeply dyed with the blue stain of dusk. Even in the city, the lilac bushes showed green tips and an occasional crocus cropped through the grass of the public-gardens, like strewn orange-peel. The evening star was a jewel in the pale green sky.

Duncan was impervious to the romance of the hour. He knew that twilight was but the prelude to night and that darkness was a shield for crime.

He looked up sharply when his visitor was admitted. She was young and flower-faced – her faint freckles already fading away into pallor. Her black suit was shabby, but her hat was garnished for the spring with a cheap cowslip wreath.

As she raised her blue eyes, he saw that they still carried the memory of country sweets . . . Thereupon he looked at her more sharply for he knew that of all poses, innocence is easiest to counterfeit.

'You say Roper sent you?' he enquired.

'Yes, Maggie Roper.'

He nodded. Maggie Roper – Sergeant Roper's niece – was already shaping as a promising young Stores' detective.

'Where did you meet her?'

'At the Girls' Hostel where I'm staying.'

'Your name?'

'Jenny Morgan.'

'From the country?'

'Yes. But I'm up now for good.'

For good? . . . He wondered.

'Alone?'

'Yes.'

'How's that?' He looked at her mourning. 'People all dead?'

She nodded. From the lightning sweep of her lashes, he knew that she had put in some rough work with a tear. It prejudiced him in her favour. His voice grew more genial as his lips relaxed.

'Well, what's it all about?'

She drew a letter from her bag.

'I'm looking for work and I advertised in the paper. I got this answer. I'm to be companion-secretary to a lady, to travel with her and be treated as her daughter – if she likes me. I sent my photograph and my references and she's fixed an appointment.'

'When and where?'

'The day after tomorrow, in the First Room in the National Gallery. But as she's elderly, she is sending her nephew to drive me to her house.'

'Where's that?'

She looked troubled.

'That's what Maggie Roper is making the fuss about. First, she said I must see if Mrs Harper – that's the lady's name – had taken up my references. And then she insisted on ringing up the Ritz where the letter was written from. The address was *printed*, so it was bound to be genuine, wasn't it?'

'Was it? What happened then?'

'They said no Mrs Harper had stayed there. But I'm sure it must be a mistake.' Her voice trembled. 'One must risk something to get such a good job.'

His face darkened. He was beginning to accept Jenny as the genuine article.

'Tell me,' he asked, 'have you had any experience of life?'

'Well, I've always lived in the country with Auntie. But I've read all sorts of novels and the newspapers.'

'Murders?'

'Oh, I love those.'

He could tell by the note in her childish voice that she ate up the newspaper accounts merely as exciting fiction, without the slightest realisation that the printed page was grim fact. He could see the picture: a sheltered childhood passed amid green spongy meadows. She could hardly cull sophistication from clover and cows.

'Did you read about the Bell murder?' he asked abruptly.

'Auntie wouldn't let me.' She added in the same breath, 'Every word.'

'Why did your aunt forbid you?'

'She said it must be a specially bad one, because they'd left all the bad parts out of the paper.'

'Well, didn't you notice the fact that that poor girl – Emmeline Bell – a well-bred girl of about your own age, was lured to her death through answering a newspaper advertisement?'

'I – I suppose so. But those things don't happen to oneself.'

'Why? What's there to prevent your falling into a similar trap?'

'I can't explain. But if there was something wrong, I should know it.'

'How? D'you expect a bell to ring or a red light to flash "Danger"?'

'Of course not. But if you believe in right and wrong, surely there must be some warning.'

He looked sceptical. That innocence bore a lily in its hand, was to him a beautiful phrase and nothing more. His own position in the sorry scheme of affairs was, to him, proof positive of the official failure of guardian angels.

'Let me see that letter, please,' he said.

She studied his face anxiously as he read, but his expression remained inscrutable. Twisting her fingers in her suspense, she glanced around the room, noting vaguely the three telephones on the desk and the stacked files in the pigeon-holes. A Great Dane snored before the red-caked fire. She wanted to cross the room and pat him, but lacked the courage to stir from her place.

The room was warm, for the windows were opened only a couple of inches at the top. In view of Duncan's weather-tanned colour, the fact struck her as odd.

Mercifully, the future is veiled. She had no inkling of the fateful part that Great Dane was to play in her own drama, nor was there anything to tell her that a closed window would have been a barrier between her and the yawning mouth of hell.

She started as Duncan spoke.

'I want to hold this letter for a bit. Will you call about this time tomorrow? Meantime, I must impress upon you the need of utmost caution. Don't take one step on your own. Should anything fresh crop up, 'phone me immediately. Here's my number.'

When she had gone, Duncan walked to the window. The blue dusk had deepened into a darkness pricked with lights.

Across the river, advertisement-signs wrote themselves intermittently in coloured beads.

He still glowed with the thrill of the hunter on the first spoor of the quarry. Although he had to await the report of the expert test, he was confident that the letter which he held had been penned by the murderer of poor ill-starred Emmeline Bell.

Then his elation vanished at a recollection of Jenny's wistful face. In this city were scores of other girls, frail as windflowers too – blossom-sweet and country-raw – forced through economic pressure into positions fraught with deadly peril.

The darkness drew down overhead like a dark shadow pregnant with crime. And out from their holes and sewers stole the rats . . .

At last Duncan had the trap baited for his rat.

A young and pretty girl – ignorant and unprotected. Cheese.

When Jenny, punctual to the minute, entered his office, the following evening, he instantly appraised her as his prospective decoy. His first feeling was one of disappointment. Either she had shrunk in the night or her eyes had grown bigger. She looked such a frail scrap as she stared at him, her lips bitten to a thin line, that it seemed hopeless to credit her with the necessary nerve for his project.

'Oh, please tell me it's all perfectly right about that letter.'

'Anything but right.'

For a moment, he thought she was about to faint. He wondered uneasily whether she had eaten that day. It was obvious from the keenness of her disappointment that she was at the end of her resources.

'Are you sure?' she insisted. 'It's – very important to me. Perhaps I'd better keep the appointment. If I didn't like the look of things, I needn't go on with it.'

'I tell you, it's not a genuine job,' he repeated. 'But I've something to put to you that is the goods. Would you like to have a shot at £500?'

Her flushed face, her eager eyes, her trembling lips, all answered him.

'Yes, please,'was all she said.

He searched for reassuring terms.

'It's like this. We've tested your letter and know it is written, from a bad motive, by an undesirable character.'

'You mean a criminal?' she asked quickly.

'Um. His record is not good. We want to get hold of him.'

'Then why don't you?'

He suppressed a smile.

'Because he doesn't confide in us. But if you have the

courage to keep your appointment tomorrow and let his messenger take you to the house of the supposititious Mrs Harper, I'll guarantee it's the hiding-place of the man we want. We get him – you get the reward. Question is – have you the nerve?'

She was silent. Presently she spoke in a small voice.

'Will I be in great danger?'

'None. I wouldn't risk your safety for any consideration. From first to last, you'll be under the protection of the Force.'

'You mean I'll be watched over by detectives in disguise?'

'From the moment you enter the National Gallery, you'll be covered doubly and trebly. You'll be followed every step of the way and directly we've located the house, the place will be raided by the police.'

'All the same, for a minute or so, just before you can get into the house, I'll be alone with – *him*?'

'The briefest interval. You'll be safe at first. He'll begin with overtures. Stall him off with questions. Don't let him see you suspect – or show you're frightened.'

Duncan frowned as he spoke. It was his duty to society to rid it of a dangerous pest and in order to do so, Jenny's cooperation was vital. Yet, to his own surprise, he disliked the necessity in the case of this especial girl.

'Remember we'll be at hand,' he said. 'But if your nerve

goes, just whistle and we'll break cover immediately.'

'Will *you* be there?' she asked suddenly.

'Not exactly in the foreground. But I'll be there.'

'Then I'll do it.' She smiled for the first time. 'You laughed at me when I said there was something inside me which told me – things. But I just know I can trust *you*.'

'Good.' His voice was rough. 'Wait a bit. You've been put to expense coming over here. This will cover your fares and so on.'

He thrust a note into her hand and hustled her out, protesting. It was a satisfaction to feel that she would eat that night. As he seated himself at his desk, preparatory to work, his frozen face was no index of the emotions raised by Jenny's parting words.

Hitherto, he had thought of women merely as 'skirts'. He had regarded a saucepan with an angry woman at the business end of it, merely as a weapon. For the first time he had a domestic vision of a country girl – creamy and fragrant as meadowsweet – in a nice womanly setting of saucepans.

Jenny experienced a thrill which was almost akin to exhilaration when she entered Victoria station, the following day. At the last moment, the place for meeting had been altered in a telegram from 'Mrs Harper'.

Immediately she had received the message, Jenny had gone to the telephone-box in the hostel and duly reported the change of plan, with a request that her message should be repeated to her, to obviate any risk of mistake.

And now – the incredible adventure was actually begun.

The station seemed filled with hurrying crowds as she walked slowly towards the clock. Her feet rather lagged on the way. She wondered if the sinister messenger had already marked the yellow wreath in her hat which she had named as her mark of identification.

Then she remembered her guards. At this moment they were here, unknown, watching over her slightest movement. It was a curious sensation to feel that she was spied upon by unseen eyes. Yet it helped to brace the muscles of her knees when she took up her station under the clock with the sensation of having exposed herself as a target for gunfire.

Nothing happened. No one spoke to her. She was encouraged to gaze around her . . .

A few yards away, a pleasant-faced smartly dressed young man was covertly regarding her. He carried a yellowish sample-bag which proclaimed him a drummer.

Suddenly Jenny felt positive that this was one of her guards. There was a quality about his keen clean-shaven face – a hint of the eagle in his eye – which reminded her of Duncan. She gave him the beginnings of a smile and was thrilled when, almost imperceptibly, he fluttered one eyelid. She read it as a signal for caution. Alarmed by her indiscretion, she looked fixedly in another direction.

Still – it helped her to know that even if she could not see him, he was there.

The minutes dragged slowly by. She began to grow anxious as to whether the affair were not some hoax. It would be not only a tame ending to the adventure but a positive disappointment. She would miss the chance of a sum which – to her – was a little fortune. Her need was so vital that she would have undertaken the venture for five pounds. Morever, after her years of green country solitude, she felt a thrill at the mere thought of her temporary link with the underworld. This was life in the raw; while screening her as she aided him, she worked with Angus Duncan.

She smiled – then started as though stung.

Someone had touched her on the arm.

'Have I the honour, happiness and felicity of addressing Miss Jenny Morgan? Yellow wreath in the lady's hat. Red Flower in the gent's buttonhole, as per arrangement.'

The man who addressed her was young and bull-necked, with florid colouring which ran into blotches. He wore a red carnation in the buttonhole of his check overcoat.

'Yes, I'm Jenny Morgan.'

As she spoke, she looked into his eyes. She felt a sharp revulsion – an instinctive recoil of her whole being.

'Are you Mrs Harper's nephew?' she faltered.

'That's right. Excuse a gent keeping a lady waiting, but I just slipped into the bar for a glass of milk. I've a taxi waiting if you'll just hop outside.'

Jenny's mind worked rapidly as she followed him. She was forewarned and protected. But – were it not for Maggie Roper's intervention – she would have kept this appointment in very different circumstances. She wondered whether she would have heeded that instinctive warning and refused to follow the stranger.

She shook her head. Her need was so urgent that, in her wish to believe the best, she knew that she would have summoned up her courage and flouted her fears as nerves. She would have done exactly what she was doing – accompanying an unknown man to an unknown destination.

She shivered at the realisation. It might have been herself. Poor defenceless Jenny – going to her doom.

At that moment she encountered the grave scrutiny of a stout clergyman who was standing by the book-stall. He was ruddy, wore horn-rimmed spectacles and carried the *Church Times*.

His look of understanding was almost as eloquent as a vocal message. It filled her with gratitude. Again she was certain that this was a second guard. Turning to see if the young commercial traveller were following her, she was thrilled to discover that he had preceded her into the station yard. He got into a taxi at the exact moment that her companion flung open the door of a cab which was waiting. It was only this knowledge that Duncan was thus making good his promise which induced her to enter the vehicle. Once again her nerves rebelled and she was rent with sick forebodings.

As they moved off, she had an overpowering impulse to scream aloud for help to the porters – just because all this might have happened to some poor girl who had not her own good fortune.

Her companion nudged her.

'Bit of all right, joy-riding, eh?'

She stiffened, but managed to force a smile.

'Is it a long ride?'

'Ah, now you're asking.'

'Where does Mrs Harper live?'

'Ah, that's telling.'

She shrank away, seized with disgust of his blotched face so near her own.

'Please give me more room. It's stifling here.'

'Now, don't you go taking no liberties with me. A married man I am, with four wives all on the dole.' All the same, to her relief, he moved further away. 'From the country, aren't you? Nice place. Lots of milk. Suit me a treat. Any objection to a gent smoking?'

'I wish you would. The cab reeks of whisky.'

They were passing St Paul's which was the last landmark in her limited knowledge of London. Girls from offices passed on the pavement, laughing and chatting together, or hurrying by intent on business. A group was scattering crumbs to the pigeons which fluttered on the steps of the cathedral.

She watched them with a stab of envy. Safe happy girls.

Then she remembered that somewhere, in the press of traffic, a taxi was shadowing her own. She took fresh courage.

The drive passed like an interminable nightmare in which she was always on guard to stem the advances of her disagreeable companion. Something seemed always on the point of happening – something unpleasant, just out of sight and round the corner – and then, somehow she staved it off.

The taxi bore her through a congested maze of streets. Shops and offices were succeeded by regions of warehouses and factories, which in turn gave way to areas of dun squalor where gas-works rubbed shoulders with grimed laundries which bore such alluring signs as DEWDROP or WHITE ROSE.

From the shrilling of sirens, Jenny judged that they were in the neighbourhood of the river, when they turned into a quiet square. The tall lean houses wore an air of drab respectability. Lace curtains hung at every window. Plaster pineapples crowned the pillared porches.

'Here's our "destitution".'

As her guide inserted his key in the door of No. 17, Jenny glanced eagerly down the street, in time to see a taxi turn the corner.

'Hop in, dearie.'

On the threshold Jenny shrank back.

Evil.

Never before had she felt its presence. But she knew. Like the fumes creeping upwards from the grating of a sewer, it poisoned the air.

Had she embarked on this enterprise in her former ignorance, she was certain that at this point, her instinct would have triumphed.

'I would never have passed through this door.'

She was wrong. Volition was swept off the board. Her arm was gripped and before she could struggle, she was pulled inside.

She heard the slam of the door.

'Never loiter on the doorstep, dearie. Gives the house a bad name. This way. Up the stairs. All the nearer to heaven.'

Her heart heavy with dread, Jenny followed him. She had entered on the crux of her adventure – the dangerous few minutes when she would be quite alone.

The place was horrible – with no visible reason for horror. It was no filthy East-end rookery, but a technically clean apartment-house. The stairs were covered with brown linoleum. The mottled yellow wallpaper was intact. Each landing had its marble-topped table, adorned with a forlorn aspidistra – its moulting rug at every door. The air was dead and smelt chiefly of dust.

They climbed four flights of stairs without meeting anyone. Only faint rustlings and whispers within the rooms told of other tenants. Then the blotched-faced man threw open a door.

'Young lady come to see Mrs Harper about the sitooation. Too-tel-oo, dearie. Hope you strike lucky.'

He pushed her inside and she heard his step upon the stairs.

In that moment, Jenny longed for anyone – even her late companion.

She was vaguely aware of the figure of a man seated in a chair. Too terrified to look at him, her eyes flickered around the room.

Like the rest of the house, it struck the note of parodied respectability. Yellowish lace curtains hung at the windows which were blocked by pots of leggy geraniums. A walnut-wood suite was upholstered in faded bottle-green rep with burst padding. A gilt-framed mirror surmounted a stained marble mantelpiece which was decorated with a clock – permanently stopped under its glass case – and a bottle of whisky. On a small table by the door rested a filthy cage, containing a grey parrot, its eyes mere slits of wicked eld between wrinkled lids.

It had to come. With an effort, she looked at the man.

He was tall and slender and wrapped in a once-gorgeous dressing-gown of frayed crimson quilted silk. At first sight, his features were not only handsome but bore some air of breeding. But the whole face was blurred – as though it were a waxen mask half-melted by the sun and over which the Fiend – in passing – had lightly drawn a hand. His eyes drew her own. Large and brilliant, they were of so light a blue as to appear almost white. The lashes were unusually long and matted into spikes.

The blood froze at Jenny's heart. The girl was no fool. Despite Duncan's cautious statements, she had drawn her own deduction which linked an unsolved murder mystery and a reward of £500.

She knew that she was alone with a homicidal maniac – the murderer of ill-starred Emmeline Bell.

In that moment, she realised the full horror of a crime which, a few months ago, had been nothing but an exciting newspaper-story. It sickened her to reflect that a girl – much like herself – whose pretty face smiled fearlessly upon the world from the printed page, had walked into this same trap, in all the blindness of her youthful confidence. No one to hear her cries. No one to guess the agony of those last terrible moments.

Jenny at least understood that first rending shock of realisation. She fought for self-control. At sight of that smiling marred face, she wanted to do what she knew instinctively that other girl had done – precipitating her doom. With a desperate effort she suppressed the impulse to rush madly round the room like a snared creature, beating her hands against the locked door and crying for help. Help which would never come.

Luckily, common sense triumphed. In a few minutes' time, she would not be alone. Even then a taxi was speeding on its mission; wires were humming; behind her was the protection of the Force.

She remembered Duncan's advice to temporise. It was true that she was not dealing with a beast of the jungle which sprang on its prey at sight.

'Oh, please.' She hardly recognised the tiny pipe. 'I've come to see Mrs Harper about her situation.'

'Yes.' The man did not remove his eyes from her face. 'So you are Jenny?'

'Yes, Jenny Morgan. Is – is Mrs Harper in?'

'She'll be in presently. Sit down. Make yourself at home.

What are you scared for?'

'I'm not scared.'

Her words were true. Her strained ears had detected faintest sounds outside – dulled footsteps, the cautious fastening of a door.

The man, for his part, also noticed the stir. For a few seconds he listened intently. Then to her relief, he relaxed his attention.

She snatched again at the fiction of her future employer.

'I hope Mrs Harper will soon come in.'

'What's your hurry? Come closer. I can't see you properly.'

They were face to face. It reminded her of the old nursery story of 'Little Red Riding Hood'.

'What big eyes you've got, Grandmother.'

The words swam into her brain.

Terrible eyes. Like white glass cracked in distorting facets. She was looking into the depths of a blasted soul. Down, down . . . That poor girl. But she must not think of *her*. She must be brave – give him back look for look.

Her lids fell . . . She could bear it no longer.

She gave an involuntary start at the sight of his hands. They were beyond the usual size – unhuman – with long knotted fingers.

'What big hands you've got.'

Before she could control her tongue, the words slipped out.

The man stopped smiling.

But Jenny was not frightened now. Her guards were near. She thought of the detective who carried the bag of samples. She thought of the stout clergyman. She thought of Duncan.

At that moment, the commercial traveller was in an upper room of a wholesale drapery house in the city, holding the fashionable blonde lady buyer with his magnetic blue eye, while he displayed his stock of crepê-de-Chine underwear.

At that moment, the clergyman was seated in a third-class railway carriage, watching the hollows of the Downs fill with heliotrope shadows. He was not quite at ease. His thoughts persisted on dwelling on the frightened face of a little country girl as she drifted by in the wake of a human vulture.

'I did wrong. I should have risked speaking to her.'

But – at that moment – Duncan was thinking of her.

Jenny's message had been received over the telephone wire, repeated and duly written down by Mr Herbert Yates, shorthand-typist – who, during the absence of Duncan's own secretary, was filling the gap for one morning. At the sound of his chief's step in the corridor outside, he rammed on his hat, for he was already overdue for a lunch appointment with one of the numerous 'only girls in the world',

At the door he met Duncan.

'May I go to lunch now, sir?'

Duncan nodded assent. He stopped for a minute in the passage while he gave Yates his instructions for the afternoon.

'Any message?' he enquired.

'One come this instant, sir. It's under the weight.'

Duncan entered the office. But in that brief interval, the disaster had occurred.

Yates could not be held to blame for what happened. It was true that he had taken advantage of Duncan's absence to open a window wide, but he was ignorant of any breach of rules. In his hurry he had also written down Jenny's message on the nearest loose-leaf to hand, but he had taken the precaution to place it under a heavy paper-weight.

It was Duncan's Great Dane which worked the mischief. He was accustomed at this hour to be regaled with a biscuit by Duncan's secretary who was an abject dog-lover. As his dole had not been forthcoming he went in search of it. His great paws on the table, he rooted among the papers, making nothing of a trifle of a letter-weight. Over it went. Out of the window – at the next gust – went Jenny's message. Back to his rug went the dog.

The instant Duncan was aware of what had happened, a

frantic search was made for Yates. But that wily and athletic youth, wise to the whims of his official superiors, had disappeared. They raked every place of refreshment within a wide radius. It was not until Duncan's men rang up to report that they had drawn a blank at the National Gallery, that Yates was discovered in an underground dive, drinking coffee and smoking cigarettes with his charmer.

Duncan arrived at Victoria forty minutes after the appointed time.

It was the bitterest hour of his life. He was haunted by the sight of Jenny's flower-face upturned to his. She had *trusted* him. And in his ambition to track the man he had taken advantage of her necessity to use her as a pawn in his game.

He had played her – and lost her.

The thought drove him to madness. Steeled though he was to face reality, he dared not to let himself think of the end. Jenny – country-raw and blossom-sweet – even then struggling in the grip of murderous fingers.

Even then.

Jenny panted as she fought, her brain on fire. The thing had rushed upon her so swiftly that her chief feeling was of sheer incredulity. What had gone before was already burning itself up in a red mist. She had no clear memory afterwards of those tense minutes of fencing. There was only an interlude filled with a dimly comprehended menace – and then this.

And still Duncan had not intervened.

Her strength was failing. Hell cracked, revealing glimpses of unguessed horror.

With a supreme effort she wrenched herself free. It was but a momentary respite, but it sufficed for her signal – a broken tremulous whistle.

The response was immediate. Somewhere outside the door a gruff voice was heard in warning.

'Perlice.'

The killer stiffened, his ears pricked, every nerve astrain. His eyes flickered to the ceiling which was broken by the outline of a trap-door.

Then his glance fell upon the parrot.

His fingers on Jenny's throat, he paused. The bird rocked on its perch, its eyes slits of malicious eld.

Time stood still. The killer stared at the parrot. Which of the gang had given the warning? Whose voice? Not Glass-eye. Not Mexican Joe. The sound had seemed to be within the room.

That parrot.

He laughed. His fingers tightened. Tightened to relax.

For a day and a half he had been in Mother Bargery's room. During that time the bird had been dumb. Did it talk?

The warning echoed in his brain. Every moment of delay

was fraught with peril. At that moment his enemies were here, stealing upwards to catch him in their trap. The instinct of the human rodent, enemy of mankind – eternally hunted and harried – prevailed. With an oath, he flung Jenny aside and jumping on the table, wormed through the trap of the door.

Jenny was alone. She was too stunned to think. There was still a roaring in her ears, shooting lights before her eyes. In a vague way, she knew that some hitch had occurred in the plan. The police were here – yet they had let their prey escape.

She put on her hat, straightened her hair. Very slowly she walked down the stairs. There was no sign of Duncan or of his men.

As she reached the hall, a door opened and a white puffed face looked at her. Had she quickened her pace or shown the least sign of fear she would never have left that place alive. Her very nonchalance proved her salvation as she unbarred the door with the deliberation bred of custom.

The street was deserted, save for an empty taxi which she hailed.

'Where to, miss?' asked the driver.

Involuntarily she glanced back at the drab house, squeezed into its strait-waistcoat of grimed bricks. She had a momentary vision of a white blurred face flattened against the glass. At the sight, realisation swept over her in wave upon wave of sick terror.

There had been no guards. She had taken every step of that perilous journey – alone.

Her very terror sharpened her wits to action. If her eyesight had not deceived her, the killer had already discovered that the alarm was false. It was obvious that he would not run the risk of remaining in his present quarters. But it was possible that he might not anticipate a lightning swoop; there was nothing to connect a raw country girl with a preconcerted alliance with a Force.

'The nearest telephone-office,' she panted. 'Quick.'

A few minutes later, Duncan was electrified by Jenny's voice gasping down the wire.

'He's at 17 Jamaica Square, SE. No time to lose. He'll go out through the roof . . . Quick, quick.'

'Right. Jenny, where'll you be?'

'At your house. I mean, Scot – Quick.'

As the taxi bore Jenny swiftly away from the dun outskirts, a shrivelled hag pattered into the upper room of that drab house. Taking no notice of its raging occupant, she approached the parrot's cage.

'Talk for mother, dearie.'

She held out a bit of dirty sugar. As she whistled, the parrot opened its eyes.

'Perlice.'

It was more than two hours later when Duncan entered his private room at Scotland Yard.

His eyes sought Jenny.

A little wan, but otherwise none the worse for her adventure, she presided over a teapot which had been provided by the resourceful Yates. The Great Dane – unmindful of a little incident of a letter-weight – accepted her biscuits and caresses with deep sighs of protest.

Yates sprang up eagerly.

'Did the cop come off, chief?'

Duncan nodded twice – the second time towards the door, in dismissal.

Jenny looked at him in some alarm when they were alone together. There was little trace left of the machine-made martinet of the Yard. The lines in his face appeared freshly re-tooled and there were dark pouches under his eyes.

'Jenny,' he said slowly, 'I've – sweated – blood.'

'Oh, was he so very difficult to capture? Did he fight?'

'Who? That rat? He ran into our net just as he was about to bolt. He'll lose his footing all right. No.'

'Then why are you—'

'*You.*'

Jenny threw him a swift glance. She had just been half-murdered after a short course of semi-starvation, but she commanded the situation like a lion tamer.

'Sit down,' she said, 'and don't say one word until you've drunk this.'

He started to gulp obediently and then knocked over his cup.

'Jenny, you don't know the hell I've been through. You don't understand what you ran into. That man—'

'He was a murderer, of course. I knew that all along.'

'But you were in deadliest peril—'

'I wasn't frightened, so it didn't matter. I knew I could trust you.'

'Don't Jenny. Don't turn the knife. I failed you. There was a ghastly blunder.'

'But it *was* all right, for it ended beautifully. You see, something told me to trust you. I always know.'

During his career, Duncan had known cases of love at first sight. So, although he could not rule them out, he always argued along Jenny's lines.

Those things did not happen to him.

He realised now that it had happened to him – cautious Scot though he was.

'Jenny,' he said, 'it strikes me that I want someone to watch *me*.'

'I'm quite sure you do. Have I won the reward?'

His rapture was dashed.

'Yes.'

'I'm so glad. I'm rich.' She smiled happily. 'So this can't be pity for me.'

'Pity? Oh, Jenny—'

Click. The mouse-trap was set for the confirmed bachelor with the right bait.

A young and friendless girl – homely and blossom-sweet.

Cheese.

THE ADVENTURE OF THE FIRST-CLASS CARRIAGE

RONALD A. KNOX, after SIR ARTHUR CONAN DOYLE

The general encouragement extended to my efforts by the public is my excuse, if excuse were needed, for continuing to act as chronicler of my friend Sherlock Holmes. But even if I confine myself to those cases in which I have had the honour of being personally associated with him, I find it difficult to make a selection among the large amount of matter at my disposal.

As I turn over my records, I find that some of them deal with events of national or even international importance; but the time has not yet come when it would be safe to disclose (for instance) the true facts about the recent change of government in Paraguay. Others (like the case of the Missing Omnibus) would do more to gratify the modern craving for sensation; but I am well aware that my friend himself is the first to deplore it when I indulge what is, in his own view, a weakness.

My preference is for recording incidents whose bizarre features gave special opportunity for the exercise of that analytical talent which he possessed in such a marked degree. Of these, the case of the Tattooed Nurseryman and that of the Luminous Cigar-Box naturally suggest themselves to the mind. But perhaps my friend's gifts were even more signally displayed when he had occasion to investigate the disappearance of Mr Nathaniel Swithinbank, which provoked so much speculation in the early days of September, five years back.

Mr Sherlock Holmes was, of all men, the least influenced by what are called class distinctions. To him the rank was but the guinea stamp; a client was a client. And it did not surprise me, one evening when I was sitting over the familiar fire in Baker Street – the days were sunny but the evenings were already falling chill – to be told that he was expecting a visit from a domestic servant, a woman who 'did' for a well-to-do, childless couple in the southern Midlands.

'My last visit,' he explained, 'was from a countess. Her mind was uninteresting, and she had no great regard for the truth; the problem she brought was quite elementary. I fancy Mrs John Hennessy will have something more important to communicate.'

'You have met her already, then?'

'No, I have not had the privilege. But anyone who is in

the habit of receiving letters from strangers will tell you the same – handwriting is often a better form of introduction than hand-shaking. You will find Mrs Hennessy's letter on the mantelpiece; and if you care to look at her j's and her w's, in particular, I think you will agree that it is no ordinary woman we have to deal with. Dear me, there is the bell ringing already; in a moment or two, if I mistake not, we shall know what Mrs Hennessy, of the Cottage, Guiseborough St Martin, wants of Sherlock Holmes.'

There was nothing in the appearance of the old dame who was shown up, a few minutes later, by the faithful Mrs Hudson to justify Holmes's estimate. To the outward view she was a typical representative of her class; from the bugles on her bonnet to her elastic-sided boots everything suggested the old-fashioned caretaker such as you may see polishing the front doorsteps of a hundred office buildings any spring morning in the city of London. Her voice, when she spoke, was articulated with unnecessary care, as that of the respectable working-class woman is apt to be. But there was something precise and businesslike about the statement of her case which made you feel that this was a mind which could easily have profited by greater educational advantages.

'I have read of you, Mr Holmes,' she began, 'and when things began to go wrong up at the Hall it wasn't long before

I thought to myself, if there's one man in England who will be able to see light here, it's Mr Sherlock Holmes. My husband was in good employment, till lately, on the railway at Chester; but the time came when the rheumatism got hold of him, and after that nothing seemed to go well with us until he had thrown up his job, and we went to live in a country village not far from Banbury, looking out for any odd work that might come our way.

'We had only been living there a week when a Mr Swithinbank and his wife took the old Hall, that had long been standing empty. They were newcomers to the district, and their needs were not great, having neither chick nor child to fend for; so they engaged me and Mr Hennessy to come and live in the lodge, close by the house, and do all the work of it for them. The pay was good and the duties light, so we were glad enough to get the billet.'

'One moment!' said Holmes. 'Did they advertise, or were you indebted to some private recommendation for the appointment?'

'They came at short notice, Mr Holmes, and were directed to us for temporary help. But they soon saw that our ways suited them, and they kept us on. They were people who kept very much to themselves, and perhaps they did not want a set of maids who would have followers, and spread gossip in the village.'

'That is suggestive. You state your case with admirable clearness. Pray proceed.'

'All this was no longer ago than last July. Since then they have once been away in London, but for the most part they have lived at Guiseborough, seeing very little of the folk round about. Parson called, but he is not a man to put his nose in where he is not wanted, and I think they must have made it clear they would sooner have his room than his company. So there was more guessing than gossiping about them in the countryside. But, sir, you can't be in domestic employment without finding out a good deal about how the land lies; and it wasn't long before my husband and I were certain of two things. One was that Mr and Mrs Swithinbank were deep in debt. And the other was that they got on badly together.'

'Debts have a way of reflecting themselves in a man's correspondence,' said Holmes, 'and whoever has the clearing of his waste-paper basket will necessarily be conscious of them. But the relations between man and wife? Surely they must have gone very wrong indeed before there is quarrelling in public.'

'That's as may be, Mr Holmes, but quarrel in public they did. Why, it was only last week I came in with the blancmange, and he was saying, "The fact is, no one would be better pleased than you to see me in my coffin." To be sure, he held his tongue after that, and looked a bit confused;

and she tried to put a brave face on it. But I've lived long enough, Mr Holmes, to know when a woman's been crying. Then last Monday, when I'd been in drawing the curtains, he burst out just before I'd closed the door behind me, "The world isn't big enough for both of us." That was all I heard, and right glad I'd have been to hear less. But I've not come round here just to repeat servants'-hall gossip.

'Today, when I was cleaning out the waste-paper basket, I came across a scrap of a letter that tells the same story, in his own handwriting. Cast your eye over that, Mr Holmes, and tell me whether a Christian woman has the right to sit by and do nothing about it.'

She had dived her hand into a capacious reticule and brought out, with a triumphant flourish, her documentary evidence. Holmes knitted his brow over it, and then passed it on to me. It ran: 'Being of sound mind, whatever the numbskulls on the jury may say of it.'

'Can you identify the writing?' my friend said.

'It was my master's,' replied Mrs Hennessy. 'I know it well enough; the bank, I am sure, will tell you the same.'

'Mrs Hennessy, let us make no bones about it. Curiosity is a well-marked instinct of the human species. Your eye having lighted on this document, no doubt inadvertently, I will wager you took a look round the basket for any other fragments it might contain.'

'That I did, sir; my husband and I went through it carefully together, for who knew but the life of a fellow-creature might depend on it? But only one other piece could we find written by the same hand, and on the same notepaper. Here it is.' And she smoothed out on her knee a second fragment, to all appearances part of the same sheet, yet strangely different in its tenor. It seemed to have been torn away from the middle of a sentence; nothing survived but the words 'in the reeds by the lake, taking a bearing at the point where the old tower hides both the middle first-floor windows'.

'Come,' I said, 'this at least gives us something to go upon. Mrs Hennessy will surely be able to tell us whether there are any landmarks in Guiseborough answering to this description.'

'Indeed there are, sir; the directions are plain as a pikestaff. There is an old ruined building which juts out upon the little lake at the bottom of the garden, and it would be easy enough to hit on the place mentioned. I daresay you gentlemen are wondering why we haven't been down to the lake-side ourselves to see what we could find there. Well, the plain fact is, we were scared. My master is a quiet-spoken man enough at ordinary times, but there's a wild look in his eye when he's roused, and I for one should be Sorry to cross him. So I thought I'd come to you, Mr Holmes, and put the whole thing in your hands.'

'I shall be interested to look into your little difficulty. To speak frankly, Mrs Hennessy, the story you have told me runs on such familiar lines that I should have been tempted to dismiss the whole case from my mind. Dr Watson here will tell you that I am a busy man, and the affairs of the Bank of Mauritius urgently require my presence in London. But this last detail about the reeds by the lake-side is piquant, decidedly piquant, and the whole matter shall be gone into. The only difficulty is a practical one. How are we to explain my presence at Guiseborough without betraying to your employers the fact that you and your husband have been intruding on their family affairs?'

'I have thought of that, sir,' replied the old dame, 'and I think we can find a way out. I slipped away today easily enough because my mistress is going abroad to visit her aunt, near Dieppe, and Mr Swithinbank has come up to town with her to see her off. I must go back by the evening train, and had half thought of asking you to accompany me. But no, he would get to hear of it if a stranger visited the place in his absence. It would be better if you came down by the quarter past ten train tomorrow, and passed yourself off for a stranger who was coming to look at the house. They have taken it on a short lease, and plenty of folks come to see it without troubling to obtain an order-to-view.'

'Will your employer be back so early?'

'That is the very train he means to take; and to speak truth, sir, I should be the better for knowing that he was being watched. This wicked talk of making away with himself is enough to make anyone anxious about him. You cannot mistake him, Mr Holmes,' she went on; 'what chiefly marks him out is a scar on the left-hand side of his chin, where a dog bit him when he was a youngster.'

'Excellent, Mrs Hennessy; you have thought of everything. Tomorrow, then, on the quarter past ten for Banbury without fail. You will oblige me by ordering the station fly to be in readiness. Country walks may be good for health, but time is more precious. I will drive straight to your cottage, and you or your husband shall escort me on my visit to this desirable country residence and its mysterious tenant.' With a wave of his hand, he cut short her protestations of gratitude.

'Well, Watson, what did you make of her?' asked my companion when the door had closed on our visitor.

'She seemed typical of that noble army of women whose hard scrubbing makes life easy for the leisured classes. I could not see her well because she sat between us and the window, and her veil was lowered over her eyes. But her manner was enough to convince me that she was telling the truth, and that she is sincere in her anxiety to avert what may be an appalling tragedy. As to its nature, I confess I am in the dark. Like yourself, I was particularly struck by the reference to the reeds by the lake-side. What can it mean? An assignation?'

'Hardly, my dear Watson. At this time of the year a man runs enough risk of cold without standing about in a reed-bed. A hiding-place, more probably, but for what? And why should a man take the trouble to hide something, and then obligingly litter his waste-paper basket with clues to its whereabouts? No, these are deep waters, Watson, and we must have more data before we begin to theorise. You will come with me?'

'Certainly, if I may. Shall I bring my revolver?'

'I do not apprehend any danger, but perhaps it is as well to be on the safe side. Mr Swithinbank seems to strike his neighbours as a formidable person. And now, if you will be good enough to hand me the more peaceful instrument which hangs beside you, I will try out that air of Scarlatti's, and leave the affairs of Guiseborough St Martin to look after themselves.'

I often had occasion to deprecate Sherlock Holmes's habit of catching trains with just half a minute to spare. But on the morning after our interview with Mrs Hennessy we arrived at Paddington station no later than ten o'clock – to find a stranger, with a pronounced scar on the left side of his chin, gazing out at us languidly from the window of a first-class carriage.

'Do you mean to travel with him?' I asked, when we were out of earshot.

'Scarcely feasible, I think. If he is the man I take him for, he has secured solitude all the way to Banbury by the simple process of slipping half a crown into the guard's hand.'

And, sure enough, a few minutes later we saw that functionary shepherd a fussy-looking gentleman, who had been vigorously assaulting the locked door, to a compartment further on. For ourselves, we took up our post in the carriage next but one behind Mr Swithinbank. This, like the other first-class compartments, was duly locked when we had entered it; behind us the less fortunate passengers accommodated themselves in seconds.

'The case is not without its interest,' observed Holmes, laying down his paper as we steamed through Burnham Beeches. 'It presents features which recall the affairs of James Phillimore, whose disappearance (though your loyalty may tempt you to forget it) we investigated without success. But this Swithinbank mystery, if I mistake not, cuts even deeper. Why, for example, is the man so anxious to parade his intention of suicide, or fictitious suicide, in the presence of his domestic staff? It can hardly fail to strike you that he chose the moment when the good Mrs Hennessy was just entering the room, or just leaving it, to make those remarkable confidences to his wife. Not content with that, he must leave evidence of his intentions lying about in the waste-paper basket. And yet this involved the risk of having his plans foiled by good-natured interference. Time enough for his disappearance to become public when it became effective! And why, in the name of fortune, does he hide something only to tell us where he has hidden it?'

Amid a maze of railway tracks, we came to a standstill at Reading. Holmes craned his neck out of the window, but reported that all the doors had been left locked. We were not destined to learn anything about our elusive travelling companion until, just as we were passing the pretty hamlet of Tilehurst, a little shower of paper fragments fluttered past the window on the right-hand side of the compartment, and two of them actually sailed in through the space we had dedicated to ventilation on that bright morning of autumn. It may easily be guessed with what avidity we pounced on them.

The messages were in the same handwriting with which Mrs Hennessy's find had made us familiar; they ran, respectively, 'Mean to make an end of it all' and 'This is the only way out.' Holmes sat over them with knitted brows, till I fairly danced with impatience.

'Should we not pull the communication cord?' I asked.

'Hardly,' answered my companion, 'unless five pound notes are more plentiful with you than they used to be. I will even anticipate your next suggestion, which is that we should look out of the windows on either side of the carriage. Either we have a lunatic two doors off, in which case there is no use in trying to foresee his next move, or he intends suicide, in which case he will not be deterred by the presence of spectators, or he is a man with a scheming brain who is sending us these messages in order to make us behave in a particular way. Quite probably, he wants to make us lean out of the windows, which seems to me an excellent reason for not leaning out of the windows. At Oxford we shall be able to read the guard a lesson on the danger of locking passengers in.'

So indeed it proved; for when the train stopped at Oxford there was no passenger to be found in Mr Swithinbank's carriage. His overcoat remained, and his wide-awake hat; his portmanteau was duly identified in the guard's van. The door on the right-hand side of the compartment, away from the platform, had swung open; nor did Holmes's lens bring to light any details about the way in which the elusive passenger had made his exit.

It was an impatient horse and an injured cabman that awaited us at Banbury, when we drove through golden woodlands to the little village of Guiseborough St Martin, nestling under the shadow of Edge Hill. Mrs Hennessy met us at the door of her cottage, dropping an old-fashioned curtsy;

and it may easily be imagined what wringing of hands, what wiping of eyes with her apron, greeted the announcement of her master's disappearance. Mr Hennessy, it seemed, had gone off to a neighbouring farm upon some errand, and it was the old dame herself who escorted us up to the Hall.

'There's a gentleman there already, Mr Holmes,' she informed us. 'Arrived early this morning and would take no denial; and not a word to say what business he came on.'

'That is unfortunate,' said Holmes. 'I particularly wanted a free field to make some investigation. Let us hope that he will be good enough to clear off when he is told that there is no chance of an interview with Mr Swithinbank.'

Guiseborough Hall stands in its own grounds a little way outside the village, the residence of a squire unmistakably, but with no airs of baronial grandeur. The old, rough walls have been refaced with pointed stone, the mullioned windows exchanged for a generous expanse of plate-glass, to suit a more recent taste, and a portico has been thrown out from the front door to welcome the traveller with its shelter. The garden descends at a precipitous slope from the main terrace, and a little lake fringes it at the bottom, dominated by a ruined eminence that serves the modern owner for a gazebo.

Within the house, furniture was of the scantiest, the Swithinbanks having evidently rented it with what fittings it had, and introduced little of their own. As Mrs Hennessy ushered us into the drawing-room, we were not a little surprised to be greeted by the wiry figure and melancholy features of our old rival, Inspector Lestrade.

'I knew you were quick off the mark, Mr Holmes,' he said, 'but it beats me how you ever heard of Mr Swithinbank's little goings-on; let alone that I didn't think you took much stock in cases of common fraud like this.'

'Common fraud?' repeated my companion. 'Why, what has he been up to?'

'Drawing cheques, and big ones, Mr Holmes, when he knew that his bank wouldn't honour them; only little things of that sort. But if you're on his track I don't suppose he's far off, and I'll be grateful for any help you can give me to lay my hands on him.'

'My dear Lestrade, if you follow out your usual systematic methods, you will have to patrol the Great Western line all the way from Reading to Oxford. I trust you have brought a drag-net with you, for the line crossed the river no less than four times in the course of the journey.' And he regaled the astonished inspector with a brief summary of our investigations.

Our information worked like a charm on the little detective. He was off in a moment to find the nearest telegraph office and put himself in touch with Scotland Yard, with the Great

Western Railway authorities, with the Thames Conservancy. He promised, however, a speedy return, and I fancy Holmes cursed himself for not having dismissed the jarvey who had brought us from the station, an undeserved windfall for our rival.

'Now, Watson!' he cried, as the sound of the wheels faded away into the distance.

'Our way lies to the lake-side, I presume.'

'How often am I to remind you that the place where the criminal tells you to look is the place not to look? No, the clue to the mystery lies, somehow, in the house, and we must hurry up if we are to find it.'

Quick as a thought, he began turning out shelves, cupboards, escritoires, while I, at his direction, went through the various rooms of the house to ascertain whether all was in order, and whether anything suggested the anticipation of a hasty flight. By the time I returned to him, having found nothing amiss, he was seated in the most comfortable of the drawing-room armchairs, reading a book he had picked out of the shelves – it dealt, if I remember right, with the aborigines of Borneo.

'The mystery, Holmes!' I cried.

'I have solved it. If you will look on the bureau yonder, you will find the household books which Mrs Swithinbank has obligingly left behind. Extraordinary how these people always make some elementary mistake. You are a man of the world, Watson; take a look at them and tell me what strikes you as curious.'

It was not long before the salient feature occurred to me. 'Why, Holmes,' I exclaimed, 'there is no record of the Hennessys being paid any wages at all!'

'Bravo, Watson! And if you will go into the figures a little more closely, you will find that the Hennessys apparently lived on air. So now the whole facts of the story are plain to you.'

'I confess,' I replied, somewhat crestfallen, 'that the whole case is as dark to me as ever.'

'Why, then, take a look at that newspaper I have left on the occasional table; I have marked the important paragraph in blue pencil.'

It was a copy of an Australian paper, issued some weeks previously. The paragraph to which Holmes had drawn my attention ran thus:

ROMANCE OF RICH MAN'S WILL

The recent lamented death of Mr John Macready, the well-known sheep-farming magnate, has had an unexpected sequel in the circumstance that the dead man, apparently, left no will. His son, Mr Alexander Macready, left for England some years back, owing to a misunderstanding with his father – it was said – because he announced his intention of marrying a lady from the stage. The young man has completely disappeared, and energetic steps are being taken by the lawyers to trace his whereabouts. It is estimated that the fortunate heirs, whoever they be, will be the richer by not far short of a hundred thousand pounds sterling.

Horse-hoofs echoed under the archway, and in another minute Lestrade was again of our party. Seldom have I seen the little detective looking so baffled and ill at ease.

'They'll have the laugh of me at the Yard over this,' he said. 'We had word that Swithinbank was in London, but I made sure it was only a feint, and I came racing up here by the early train, instead of catching the quarter past ten and my man in it. He's a slippery devil, and he may be half-way to the Continent by this time.'

'Don't be downhearted about it, Lestrade. Come and interview Mr and Mrs Hennessy, at the lodge; we may get news of your man down there.'

A coarse-looking fellow in a bushy red beard sat sharing his tea with our friend of the evening before. His greasy waistcoat and corduroy trousers proclaimed him a manual worker. He rose to meet us with something of a defiant air; his wife was all affability.

'Have you heard any news of the poor gentleman?'

she asked.

'We may have some before long,' answered Holmes. 'Lestrade, you might arrest John Hennessy for stealing that porter's cap you see on the dresser, the property of the Great Western Railway Company. Or, if you prefer an alternative charge, you might arrest him as Alexander Macready, alias Nathaniel Swithinbank.' And while we stood there literally thunder-struck, he tore off the red beard from a chin marked with a scar on the left-hand side.

'The case was difficult,' he said to me afterwards, 'only because we had no clue to the motive. Swithinbank's debts would almost have swallowed up Macready's legacy; so it was necessary for the couple to disappear, and take up the claim under a fresh alias. This meant a duplication of personalities, but it was not really difficult. She had been an actress; he had really been a railway porter in his hard-up days. When he got out at Reading, and passed along the six-foot way to take his place in a third-class carriage, nobody marked the circumstance, because on the way from London he had changed into a porter's clothes; he had the cap, no doubt, in his pocket. On the sill of the door he left open, he had made a little pile of suicide messages, hoping that when it swung open these would be shaken out and flutter into the carriages behind.'

'But why the visit to London? And, above all, why the visit to Baker Street?'

'That is the most amusing part of the story; we should have seen through it at once. He wanted Nathaniel Swithinbank to disappear finally, beyond all hope of tracing him. And who would hope to trace him, when Mr Sherlock Holmes, who was travelling only two carriages behind, had given up the attempt? Their only fear was that I should find the case uninteresting; hence the random reference to a hiding-place among the reeds, which so intrigued you. Come to think of it, they nearly had Inspector Lestrade in the same train as well. I hear he has won golden opinions with his superiors by cornering his man so neatly. *Sic vos non vobis*, as Virgil said of the bees; only they tell us nowadays the lines are not by Virgil.'

THE MURDER ON THE OKEHAMPTON LINE

VICTOR L. WHITECHURCH

The solution of the murder on the Okehampton line was, at best, only partial, and yet there can be no doubt whatever that Godfrey Page penetrated the mystery as deeply as it could be penetrated and that his theory was correct; in fact, though some links in the chain of evidence were missing, there was quite sufficient to prove that my brother-in-law had fathomed the leading points.

He was not pressed into the investigation, but took it up out of sheer curiosity.

I had been dining at his house one night and he had sent out for the last edition of the evening paper. I think there was a railway strike or something of the kind going on that interested him. But however that might be, his attention was caught directly he opened the paper with the following paragraph, which he handed me to read:

MURDER ON THE OKEHAMPTON LINE!

(A Railway Mystery)

On the arrival of the last train from Exeter to Okehampton at the latter station last night, a gruesome discovery was made. A porter on the platform noticed a gentleman seated in the corner of a third-class compartment and, as he made no attempt to get out of the carriage, opened the door to wake him, thinking he might be asleep. To his horror he discovered that the man was dead and a subsequent examination revealed the fact that he had been stabbed in the heart with some sharp instrument. There were signs of a struggle in the carriage.

The murdered man was dressed in a dark blue suit with a soft felt hat, but there was absolutely nothing on him to lead to his identification – not a scrap of paper of any sort.

That robbery was not the object is proved by the fact that some five or six pounds in gold and silver and his watch and chain were still on him.

Although the police were communicated with at once nothing further has been ascertained up to going to press. The body has been removed to the White Hart Hotel and there awaits identification.

'Here's a mystery if you like,' said Godfrey Page. 'Let me see, the last down train arrives at Okehampton at ten-fifty.

It's the one that leaves Waterloo at five-fifty and Exeter, St David's, at ten-thirty. Of course, the great question is – where did he get into the train and whereabouts on the journey was he murdered?'

'And who he was?' I added.

'Exactly. Do you know, I've half a mind to run down tomorrow and have a look at things. Would you care to come?'

'Well,' I said, 'I think I could spare the day.'

'It means two days. We'll go down tomorrow morning by the ten-thirty express from Paddington. I've been wanting to have a run on that train for a long time.'

'But Okehampton is on the L & SW Railway,' I ventured to suggest.

'I fancy I'm aware of that,' he replied snappishly, 'but I tell you I want a run on the Great Western. I've got a friend at Paddington, too, who'll give me a leg up. I'll write to him tonight. Meet me at Paddington at ten-fifteen under the clock.'

I found him waiting for me when I arrived, holding in his hand a newspaper and a letter.

'It's all right,' he said; 'I've got a line of introduction to the officials at St David's in case I want information. And there's a whole column about the case in this morning's paper. We'll read it as we go down.'

He spent the rest of the time before starting in noting the name of the engine, the number of the coaches, and other details of the express, and then we found ourselves in a comfortable carriage, speeding westward.

'Now,' he said, when we had read the paper, 'you see, there are several new points in the case. Let's try and sum them up.

'First of all, the identity of the murdered man is still unknown. Secondly, you see, the crime must have been committed between Exeter and Okehampton, because the guard of the train remembers speaking to the man at Exeter. It appears that the guard put his head in the window just before the train started and said: "Where are you for, sir?" To which the man made a singular reply. He answered: "Where does this train go to?" Upon the guard saying "Okehampton," he simply replied, "All right." Now this seems to show that he was in a train *the destination of which he didn't know.*'

'And the next point evidently touches the murderer,' I said.

'Yes; I think so, too. Two men got off the train at Yeoford junction, telling the ticket-collector that there had been no time for them to get a ticket at St David's and paying him the fare. These two men seem to have disappeared. They could not have got away by train, for that was the last one at the junction that night. But it's only a seven or eight miles' walk back to Exeter, and that's probably how they've eluded search.

'Now, you see, this gives us two more points. First, if these two men committed the crime, they did it between Exeter and Yeoford; and secondly, the fact of their having no tickets proves our theory correct that the murdered man was in a train that was strange to him.'

'How so?'

'Because *they* didn't know where they were going either. They must have been following him. They saw him get into the Okehampton train and they got in after him.'

'But the guard said he was alone when he saw him at St David's and spoke to him.'

'Very likely. But the train had not quite started. There was time for them to get in – if not in his compartment in another one. And there *is* such a thing as walking along the footboard of a train in motion, and getting into another compartment. I've done it lots of times.

'Now,' he went on, 'acting on these theories, the next question is – what made the murdered man get into the Okehampton train, and where was he before he got in? Perhaps our good friend Bradshaw will help us.' He opened the book and consulted its pages carefully. 'I won't say what I think yet,' he remarked presently, 'but I've a sort of an idea. There's an island platform at St David's.'

'What on earth's that?'

He looked at me scornfully.

'An island platform is one between two lines, so that trains run on either side of it. But now I'm going to enjoy the run.'

I scarcely saw where the enjoyment came in. He was not still for five minutes together. At every station his head went out of the window, once or twice when we slowed down he grew impatient, but brightened up when he timed a mile in fifty-seven and three-fifths seconds. He made notes of all sorts of things and generally fidgeted during the whole journey.

'It's been a glorious run,' he exclaimed as we drew up at St David's. 'One hundred and ninety-four miles without a stop, and a minute ahead of scheduled time in spite of that signal against us at Taunton and the slowing down for the PW operations.'

'What's "PW"?' I asked.

'Permanent way, you ignoramus. Stop a minute. I want to speak to the driver.'

He was back in a few minutes.

'Our train leaves for Okehampton at three twenty-five,' he said. 'Now, we'll just have a chat with one of the officials here to begin with.'

We found our way to one of the officials, and Godfrey

Page presented the letter of introduction.

'Ah, I've heard of you, Mr Page,' he said. 'You unearthed that strange affair at Warchester, didn't you? Well, I see you've come down to have a look at this Okehampton mystery. Can I do anything for you?'

'Not at present,' said my brother-in-law, 'except to tell me if the train in which the murder took place wasn't a bit late in starting from St David's.'

'Aha,' laughed the other, 'we Great Western men always like to get a rise out of the South-Western, you know. Yes, she *was* three or four minutes late.'

'That's all I want to know. It confirms me in a little theory, though. If I find out anything further at Okehampton I shall trouble you again.'

'Certainly. Anything we can do for you, please ask me. But it seems to me that it is a South-Western job, Mr Page.'

'Ah! I'm not so sure that your line isn't mixed up in it!'

Arrived at Okehampton we quickly found our way to the hotel. Godfrey Page made himself known to the detective-inspector on the premises and we were ushered by him into the room where the body of the murdered man had been taken. He lay in the bed, quiet and serene, with quite a smile upon his face.

He was a man of some five and thirty years of age, with very dark moustache and beard and a bronzed countenance which even death had not been able to stamp with pallor.

'Are there no marks about him?' asked Godfrey Page of the inspector.

'Only this,' and he turned down the sheet and showed the man's right arm, on which a small dragon was tattooed in black and red.

'Hm!' said my brother-in-law, 'looks as if he'd been in the Far East. Only a Chinese or Japanese artist could have done that.'

'Yes,' said the inspector, 'there was a silver dollar along with his money, too, which corroborates that.'

'Were there no marks on his clothes?'

'No.'

'May I look at them?'

'Here they are.'

The inspector narrowly watched Godfrey Page as he turned over garment after garment till he arrived at the shirt. It was an ordinary white one, but with a nasty red stain upon it that told its own tale.

'It's no use,' said the inspector, 'there's no name upon it.'

'By George, though, there's something else. Look, have you noticed this?'

And he pointed to a faint pencilling inside the starched linen cuff.

'What is it?' asked the inspector. 'Looks like a pencilled

note. Strange we never noticed it.'

'You gentlemen don't always look everywhere. But I'll just jot that down, please. It's interesting.'

And he entered the following in his notebook, a copy of what had been scrawled on the dead man's shirt cuff: 242, E3 Great Marlow.

'I'll wire to Great Marlow at once,' said the inspector; 'it looks like a clue. It may be he's known there. It might even be the number of a street he knows, or something of that kind.'

'It might be,' returned Godfrey Page dryly. 'I'll only detain you one moment. Was anything else found on him besides money?'

'Only this knife.'

It was an ordinary, rather large, clasp knife. My brother-in-law opened it.

'The big blade's broken,' he said, 'and freshly done, too. Ah, and see how loose it is.'

'Now, sir,' said the inspector impatiently, 'if you've quite finished we'll go. I hope you won't mention what you've seen.'

'Not I. And you're really going to investigate at Great Marlow?'

'Certainly!'

'Ah! Perhaps the bit of blade broken off that knife lies

somewhere by Great Marlow.'

The inspector stared at him with astonishment.

'I've heard of you as a sort of private detective where railways are concerned,' he said, 'but, if you'll excuse my saying so, you don't seem to know much about this kind of thing.'

'And perhaps you are as strangely ignorant of railways,' retorted Godfrey Page, 'but I don't bear you any malice. If I'm ever in a position to help you, I will.'

'Now,' he said to me, as we regained the street, 'there's just time for us to make a little purchase, and then we'll catch the five-twelve train back to Exeter.'

And, taking me into an ironmonger's shop, he bought a small screwdriver and put it into his pocket.

Arrived at Exeter we sought out the friendly GW official, and my brother-in-law at once began:

'I'm going to ask you for some rather curious information. We shall stay the night at Exeter, and if you can get it by tomorrow I shall be much obliged.'

'What is it, Mr Page?'

'Find out on what train the third-class coach numbered 242 was running the night before last, and where it is to be found tomorrow.'

The official promised to do so.

Godfrey Page refused to say another word on the subject

that night. The next morning we went to St David's and sought out our friend.

'Well?' asked the 'railwayac'.

'I've got you the information, but I don't see how it will help you. Number 242 third coach is one that at present is kept at Plymouth as a spare carriage in case there is an abnormal number of passengers for the Paddington express. The night to which you refer it ran—'

'On the eight-twenty p.m. from North Road, Plymouth, arriving here at 10.03.'

'How on earth did you know that, for it's quite true?'

'It was only my little theory,' said Page, with a smile, 'but go on.'

'It was put on to the up-corridor express at Plymouth because some passengers, arriving by a P&O steamer, increased the demand for room on that train. You know, perhaps, that if we have over twenty-four P&O passengers we run a "boat special", but not if we take them by ordinary express. On this occasion only sixteen travelled to London.'

'And where is number 242 now?' asked Page impatiently.

'Here.'

'Here?'

'Yes. It was running back to Plymouth last night and I took the liberty of detaining it here because you seemed interested in it.'

Godfrey Page was jubilant.

'Let's go and see it at once,' he said, drawing the screwdriver out of his pocket.

'What do you want that for?' asked the official.

'You'll see,' was the only reply he would make.

We very soon reached the siding where the third-class carriage was standing. Page counted down the fifth compartment and climbed in. We followed.

'Now,' said he to me, 'what do you see? Notice that!' And he pointed above the door. There I read as follows: 242, E. 'All the compartments are lettered, you see,' went on Page, 'and E, of course, is the fifth compartment from the end, commencing with A. Now look at those photographs!'

As is customary in Great Western carriages there were photographs of places of interest along the line over the seats.

'Great Scott!' I exclaimed.

'Great Marlow! you mean,' said my brother-in-law triumphantly, for there, before me, was a photograph of that picturesque Thames town.

'Now,' said Godfrey Page, 'I'll give you my theory, and then we'll see if it's correct.

'A man, travelling in a train the destination of which he is seemingly ignorant of, is found murdered. Not a single scrap of paper of any kind remains upon him to prove his identity.

His money being left proves that robbery of *that* was not an object. The two men whom we assume committed the crime were following him, and he was flying from them. He was evidently acquainted with China or Japan, and his bronzed face suggested a recent return from abroad.

'Let us assume that he landed at Plymouth from the P&O boat and took the eight-twenty express to Paddington, travelling alone in this compartment. Let us further assume that he discovered that his enemies were on board the same train, having watched for his arrival at Plymouth, and further that he had in his possession some very important paper or letter that it was their object to obtain.

'He knows he is watched and is in danger. First, then, he hides the paper and scribbles the key to finding it again on his wristband. Then, as the train draws up at 10.03 on the left-hand side of the island platform, here he sees another train, the Okehampton one, which ought to have been starting at that very moment, standing on the other side of the platform. Thinking to escape, he rushes across and takes a seat in it. But he is observed by his followers, and they do the same. Then the murder takes place, and they search in vain for the hidden paper.'

'But where did he hide it?'

'Behind this picture of Great Marlow,' said Godfrey Page, commencing to unscrew the panel of it. 'He broke the blade of his knife in doing what I'm doing now.'

Breathlessly we waited while the four screws were withdrawn. Then the panel was removed, and out dropped a large sheet of thin tracing paper, many times folded. We undid it carefully.

'A map,' exclaimed the railway official.

'Yes, but what a map! Look, Tom!'

'A plan of a fortress apparently,' I said.

'A plan of Port Arthur!' cried Godfrey Page.

There, sure enough, was the map of a fortress, with guns and other points marked out with care, and brief explanations in French.

'I'll tell you what,' said Godfrey Page, as he commenced screwing up the panel, 'it's my opinion that we three had better keep this little discovery to ourselves. For, depend upon it, even if we handed this over to the police, the murderers would never be discovered.'

'Why not?'

'Because in all probability they are police themselves.'

'Russians?'

'Exactly so. He met with a spy's fate.'

'But who was this map intended for?'

'My dear fellow, our government would have paid well for it, eh?'

On further consultation we agreed to say nothing to the

police. Just before we took the train back to Paddington, Godfrey Page said to our friend the official: 'By the way, they take tickets at Reading from the passengers in the eight-twenty p.m. from Plymouth? You might try and find out if three fewer tickets than were issued at Plymouth were collected that night?'

'All right, Mr Page, I'll drop you a line.'

On our way home my brother-in-law was much puzzled how to act. He had retained the map in his possession, and he was talking of destroying it when suddenly an idea occurred to him.

'Tom,' he said, 'do you ever come across Colonel Sylvester now?'

'Occasionally I meet him at the club.'

'Ah! Isn't he something to do with the Secret Service?'

'Yes.'

'Good. Let's sound him. Ask me to meet him at your place to dinner and leave the rest to me.'

A few days later the dinner came off. We three men were lazily smoking our cigars afterwards when Godfrey Page exlaimed: 'Mysterious affair that at Okehampton the other night.'

'Very,' said the Colonel, with a quick look at him.

'I was down there a day or two afterwards.'

'Indeed!'

'I made an interesting discovery.'

'What?'

'I found a curious thing in a railway carriage.'

'May I ask what?'

'This map,' replied Godfrey Page, taking it out of his pocket.

The Colonel seized it eagerly.

'Good heavens!' he said. 'Have you told anyone of this?'

'Only two beside ourselves know it.'

'For goodness' sake say nothing, Mr Page. If the Russian police knew you had that map, they'd – they'd—'

'Murder me as they did the man who brought it to England, eh?'

The Colonel was pale and trembling as he laid a hand on Godfrey Page's arm.

'Tell me,' he said, 'the police know nothing of this?'

'Nothing.'

'What do you propose to do with it?'

'I thought *you* might find it more useful than I should,' he said significantly.

The Colonel put it in his breast-pocket with a sigh of satisfaction.

'You are a wise man, Mr Page,' he said. 'I am extremely obliged to you.'

'I wonder,' remarked my brother-in-law a day or two later,

'how the inspector got on at Great Marlow? By the way, I've had a letter from Exeter. There *were* three tickets from Plymouth to London missing at the collection at Reading!'

THE MYSTERY OF THE BLACK BLIGHT

FRANCIS LYNDE

The wreck at Lobo Cut, half-way between Angels and the upper portal of Timanyoni Canyon, was a pretty bad one. Train Six, known in the advertising folders as 'The Fast Mail,' had collided in the early-morning darkness with the first section of a westbound freight which, though it was an hour and fifty minutes off its schedule time, had run past Angels without heeding the 'stop for orders' signal plainly displayed.

Ten minutes after the crash, the second section of the freight had shot around the hill curve to hurl itself, a six-thousand-ton, steel-pointed projectile, into the rear end of the first section, and the disaster was complete. Somewhere under the smoking mountain of wreckage marking the spot where the Mail and first-section locomotives had locked themselves together, reared, and fallen over into the ditch, two firemen and an engineer were buried. Out of one of the crushed mail-cars two postal clerks were taken; one of them to die a few minutes after his rescue, and the other bruised and broken, with an arm and a leg dangling, as he was carried out to safety.

At the other point of impact there had been no loss of life, though the material damage was almost as great. The engine of the second section had split its way sheer through the first-section caboose – which, in the nature of things, had no one in it to be killed – and through two of the three merchandise-cars next in its plunging path. With a mixed chaos of groceries, farming implements, and splintered timbers for its monument, the big mogul had burrowed into the soft side bank of the cutting as if in some blind attempt to bury itself out of sight of the havoc it had wrought.

On the Thursday morning of this, the worst of a series of accidents thickly bestudding that fateful month of August, Maxwell, the general superintendent, chanced to be two hundred miles away to the eastward. His service-car was in the Copah yards, and he was asleep in it when the nightwatchman came down from the despatcher's office to rouse him with the bad news.

What could be done at such long range was done instantly and with good generalship. The wires were working with Brewster, the division headquarters in Timanyoni Park. With his own hand Maxwell sent the orders to Connolly, the despatcher, to Fordyce, the trainmaster, and to Bascom, the master mechanic. A relief train was to be made up with all haste to take the doctors to the wreck, and to convey the passengers of Number Six back to Brewster. Following the relief train, but giving it precedence, should go the wrecking-train. The superintendent even went so far as to specify the equipment which should be taken: the heavier of the two wrecking-cranes, a carload of rails for temporary tracking, and two or three water-cars for the extinguishing of the fire.

These things done, and the arrangements made to start his own special immediately for the scene of disaster, the superintendent had the fine courage, in the face of this last and most unnerving of many disheartenments, to return to his car and to go back to bed. He had been up very late in conference with his president, Ford, and he knew that the demands awaiting him at the end of the five-hour run to Lobo Cut would call for all the reserves of strength and energy he could hope to store up during the distance-covering interval.

Much good work had already been accomplished when Maxwell's special, feeling its way past the four long freights and the midnight passenger, all held up at Angels, came upon the scene of destruction among the foothills at an early hour in the forenoon. The relief train had come and gone, bearing away the unhurt, the injured, and the dead. A temporary working-track had been laid through the cut, and the mighty one-hundred-and-fifty-ton steam crane, its movements directed by a big, rather flashily dressed man with an accurately creased brown hat pulled down over his brows, was reaching its steel finger here and there in the debris and plucking the derelict freight-cars out of the way.

Up at the other end Fordyce, the trainmaster, was working with another crew, using a mammoth block-and-tackle, with a detached locomotive for its pulling power. When Maxwell came on the ground, Fordyce, a gnarled little man with a twist in his jaw and a temper like the sparks from an emery wheel, was alternately cajoling and cursing his men in a praiseworthy attempt to make his block-and-tackle outheave the master mechanic's powerful crane.

'Yank 'em – yank 'em, men! Get that rail under there and heave! Wig it – *wig it*! Now get that grab-hook in here – lively! Don't let them fellows at the other end snake two to our ONE!'

Maxwell stopped to exchange a word or two with the sweating trainmaster and then passed on down the wreck-strewn line. At the master mechanic's end of things he came upon Benson, chief of construction, who had accompanied the wrecking-train from Brewster only because he had happened to be on the way to Angels and saw no other probable means of reaching his destination.

'Pretty bad medicine – the worst of the lot,' commented the young chief of construction, when, tramping soberly, they came to the place where the two great locomotives, locked in their death grapple, were nuzzling the clay bank of the cutting.

Maxwell's teeth came together with a savage little click.

'A few weeks ago, Jack, we were scared stiff for fear the "Big-Nine" crowd of stock-jobbers would succeed in doing something to put us on the panic-slide. Now we are doing it ourselves, just about as fast as we can. Is it true that there were four killed?'

'Yes; both firemen, and Bamberg, the engineer of the freight. The other man was a postal clerk; and his mate had an arm and a leg broken.'

'Many injuries?'

'Astonishingly few, when there was such a good chance for a general massacre. Both men on the second-section engine jumped, and both were hurt, though not badly. There was nobody in the split caboose when it was hit. On the Mail, Cargill, who was running, got off with a pretty bad scalp wound. An express messenger had his foot jammed; and the train baggageman had a lot of trunks shaken down on him. In the coaches there were a few people thrown out of their seats and hurt by the sudden stop; but in the sleepers there were a good many who slept straight through it, incredible as that may sound.'

'I know,' said Maxwell; 'I've seen that happen more than once, when the Pullmans stayed on the rails.' Then, with a slight backward nod of his head he changed the subject abruptly. 'Bascom – has he been handling it all right?'

'He's a dandy!' said Benson. 'Personally, I'd about as soon associate with any one of a dozen Copah tin-horns that I could name as to foregather with Mr Judson Bascom. But he's on to his job, all right. He laid this temporary track himself; I haven't butted in at all, either here or at Fordyce's end.'

'How did you happen to get here? I thought you were up Red Butte way,' said the superintendent.

'I was; but I came down to Brewster on Six last night, meaning to go through to Angels. While we were changing engines I ran upstairs to get some maps and papers out of my office, and took too long about it; the train got away from me and I chased out with the wreck-wagons. That's how near I came to being mixed up in this thing myself.'

'And you want to go on to Angels now?'

'Yes; when I get a chance. Those irrigation people in Mesquite Valley are howling to have an unloading spur built up from the old copper-mine track, and I thought I'd go and look the ground over.'

The superintendent's frown was expressive of impatient dissatisfaction.

'That Mesquite project is another of the grafts that are continually giving this country a black eye, Jack. It's "bunk", pure and simple. Everybody who has ever been in the Mesquite knows that you couldn't raise little white beans in that disintegrated sandstone!'

'It'll do for an excuse to rake in a few hundred thousand Eastern shekels,' Benson remarked. 'There will be plenty of "come-ons" to buy the land when the dam is built.'

Bascom's great crane was poising a crushed and mangled box-car in air, and when the crooking steel finger swung its burden aside and dropped it with a crash out of the way, Maxwell turned upon his heel.

'I have my car here, and I'm going back to Angels to do some wiring,' he said. 'Come along, if you want to see those irrigation people. But I'll tell you right now, I won't approve any recommendation for more track-laying for them.'

They had walked possibly half the length of the long blockade when a noisy automobile, dust-covered and filled with men, drew up on the mesa flat above the wreck. Benson looked up with a scowl.

'There's another gang of those newspaper ghouls!' he commented, as two of the three men in the tonneau got out and began to unlimber their cameras and tripods. 'It's no picnic to drive a car from Brewster over the range, to say nothing of the danger; and this is the second squad since daylight. There have been enough pictures taken of this wreck to fill all the newspapers between New York and San Francisco for a week!'

Maxwell's smile was a mere teeth-baring.

'Yes; we're getting the advertising all right,' he said. 'We've been getting it for a month or more.' Then, as they tramped on out of the wreck raffle and headed for the waiting office-car: 'I had a talk with Ford last night; that is what took me to Copah. We're in bad, Benson. Ford says they've taken to calling us "the sick railroad" on the Stock Exchange, and our securities are simply going to the puppies. Another month like this one we've just stumbled through will either wipe us from the map or clean us up definitely and put us into the hands of a receiver.'

'Does Ford say that?' gasped the young chief engineer.

'He said a good bit more than that. He still insists that these troubles of ours are helped along from the outside; that they are in reality just so many moves in the game that a certain Wall Street pool is playing to get control of our road. I tried to show him how impossible it was; how the entire slump in discipline which causes all the trouble is merely one of those crazy epidemics that now and then sweep over the length of the best-managed railroads on earth.'

'And he wouldn't believe it?' queried Benson.

'No; the last thing he said to me as his train was pulling out proved that he didn't. He intimated that there wasn't any "act-of-God" verdict to be brought in, in our case, and told me to go back to Brewster and dig until I found the real cause.'

By this time they had reached the service-car special, and Maxwell passed the word to his engineer to back up the line to Angels. When the wreck and the wreckers had vanished beyond the hill curves, Benson filled his short pipe and at the lighting of it asked another question.

'I've been wondering if we couldn't get a little expert help on this thing, Maxwell. Have you tried to interest Mr Sprague in this discipline business?'

The superintendent shook his head.

'Sprague isn't going around doing odd jobs in psychology for anybody and everybody,' he deprecated. 'He is a government chemist, and he is out here on the government's business. Besides, it isn't a case for a detective; even for the best amateur detective in the bunch – which is easily what Sprague might claim to be, you'd say. You see, there isn't anything special to detect. What we need is a doctor; not a plainclothes man.'

Benson's left eye closed itself slowly in qualified dissent.

'What does Mr Sprague himself have to say about it?'

he queried.

'He hasn't said anything. In fact, I haven't seen him for over two weeks. He's been out with Billy Starbuck, gathering soil specimens; they are still out somewhere, I don't know just where.'

Neither of the two men riding the rear platform of the backing service-car spoke again until the car stopped with a jerk at the edge-of-the-desert station with the celestial name, which had once been the headquarters of the original Red Butte Western Railroad. Then Benson summed up the situation in a couple of terse sentences.

'If we don't do something, and do it quick, there is a bunch of us so-called railroad bosses on this high-line who may as well pack our dufflebags and fade away into the landscape. Three wrecks within a week; and this last one will cost a hundred thousand cold iron dollars before we're through with the lawyers; I'll be hanged if I wouldn't call in the doctor – some doctor – any doctor, Maxwell. That's my ante. So long; see you a little later about this Mesquite business, if you're still here.' And he put a leg over the platform railing and went away.

Three minutes later, when the superintendent had crossed the station platform and was on his way around to the door opening into the operator's office, two men mounted upon wiry range horses rode down the single remaining street of the dead-alive former railroad town, pointing for the station.

One of them, a good-looking youngish man with a preternaturally grave face and the shrewd, thoughtful eyes that tell of days and nights spent afield and alone with the desert immensities, was the superintendent's brother-in-law by courtesy. The other, a gigantic athlete of a man, whose weight fairly bowed the back of the stout horse he rode, was Mr Calvin Sprague.

Maxwell paused when he saw and recognised the two horsemen. But when they came up, the weight of the recent disaster made his greeting a rather dismal attempt at friendly jocularity.

'Well, well!' he said, gripping hands with the athlete; 'Billy certainly had it in for you this time! Rode you over the range, did he? I'll bet you'll never have the nerve to look a horse in the face again, after this. Where on top of earth have you two been keeping yourselves for the last fortnight?'

'Oh, just sashayin' round on the edges,' drawled Starbuck, replying for both; 'gettin' acquainted with the luminous landscape, and chewin' off chunks of the scenery, and layin' awake nights to soak up some of the good old ozone.'

'Ozone!' chuckled the big man; 'I'm jammed gullet-full of it, Dick, and I have a hunch that it's going to settle somewhere below the waist line and make me bow-legged for life. King David said that a horse is a vain, thing for safety, but I can go him one better and say that it's the vainest possible thing for just plain, ordinary, everyday comfort. I'm a living parenthesis-mark – or a pair of 'em, if you like that better.' Then without warning and almost without a break: 'Where is the wreck, this time?'

Maxwell's frown was a little brow-wrinkling of curious perplexity.

'You've just ridden down from the hills, haven't you? How do you know there is a wreck?'

'That's too easy,' laughed the expert, waving a Samsonic arm toward the five side-tracked trains held up in the Angels yard. 'If you didn't have your track cluttered up somewhere, those trains wouldn't be hanging up here, I'm sure. Is it a bad one? – but you needn't answer that; I can see at least one dead man in your eyes.'

'There are four of them,' said the superintendent soberly, 'and some others desperately hurt. We're in a bad way, Sprague. This is the third smash within a week.'

Sprague dismounted stiffly and secured his saddle-bags containing the soil specimens gathered at the price of so much discomfort.

'Starbuck,' he said whimsically, 'I'm willing to pay the price of a hundred-dollar guinea-pig, if necessary, to have this razor-back mustang shipped home in a palace stockcar to his stable in Brewster. Mr Maxwell's office-car is good enough for me from this on.'

Starbuck smiled grimly and took the abandoned horse in charge. 'I'll take care of the bronc',' he agreed; and the big man limped around the station to board the service-car while Maxwell went into the office to do his telegraphing.

When the superintendent returned half an hour later he found his self-invited guest lounging luxuriously in the easiest of the big wicker chairs in the open compartment of the car, smoking the fattest of black cigars and reading a two-days-old Denver paper.

'This is something like,' he said. 'I was never cut out for a pioneer, Richard; Starbuck has proved that to my entire satisfaction in these last two weeks. But that's enough of me and my knockings. Sit down and tell me your troubles. I see the papers are making space-fillers out of your railroad to beat the band. Are you ready to come around to my point of view yet?'

Maxwell sat down like a man who was both worried and wearied.

'The Lord knows, I wish I could come around to your point of view, Calvin. If I could see any possibility of charging these things to outside influences . . . But there isn't any. The trouble is purely local and internal – and as unaccountable as the breaking out of an epidemic when the strictest kind of quarantine has been maintained.'

Sprague smiled incredulously.

'There never was a case of typhoid yet without its germ to account for it, Dick,' he asserted dogmatically.

'I know; but that theory doesn't hold good in the psychological field. We've got a good set of men, Sprague. To a degree which you don't often find in modern railroad consolidations, we've had that precious thing called *esprit de corps*. We've never had any labour troubles since Lidgerwood's time, and there are no grievances in the air to account for the present let-down. Yet the let-down is with us. Almost every day some man who has hitherto proved trustworthy falls down on his job, and there you are.'

'You've tried all the usual remedies, I suppose?'

'I should say I had! I've stormed and cursed and pleaded and reasoned until I'm worn out! If I fire a bunch of them, I have to hire a new bunch, and inside of a week the new men have caught the disease for themselves. One bad wreck will make a hundred trainmen uncertain and jumpy, and a second one will turn half of the hundred into irresponsible lunatics. You'd have to mix and mingle with the force as I do to understand the condition things have gotten into. It's horrible, Calvin. It is like the black blight that you have seen spread through a well-kept orchard.'

'There is a cause,' said the expert, settling himself solidly in his chair. 'I tell you, Dick, there's a germ in the air, and that second mentality of mine that you are so fond of poking fun at tells me that in the case of your railroad orchard the germ has been deliberately planted. You say it's impossible: I've a good notion to let the soil-testing rest for a few minutes and show you.'

'If I thought there was the least chance in the world that you could show me—'

'Is that a challenge? By Jove! I'll take you. When can you get me back to Brewster?'

'As soon as the track is cleared. We ought to be able to get through by noon.'

The expert got up, shook the riding kinks out of his legs, and threw the newspaper aside.

'I'm going out to walk around for a bit, and after a while I'll ask you to take me down to this wreck,' he said; and Maxwell, who had a deskful of work awaiting him, nodded.

'Say, in an hour?'

'An hour will do; I'll show up within that time.'

Later, the superintendent, wading through the files of business correspondence which always accompanied him in his goings to and fro on the line, had window glimpses of Sprague strolling up and down beside the waiting trains in the yard or standing to chat with some member of the loafing crews.

The glimpses were provocative of good-natured incredulity on the part of the desk-worker. Thrice during the summer of warfare Sprague had been able to step into the breach, each time with signal success. But in each of the three former instances there had been tangible causes with which to grapple; flesh-and-blood criminals to be ferreted out and apprehended. Maxwell, glancing out of the window again, shook his head despondently. What could the keenest intelligence avail in the case of an entire railroad suffering from an acute attack of nervous disintegration and recklessness? Nothing, the superintendent decided; there was nothing for it but to settle down upon a grim determination to outlive and worry through the period of disaster; and he was still grinding away at his desk with that thought in the back part of his mind when Sprague came in and announced his willingness to be taken on to the wreck.

Maxwell gave the necessary order, and in due time the one-car special had repassed the few miles intervening between Angels and Lobo Cut, to come to a stand on the curve of hazard. Sprague was lighting a fresh cigar preparatory to a plunge into the track-clearing activities, and Maxwell looked up from his work.

'Want me to get off with you?' he asked.

'No; it's the very thing I don't want,' declared the expert briefly; and therewith he went out to drop from the car-step and to take the plunge alone.

In the two hours which had elapsed since the departure of the superintendent's car the track-clearers at both ends of the wreck had made astonishingly good progress. Step by step the master mechanic had worked his big crane up the line, tossing the derelicts aside or righting them upon the rails, as their condition warranted; and further along Fordyce, with his huge tackle and its pulling locomotive, had been equally enthusiastic.

It was Sprague's boast that his methods of investigation, in the field of his hobby, as in all others, were purely scientific; and he insisted that the true scientist and the most successful is the one who can best qualify as a shrewd and wholly impartial observer.

Where another man might have asked questions, he stood aside and looked on and listened. In the fierce toil of track-clearing no one seemed to pay any attention to him, and the picture which presented itself was a life-sketch of the railroad force *in petto* and in the raw. The big onlooker took his time and made his mental jottings thoughtfully, strolling from one group to another and lingering longest near the hot boiler-cab of the great crane where a wizened human automaton in dirty overalls and jumper jerked the levers and spun the wheels of the hoist in obedience to the signals given by the flashily dressed master mechanic.

It wanted less than a quarter of an hour of noon when the final obstruction was heaved aside, and the track gang, which had been following the wreckers, trued and spiked the distorted rails of the main line into place. Sprague closed his mental notebook and went back to join Maxwell.

In the office-car the porter-cook had laid the table for the midday meal; and the superintendent and his guest ate it in transit, the office-car special being the first of the halted trains to pass westward over the newly cleared line.

'Well?' said Maxwell interrogatively, when the meal had progressed to the meat and vegetables without comment on the part of the one who had lifted the challenge.

'You've got the disease, all right; it's with you, and in the epidemic form, too. Its expression came out emphatically every now and then in that track-clearing hustle. One little snappy, snarly fellow lying under a box-car to make the hoisting-hitch voiced it precisely when his mate yelled at him to come out, that the hitch might slip. He yapped back, "Who the hell and blinkety-blank blankation cares!" That's one form your disease is taking, and you'd say it would account for a good many of the smashes.'

'Well?' queried the superintendent again. 'You didn't stop at that?'

'No; I made a few other preliminary observations which may or may not prove up. Give me a little time; and when we get back to Brewster, detail that ex-cowboy "relief operator" of yours, Tarbell, to run errands for me. If I can't show you good, tangible results within the next forty-eight hours or so, you may discharge me and hire a Pinkerton.'

'You'll fail,' said Maxwell gloomily. 'I've been through a sickness of this kind before. There's no cure for it. It has simply got to run its course and wear itself out.'

'That's what they used to say about cholera and the plague and yellow-fever, and all those things,' laughed the man from Washington; but he did not go any further into the matter of theories.

The run of the special train to Brewster was made without incident, and from the station Sprague went directly across to his hotel.

'I'm going over to clean up,' he announced. 'By and by, when you get around to it, send Tarbell over and tell him to wait in the lobby for me.'

It was possibly an hour later when the young man who resembled William Starbuck sufficiently to pass for the mine owner's younger brother, got out of his chair in the quietest corner of the Hotel Topaz lobby and crossed to the elevators to meet the government chemist.

'How are you, Archer?' was the renovated soil-gatherer's greeting. And then, as he led the way back to the quiet corner from which the young man had been keeping his watch upon the elevators: 'We're up against it good and hard, this time, young man. Your boss has stumped us to prove a thing which he says can't be proved. Sit down and let's see if we can't start the thin edge of a wedge. I'll do the hammering and let you hold the wedge, and you can squeal if I strike off and hit you. How long has this case of bad railroading, which is smashing things right and left, been going on?'

The young fellow who was on the railroad payrolls as a 'relief operator' took time to consider.

'A month or better.'

'How did it begin?'

'I don't know. One way 'r another, the boys've just seemed to be gettin' sort o' careless and losin' their grip. After two or three wrecks had happened, it was all off. Half o' the men've taken to runnin' on their nerve, and the other half act like they don't care a durn.'

'Is it only in the train service?'

'Lord, no; it's mighty near everywhere. It's sort of a dry rot; cars go without repairin', engines burn out, and twice within the last week the roundhouse has caught fire. You'd think every man on the road had just turned loose all holts and didn't give a cuss whether he ever got 'em again or not.'

'What do the men themselves say about it?'

'There's a heap o' kickin' and knockin'. Some say it's Mr Maxwell. When he gets good and mad and fires a bunch of 'em, they raise a rookus about it; and when he lets the next bunch down easy, they kick the other way.'

Sprague sat back in the big leather-upholstered lobby chair and for a time seemed to be absorbed in a study of the rather over-massive beam arrangement of the ceiling. Suddenly he turned to ask: 'How much of a prohibition country is this, Archer?'

Tarbell laughed.

'I reckon you don't need to ask that, with three saloons in every block in Brewster. We haven't got the water-wagon bug much out here. They say it don't breed well this side o' the main range.'

'Much drinking among the railroad men?'

'Well – m – m – not so you could notice it. There's a rule against it.'

'While they're on duty, you mean?'

'Any old time.'

'Is that rule enforced?'

'Mr Maxwell allows it is. He's sure some Ranahan when it comes to buckin' the booze-fighters.'

'Still, there is more or less drinking among the men; you know there is, don't you, Archer?'

The young man grinned soberly.

'I ain't tellin' no tales out o' school, Mr Sprague, not me,' he drawled.

'Get rid of that notion,' said the big man sharply. 'You are working for Mr Maxwell and his rules are your law and gospel. I'll tell you what I've seen, and then you can tell me what you've seen. I counted sixteen men in one place on this railroad today who, within the half-hour that I was looking on, stopped work either to hit or to pass a pocket-flask. Now go on.'

'If you hold me up that-away, I reckon maybe there *is* a good many empty bottles layin' round on the right-o'-way – more'n what the passengers throw out o' the car windows,' was the reluctant admission.

'And more than there used to be, say, two or three months ago?'

'Yes; right smart more.'

'I thought so. We don't need to look any further, Archer, for the disease itself. Your "dry rot" is very pointedly a wet rot. Booze and the running of a railroad are two things that won't mix. Now we'll come to the nib of it. Why is there more drinking now than there used to be?'

The younger man took time to think about it before he said: 'You got me goin'; I don't know the answer to that.'

'I didn't suppose you did,' was the curt rejoinder. 'But you are going to learn the answer, Archer, my son. It is now four o'clock; by half past seven this evening I want you to be back here prepared to tell me who has been letting down the fences for the railroad men in this matter of drinking.'

'Holy Smoke!' exclaimed the ex-cowboy, jarred for once out of his plainsman calm, 'how am I goin' to do that, Mr Sprague?'

'That is for you to find out, my boy. If you don't use your brain you'll never know whether or no you've got any. That's all – until half past seven. You'll find me here at the hotel.'

It was an even hour before the time appointed for Tarbell's return when Maxwell joined the chemistry expert at the table in the Topaz café where they usually sat when they could dine together.

At the unfolding of the napkins Sprague said: 'I've found your germ, Dick, and things are beginning to develop. What do you think of that?' – passing a bit of dingy coarse-fibred paper across the table.

Maxwell opened the paper and read the ill-spelled typewritten note it bore.

Mr Spraig:
Weer onto you with both feet, keep youre fingers out ov the geers or maybe youll git em mashed.
A well-Wishur.

'Where did that come from?' asked the superintendent, plainly amused.

'It was pushed under the door of my room upstairs about half an hour ago. The man who left it was short, thick-set, smooth-shaven, and he wore a pepper-and-salt suit and a slouch hat. Also, his breath smelled of whiskey.'

'You expect me to recognise the description?'

'I didn't know but you might.'

'I don't,' Maxwell denied. Then his smile of amusement changed to one of amazement. 'How could you know all these things about this man if you were on the other side of a closed door, Calvin?'

Sprague laughed. 'See how easy it is to jump to conclusions,' he derided. 'I wasn't on the other side of a closed door; I was in the corridor when the fellow passed me, looking for the number on the door. I saw him leave the note. I'll ask one question, and then we'll dismiss that phase of the case. Is the wrecking-train back from Lobo yet?'

'Yes; it came in about four o'clock with the string of crippled cars. But you say you have found the germ; does that mean that you are going to prove up on your assertion about the epidemic?'

'I can't tell what it means yet; but I can tell you the name of the germ. It's whiskey.'

'Drinking among the men?'

'Worse than that; drunkenness among the men. Enough of it, I should say, to account for all of your troubles and then some.'

'Oh, you're off – way off!' objected the harassed one irritably. 'I know there is some drinking; in a wide-open country like this it is almost impossible to stamp it out entirely. But to account for the epidemic in that way, you'd have to imagine every other man in the service carrying a pocket-pistol on the job!'

'And you think that couldn't happen without your knowing it, eh? A little further along I may have some statistics to show you; but just now I'm looking not so much for the germ as for the germ-carrier.'

Maxwell smiled wearily.

'Still sticking to the theory that the blight is imported, are you? It's the only time I've ever known you to be "yellow", Calvin. I can imagine some wild-eyed newspaper reporter hatching such an idea, but not you. Think of the absurdity of a bunch of Wall Street stock-jobbers trying to get at us in any such indirect way as that – shipping whiskey in here to demoralise our working force! Pshaw! When these fellows get busy and go to work, they want action – quick action.'

The expert put down his knife and fork and sat back in his chair.

'You are so close to the thing that you are continually losing the perspective, Dick,' he said earnestly. 'You are going on the supposition that those New York looters are trying first one thing and then another. That doesn't follow at all. For all you know, they may be gunning for you in half a dozen different ways this blessed minute – as they probably are. Assume, for the sake of the argument, that this whiskey scheme could be worked; I know you say it can't, but suppose it could: can you conceive of any expedient that would be more certain to kill your traffic, wipe out your earnings, smash your securities, and put you on the toboggan slide generally?'

'Oh, no; if it could be worked.' Maxwell's answer this time was less confidently derisive.

'All right; now that you've come that far, I'll say this: it can be worked, and I'm here to tell you that it has been worked. Your railroad is practically an inebriate asylum in the making, right now, Richard. Half of your force has already fallen off the water chariot, and the other half is scared to death at the thought of what the drunken half may do.'

Maxwell pushed away his dessert untasted.

'You have the proof of this, Calvin?' he broke out.

'I have some proof, and Tarbell is getting more. You've been blind. You didn't want to admit that your house of discipline was tumbling about your ears, and you've been shutting your eyes to the plain facts. For example: you may or may not be the only man in the service who doesn't know that those two freight engineers – the one who was killed and the other who overran their orders and smashed into the passenger at Lobo Cut this morning were just plain drunk!'

'What's that? It – it can't be, Calvin!'

'But it *is*,' insisted the big man across the table. 'It is common talk among your own men; so common that it reached out and hit me – an outsider.'

The superintendent drank his small coffee at a single gulp and flung his napkin aside.

'I'll get 'em!' he gritted savagely. 'I'll get the last damned booze-fighter in the bunch!' And then: 'Good God, Sprague; how could anything like this go on without my knowing it?'

'You would have found it out, sooner or later, of course. But you're a railroad man yourself, and you ought to know railroad men well enough to take into consideration that sort of loyalty among them which keeps them from "peaching" on one another. Even Tarbell had to be jarred before he would admit that he knew about it. I can imagine that there has been a sort of generous conspiracy among the men to keep you from finding out.'

'That's all right; I know now, and I'll sift them out; I'll go through the whole blamed outfit with a club! I'll—'

The man who had called out this upbubbling of righteous wrath was chuckling softly.

'You won't do anything that you say you will,' he

interrupted good-naturedly. 'You stumped me to take the case, and I've taken it; which means that you're under the doctor's orders. When you have cooled down a bit, you'll see very clearly that the worst thing you could do at this particular crisis would be to start a division-wide scrap with the rank and file.'

'But, good Lord, Sprague; I've got to do something, haven't I?'

'You surely have; and that something is to help me find the germ-carrier. Somebody has been taking down the bars for your men; who is it?'

'I don't know any more than a goat. I can't yet believe that it is the work of any one man.'

'Possibly it isn't; there may be a good many. But I'll chance a guess that someone in authority is setting the pace. Leave that for a moment and we'll take up something else. You have two daily papers here in Brewster: I've noticed that one of them, *The Tribune*, is friendly to your road. How about the other, *The Times-Record*?'

'It is supposed to be independent, with a slant against corporations and "the system", whatever that may be.'

'Um,' said the scientist. 'Before I went out on this last trip with Billy, I remarked that this other paper was giving a good bit of space to your road troubles in its news columns, and a good bit of its editorial space to criticisms of the Ford management. It occurred to me then that there might be a reason. How is the paper organised?'

'It is owned by one of our near-millionaires; a retired ranchman named Parker Higginson, who has dabbled in real estate, in mines, and latterly in politics. His grouch against the railroad is purely personal. He has asked favours that I couldn't legally grant; and on one occasion he took offence because I told him that a newspaper man should be the last person in the world to invite us to become law-breakers.'

'And his editor?' queried the expert.

'Is a bird of the same feather; a rather "yellow" little fice named Healy.'

Sprague looked rather dubiously at the two cigars which the waiter was tendering on a server. 'No, I think not, George,' he said, waving the cigars aside and feeling for his own pocket-case of stronger ones. And then to Maxwell: 'This is all very nourishing. It may help out more than you suspect. Later in the evening I may ask you to call with me at the office of *The Times-Record* – though we may not have to go that far up the ladder to find what we are looking for. In the meantime, Tarbell is waiting for us out yonder in the lobby. Suppose we go and see what he wants.'

They found the young man, who looked like a younger brother to Starbuck, and who had made his record chasing cattle thieves in Montana, methodically rolling a cigarette in the loggia alcove, and Sprague began on him briskly.

'Spit it out, Archer; what have you found?'

'I didn't make out to find what you sent me after,' was the half-evasive reply.

'All right; tell us what you did find.'

The young man dropped his cigarette and looked up with a glint of stubbornness in his stone-grey eyes.

'If it's just the same to you, Mr Sprague, I'd a heap ruther not,' he said.

Sprague reached out and turned the lapel of Tarbell's coat, exposing the small silver star of a deputy sheriff.

'You took an oath when you got that, Archer; and Mr Maxwell pays you for wearing it.'

Tarbell threw up his head defiantly. 'Deputy or no deputy, I ain't goin' to name no names,' he began slowly. 'But here's what I found out: I been in twenty-three saloons and dives since you told me to go chase, and I counted thirty-one railroad men in 'em. Not all of 'em was drinkin' or gamblin', but some of 'em was.'

Sprague turned to Maxwell.

'You see, I knew what I was talking about.'

The superintendent was shaking his head.

'As openly as that!' he exclaimed. 'I must have been the blindest fool in all this hill country!'

Tarbell chipped in quickly. 'It ain't been that bad for

very long. But it's just as Mr Sprague says; it's spreadin' like murrain on a dry range. I saw men in them places this evenin' that I'd a swore never got off the water-wagon. I ain't namin' no names.'

'Mr Maxwell isn't asking you to give anybody away,' the expert qualified. And then: 'Had your supper?'

Tarbell nodded. 'I had a hand-out in one o' the saloons.'

'Good. Then I'll give you another job. Look around town for a man about Mr Maxwell's build, only about twenty pounds heavier. He is between twenty-five and thirty years old, wears a slouch hat soft grey in colour, dresses in pepper-and-salt, is clean-shaven, red-faced, blue-eyed, and walks with a little hitch to his left leg which isn't quite a limp. When you catch up with him, find out who he is and come and tell me. I'll be over at Mr Maxwell's office.'

Tarbell vanished, rolling a fresh cigarette as he went, and Sprague thrust his arm in Maxwell's.

'I'll go over to your shop with you,' he said. 'I know you're anxious to climb back into the working saddle. I'm not going to bore you; I merely want to have a little talk with that irreproachable chief clerk of yours, Harvey Calmaine.'

A little later they climbed the stair to the office floor of the railroad building together, and Maxwell went on down the corridor to the despatcher's room. When he came back to his own office a half-hour later and found Sprague and young

Calmaine figuring together at the chief clerk's desk in the outer room, he went on to his own inner sanctum without disturbing them.

It was perhaps another half-hour further along when the expert, who had been patiently going over a mass of statistics with the alert, well-groomed young fellow who served as the superintendent's right hand, sat back in his chair and relit the fat black cigar which had been suffered to go out many times during the figuring process.

'It seems that a good many things besides wrecks have been happening in the past few weeks, Mr Calmaine,' he suggested musingly. 'In that short interval you have had many changes in the force, especially in the motive-power department. I don't know whether you have remarked it, but fully half of the men in the shops and roundhouses are new men. And that is the department in which the sickness seems to be the worst. Your maintenance costs have increased three hundred per cent over the same period last year.'

'I know it,' admitted the chief clerk. 'It is the more marked because Dawson, our former master mechanic, made such phenomenally good records.'

'I remember Dawson,' said the big man, slipping easily from the statistics into the humanities. 'He was here the first time I came over the road, early in the summer. Has he left the Short Line?'

'He has been promoted. He is superintendent of motive power on the east end of the South-western.'

'That is recent, isn't it?'

'Yes; it was only a few weeks ago.'

'And you have a new man as department chief?'

'We have – Judson Bascom. You may remember him as the man who ran the special train for you and Mr Maxwell the day you made the blind trip to Tunnel Number Three. He is a sort of slave-driver and seems to have a good deal of trouble with his men – is continually hiring and firing, you'd say, from the appearance of his payrolls.'

The big expert's eyes narrowed.

'Was he also promoted from some other place on the sytem?' he asked.

'No; he is a new man. I don't know where he got his experience; somewhere in the East, I suppose.'

'Another question,' put in Sprague. 'Does Mr Maxwell have the appointment of his own motive-power chief?'

'No; this appointment was made in New York – by the executive committee, I imagine.'

'Somebody's nephew or brother-in-law?' queried the chemist, with a twinkle in his eye.

'I don't know about that. I guess it happens that way, once in a while, on any railroad. But Bascom is all kinds of capable.'

Sprague shook his head. 'The true test of capability is always in the final result, my son,' he said reflectively; adding, 'and results nowadays are usually measured in dollars and cents. As an outsider, I should say that this Mr Bascom is a pretty expensive man to have around, judging from his cost sheets. He drinks some, doesn't he?'

The young chief clerk closed one eye gravely.

'I'm not supposed to know anything about that, Mr Sprague.'

'No, of course not. As you might say, it's nobody's business but Mr Bascom's. By the way, what is that whistle blowing so persistently for?'

Calmaine leaped out of his chair as if it had been suddenly connected with the grounding wire of a forty-kilowatt generator.

'By George! It's a fire!' he exclaimed; and the sound of hurrying feet in the corridor confirmed the surmise. Maxwell's door opened at the same instant, and the three rushed out to join the crowd which was already streaming across the yard tracks toward the company's shops.

The fire was in the shops, originating in the boiler-room; and, thanks to the timely alarm and the comparative earliness of the hour, it was soon extinguished. Investigation, promptly instituted on the spot by the superintendent, proved that it was the result of pure carelessness. Some of the mechanics had washed their overalls and had hung them too near the sheet-iron stack in the fire-room; that was all.

Sprague lingered at Maxwell's elbow while the investigation was going on, and he appeared to be a more or less perfunctory listener when Bascom, oozing wrathful profanity at every pore, told the superintendent what he would do to the careless clothes-driers when they should show up in the morning. But later, after the return to the headquarters offices, the man from Washington sat for a long time in Maxwell's easiest chair, smoking steadily and with his gaze fixed upon the disused gas chandelier marking the exact centre of the ceiling.

It was not until after Maxwell had finished his quota of night work and was closing his desk that Tarbell came in to make a whispered report to the big man apparently dreaming in the easy-chair.

Sprague listened, nodded, and rose to join the office-closing retreat.

'That is about what I thought, Archer,' he said soberly. 'Now I have one more little job for you, and when it is done we'll call it a go for tonight. Come around to my laboratory with me and I'll explain it to you.' And when the four of them reached the plaza-fronting street he excused himself to Maxwell and the chief clerk and went, with Tarbell at his elbow, to the little second-floor den in the Kinzie Building where his experiments in soil analysis were conducted.

Reaching the back room which served as the laboratory proper, Sprague provided his follower with half a dozen small bottles, empty and tightly corked.

'There you are,' he said, from which it may be inferred that the nature of the remaining 'job' had been explained on the way up from the railroad headquarters. 'Do it neatly, Archer, and don't let them catch you at it. Everything will have quieted down by this time, and you shouldn't have any trouble. I'll wait for you here.'

Tarbell was gone possibly half an hour, and when he returned the bottles they were filled, two of them with a black-brown liquid, thick and viscous, and four with what appeared to be specimens of more or less dirty water. Each bottle was carefully marked on the blank label pasted upon it. Sprague stood them in a row on the laboratory working-table.

'I shall be busy here for twenty or thirty minutes,' he said. 'I don't want to ride a willing horse to death, but I'd be glad if you'd go by the hotel and ask Mr Maxwell to wait up for me. I want to see him before he goes to bed.'

Tarbell nodded, but he hesitated about going.

'I got a hunch that we ain't doin' all the shadow work by our little lonesomes, Mr Sprague,' he ventured to say. But before he could go on, Sprague lifted a finger for silence, made a whirling half-turn with a swiftness marvellous in so huge a body, and flung himself through the open door into the unlit outer office-room to which the laboratory was an inner extension.

There were sounds of a collision, a fall, and a brief struggle before Tarbell could get action. At the end of it Sprague came back into the laboratory, dragging a thickset, square-shouldered man in pepper-and-salt clothes; a man with a clean-shaven red face down the side of which a thin line of blood was trickling.

'You were eminently correct, Archer,' said the expert, slamming his unresisting burden into a corner of the room after he had deftly gone through the pepper-and-salt pockets for weapons with the result of turning out a cheap revolver, and a wicked-looking knife. 'I'm sorry I can't keep my word and let you go to bed, but the plot has thickened a little too rapidly. Go around to the Topaz and ask Mr Maxwell to wait. Then come back here and keep this fellow quiet while I do my work.'

When Tarbell went out, Sprague quickly stripped his coat and went to work at his laboratory table. For some little time the man in the corner lay as he had been cast, and the worker at the table paid no attention to him. But a few minutes before Tarbell's return, the red-faced man gasped, gurgled, and sat up to hold his head in his hands as one trying to remember what had happened to him. Presently he looked up, and after a long stare at the big figure of the man at the work table, he found his voice.

'Say, guv'ner, wot am I doin' here?' he asked huskily.

Sprague, who was skilfully dropping a fuming yellow liquor from a glass-stoppered bottle into a beaker, replied without turning his head.

'If anybody should ask, I should say you are waiting for an officer to come and take you to jail.'

'Who, me? Wot have I been doin'?' queried the husky one, in the anxious rasp of a deeply aggrieved victim of circumstances.

'You've been shoving threatening letters under my door in the Hotel Topaz, for one thing,' said Sprague, still busy with his experiment.

'Who me? My Gawd – just lissen to 'im!' wheezed the red-faced man, as if appealing to some third person invisible.

A silence followed during which the crouching man's feet drew themselves by imperceptible fractions of an inch at a time into position for a tackling spring. Sprague did not look aside, but when the leg muscles of the man began to bulge as if testing themselves for the leap, the worker at the table spoke again.

'I shouldn't try it if I were you. This stuff that I am fooling with is nitric acid, ninety-eight per cent pure. If any of it should happen to get spilled on you, there wouldn't be sweet oil enough in this town to put the fire out.'

'My Gawd!' gasped the red-faced one, suddenly sticking his feet out in front of him again; and just then Tar bell came in.

'I'll be through in a minute, Archer,' said the experimenter at the work-table, still without looking around. 'Did you find your man?'

'Yes; and Starbuck is with him. What do you want me to do with this geezer?'

'Nothing. I'll fix him when we're ready to go.'

'I've got a pair of handcuffs,' Tarbell suggested.

'They won't be needed – not for this one.'

Tarbell dragged out a chair and sat down, tilting comfortably against the wall and staring half-absently at the man in the corner. 'Before I'd let any bare-handed man take my arsenal away from me and slam me around like that,' he murmured, quite impersonally.

The man on the floor lifted the challenge promptly.

'Lemmie git up and gimme half a chanst,' he croaked. 'I won't hurt you none if you don't git in the way o' that door.'

'Not this evenin',' said Tarbell succinctly; and there the matter rested until Sprague put his beakers and test-tubes aside, and, resuming his coat, took a flat black box from a shelf and slipped it into his pocket.

'Now we're ready,' he announced; and then he turned to the captured spy. 'We're going to leave you here in the dark for a little while, and there will be nothing between you and a get-away but a small matter of fear. After we turn the lights off I shall leave a few bottles of stuff around where they will do the most good. If you should happen to upset one of them in moving about, it's goodbye. If it doesn't burn you to death, you'll stifle.'

'My Gawd!' said the captive; and he was still saying it over softly to himself when they switched off the lights, shut the office doors, and went away.

'There is a good example of the power of matter over mind, Archer,' said Sprague whimsically, when they reached the street. 'If that fellow would use his reason even a little bit he'd know that I hadn't made any very elaborate preparations to hold him; there wasn't time between the turning off of the lights and our leaving. Yet I'll bet a small chicken worth twenty-five dollars that we find him still crouching in his corner and afraid to move when we go back. He saw me using acid in my little experiment; saw the fumes and probably got a whiff of them. That was enough.'

They found Maxwell and Starbuck sitting on the hotel porch, smoking. Sprague took the superintendent aside.

'It's rather worse than I thought it was, Dick,' he began,

when they had drawn their chairs a little apart. 'That is my excuse for keeping you up so late. We have one of the conspirators under a sort of mental lock and key over at my place in the Kinzie Building, but he is only a hired striker, and I'd like to flush the big game. Are you good for a watch-meeting – you and Starbuck? It may last all night, and nothing may come of it, but it's worth trying.'

Maxwell spread his hands.

'Whatever you say, Calvin,' he acquiesced. 'After the jolt you've given me tonight, I can only get into the harness and pull when you give the word.'

'All right. We'll take Tarbell for a guide. Tarbell, you know your way around in the shops pretty well, don't you?'

'I reckon so,' was the young man's reply.

'We want to go to the foundry, or to some place near by where we can keep an eye on the pickle shed. Can you get us there without arousing curiosity?'

'Sure,' said Tarbell.

'Good. Pitch out,' was the curt command, and the four of them left the hotel to make a circuit through ill-lit streets and around the lower end of the eastern railroad yard to come at the long line of shop buildings from the rear.

On the way Maxwell enquired curiously: 'What do you know about pickling-sheds, Calvin?'

'I know that every well-regulated foundry has one where

castings which are to be machined are treated with acid to take the hard sand-scale off.'

'And why, just why, are you anxious to get a near-hand view of ours, at this time of night?'

'I'm hoping we shall find the answer to that in your foundry yard, Dick. If we don't, the joke will be on me.'

The approach to the locomotive-repairing section of the railroad plant was made through a riverbank yard littered with slag dumps, piled flasks, and heaps of scrap iron. There was no moon, and when they got among the lumber sheds in the rear of the car-shops the darkness was almost tangible. But Tarbell knew the ground, and when he finally called a halt the twin cupola stacks of the foundry loomed before them in the darkness and the acrid smell of the warm, moist moulding sand was in the air.

When the pickling-shed had been located for him, Sprague chose the waiting-place under a flask shelter directly opposite and the silent watch began. For a weary half-hour nothing happened. Though the month was August, a cool wind crept down from the Timanyoni snow peaks, and the splash and gurgle of the nearby river added its suggestion of chill to the moonless night. Over in the western yards the night crew was making up the midnight freights; but with the buildings of the plant intervening, the noises of the shifter's exhaust and the clankings and crashings of the shunted cars came faintly to the ears of the watchers.

On the even hour of one the watchman made his round. They could see his lantern twinkling through the windows of the shops, and later he made a circuit of the outbuildings. His route led him finally through the foundry, and as he came out the light of his lantern fell upon the piled castings and the pickling-troughs, and on the carboys of vitriol. There were four of the boxed acid-holders standing under the shed. Sprague drew down his left cuff and made pencil marks on it in the darkness when the watchman passed on.

It was possibly fifteen minutes after the watchman had disappeared when Maxwell broke the strained silence with a whisper.

'Duck!' he said to Starbuck, who was standing up. 'Dunkell's coming back – without his lantern!'

Sprague spread his arms and crushed the other three back into the shadows. 'It isn't the watchman this time – be ready!' he whispered; and as he said it the figure of a man appeared coming down the littered roadway from the blacksmith shop.

Though he walked in darkness there was no incertitude about the man's movements. Turning abruptly out of the material-road he went straight to the foundry shed. A moment later a beam of white light played steadily upon the acid carboys, a sheltered beam which seemed to come from a tiny electric searchlight. Plainly they saw a pair of hands place a large bottle on the ground, remove the stopper, and fix a tin funnel in the neck. Then one of the carboys was tilted, presumably by the same pair of hands, though the hands were invisible now, and a thin stream of the yellow acid gurgled through the funnel.

When the bottle was filled the carboy slowly righted itself; the hands came in view again to remove the funnel and to replace the stopper; and then the searchlight went out with the faint snap of an electric switch. Almost at the same instant the watchers saw the figure of the man fading away into the inner and darker blackness of the foundry.

'We've got to follow him, Tarbell,' said Sprague, hurriedly; 'and we lose out if he discovers us. Can you pilot us?'

'I can,' asserted Maxwell, and under the superintendent's lead the shadow race was begun.

Happily, there was a noisy diversion to make the secret pursuit feasible. The train-making clamour had come down from the western yards, and for the moment the yard crew was working on the freight-house tracks opposite the shops. Under cover of the outdoor clamour the four pursuers were able to close up on the bottle-carrier until they were treading almost in his footsteps. The route led through the foundry floor to the machine shop. On the erecting pits were two locomotives, apparently ready to be hauled out and put into service after their period of back-shop repairs.

Into the cab of one of the engines the bottle-bearer climbed, first placing his burden carefully in the gangway. A little later they heard him climbing over the coal in the tender, heard him remove the cover of the water manhole, and heard the glug-glug of liquid issuing from a bottleneck.

Sprague silently drew a small square object from his pocket, the little flat black box he had caught up as he was leaving his office in the Kinzie Building. Then he whispered to Tarbell: 'Cover him, Archer, and don't hesitate to shoot if you need to: ready!' At the word there was a blinding burst of illumination and the report of a flashlight cartridge, followed instantly by the crash of the breaking bottle, silence, and black darkness. Then Sprague's mellow voice boomed into the stillness.

'Come down, Mr Bascom. We've got your picture, and a man who doesn't often miss what he shoots at is covering you with his gun.'

It was a grim little group of five which gathered in the master mechanic's room in the office wing of the machine shop a few minutes after the flashlight photograph had been taken in the erecting shop. Bascom's ruddy flush was gone when he sat down heavily in his desk chair; but his natty brown crush hat was pushed back, and the gleam in his small, lynx-like eyes was not of fear.

'Just name the kind of a hand-spring you'd like to have me turn, gentlemen,' he said, half-sardonically, when Tarbell had switched on the second circuit of incandescents. 'I'm not much of an acrobat, but I'll do the best I can to amuse you.'

It was Sprague who did the talking for the prosecution.

'We want to know first who is with you in this job of inside worm-eating, Mr Bascom,' he said coolly.

'Nobody,' came the prompt lie.

Sprague's smile was affable. 'I'm sure you'll make one exception,' he urged; 'a man named Murtagh, who was for a little time one of your shop machinists and who is now a press-repairer on *The Times-Record*.'

Bascom sat up and swore a savage oath.

'So that damned scab has welshed, has he?' he grated.

Sprague branched off and began again, this time in the straitly criminal field.

'How many locomotives have you treated with the acid cure, first and last, Mr Bascom?'

'Enough so you'll still be resetting flues in 'em a year from now.'

This time it was Maxwell's turn to swear, and for a minute or two the air of the office was sulphurous. When the atmosphere had cleared again, Sprague went on.

'I presume that your defence in court will be that you were

trying an experiment to neutralise the effect of the alkaline water of this region?'

Bascom grinned appreciatively. 'You're an expert chemist yourself, Mr Sprague. The water in this country, outside of the Park, *is* pretty badly alkaline, as you probably know.'

'But that defence will scarcely explain why you put acid in the oil which is used for lubricating the internal parts of the engines – cylinders and valves,' Sprague cut in quietly.

The master mechanic's chair righted itself with a crash, and the crash punctuated another blast of bad language directed at the man who had been left crouching in the corner in Sprague's uptown laboratory.

'So Murtagh gave you that, too, did he?' Bascom finished. 'It's your lead, Mr Sprague; what do you want me to play?'

'Names,' said the expert curtly.

'But if I say I was playing a lone hand?'

'We should know you were lying. This acid business may be all your own; but there are other things. You've had plenty of help in the drink-fest and the demoralisation game, Bascom.'

The big master mechanic's lips shut like the jaws of a steel trap. But after a time he said: 'What do I get if I spout on the others?'

'A chance to get out of the country – eh, Maxwell?'

The superintendent nodded. 'Yes; if he can get away before

I can find a gun to kill him with.'

Bascom reached into his desk, found a scratch-pad and tossed it over to Starbuck. 'Take 'em down,' he said briefly; and then followed a blacklist that was simply heartbreaking to Richard Maxwell, a man who had built his reputation as a railroad executive, and would have staked it instantly, upon the loyalty of his rank and file. Shop foremen, roundhouse bosses, bridge men, yard foremen, section bosses, a travelling engineer, a clerk here and a telegraph operator there – the list seemed endless.

When Bascom paused, Sprague began again.

'What was the plan, Bascom, as it was outlined to these others?'

The master mechanic's smile showed his fine even teeth.

'To make this jerk-water railroad a little easier to work for,' he sneered. 'When we found the right kind of a man we made him believe that the discipline was keyed up too damned tight and showed him how he could loosen up a little, if he felt like it. Murtagh was barkeep' and handed out the bug-juice. That's all there was to it.'

'Not quite all,' said Sprague evenly. 'You got Murtagh his job on *The Times-Record* in order to have him handy without being too much in the way or too much in evidence. How much do the *Times-Record* people know about the scheme for smashing the Nevada Short Line securities from the inside?'

Bascom laughed hardily.

'You'll never catch a newspaper man,' he said. 'But I'll tell you this: Parker Higginson is a pretty smooth politician, and he's got a mighty long arm when it comes to reaching for the thing he wants. He was the man who got me my job here, and I'll bet those New York people who appointed me don't know yet why they did it. Another thing: when I'm gone, Higginson will still be here – don't you forget that!'

'We'll try to remember it,' Sprague promised. Then he looked at his watch. 'The overland passenger, westbound, will be here in a few minutes, and when it goes, you may go with it, Mr Bascom. But first we want a few more names, the names of the New York people who are behind both you and Mr Higginson.'

Bascom got up, went to a wardrobe in one corner of the office, and dragged out two heavy suitcases.

'I've been fixed for this for some little time,' he volunteered. 'Send Murtagh to the stone-pile for splitting on us, and I won't make any claim for the half-month's salary that's due me. As to the names of the big fellows, I only wish I knew them, Mr Sprague. If I did, I'd go east instead of west and make somebody come across with big money. As it is, I guess it's South America for mine. Good night, all. I wish you luck with the booze-fighters, Mr Maxwell. You'll have a bully good time loading some of them back on to the water-automobile.' And he went out into the night with a suitcase in either hand.

'Talk about cold gall!' said Starbuck, when the door closed behind the retreating figure of the big master mechanic; 'Great Cat! That fellow's got enough to swim in.' Then he turned to Sprague. 'Is the show over?'

The man from Washington laughed genially.

'That is for Maxwell to say. We might go uptown and give those newspaper people a bad quarter of an hour, though I doubt if we'd make any money at it.'

Maxwell looked up quickly.

'You think they're in it, Calvin? Bascom wasn't lying about that part of it?'

'Yes; they are in it up to their necks. I suppose it's politics for Higginson. Haven't I heard somewhere that he is one of the State bosses?'

'You might have,' drawled Starbuck. 'He's It, all right.'

Sprague stood up, and yawned sleepily.

'Perhaps, a little later on, we can throw a scare into this Mr Parker Higginson,' he suggested. 'Just now, I'm for the hotel and a few winks of much-needed sleep. Tarbell, you go up to my office and get Murtagh. Have him locked up on a charge of – oh, any old charge will do; breaking into my office tonight, if you can't think of anything better. If we can manage to hold on to him for a while, we may be able to keep this Mr Higginson quiet while Maxwell is straightening out his booze-fighters. Let's go.'

'Hold on, just a minute,' pleaded Maxwell. 'There are three of us here who have seen the wheels go round, and I don't forget that I was the one who said there weren't any wheels. How in the name of all that is wonderful have you been able to work this puzzle out in less than twelve hours, Sprague?'

The big chemistry expert sat down again and locked his hands behind his head.

'My gosh!' he said; 'have I got to open up a kindergarten for you fellows when I'm so sleepy that I don't know what I'm going to have for breakfast tomorrow morning? It was easy, dead easy. Half an hour with those delayed train crews at Angels this morning showed me that the discipline strings were all off; one of the freight conductors even offered me a nip out of his pocket-flask when I intimated that I was thirsty. With that for a pointer, I had my eyes open at the wreck, and what I saw there you all know. Moreover, I noticed that the pocket-flasks were all alike, as if they'd all been handed out over the same bar. All straight, so far?'

'Go on,' said Maxwell.

'I got my first pointer on Bascom at the wreck, too. I saw that the men in the trainmaster's gang didn't drink when the boss was looking, a condition which didn't apply in the other crew. Again, I noticed that Bascom took his track-clearing privilege with a large and handsome disregard for the salvage. He didn't care how much property was destroyed in the process, and once I saw him give the signal to the crane engineer to drop a car loaded with automobiles – which was promptly done and the autos properly smashed.'

'The cold-blooded devil!' growled the superintendent.

'When we reached town, Tarbell here promptly confirmed my guess about the whiskey; and in the evening Calmaine helped some more by going with me over the payrolls for new names, and over the cost-sheets for increases. Naturally, we dwelt longest upon the motive-power and repair department, with its huge increases, and it so happened that my eye fell upon the various charges for vitriol in carboys. I asked Calmaine what use a railroad shop had for so much sulphuric acid, and he told me it was used to pickle castings. Afterward I sent Tarbell out to bring me samples of water from the tanks of the crippled locomotives on the shop-track and of the oil in their cylinder-cups. Analyses of both, which I made on the spot, showed the presence of sulphuric acid in the water, and also in the oil.'

'Still, you didn't have any cinch on Bascom,' Starbuck put in.

'No, but things were leaning pretty heavily his way. Tarbell had traced Murtagh for me and had found out the one thing that I needed to know; namely, that Murtagh had been "placed" on *The Times-Record* by Bascom's recommendation. Murtagh was the man who put the threatening note under my door; the note was printed on a scrap of scratch-paper – copy paper – of the sort that you rarely find outside of a newspaper office. Here I simply put two and two together. Bascom had been conferring with Higginson, or his editor, or both of them, and telling them of my rubber-necking at the wreck. They had agreed among themselves that I'd better be warned off the grass, and they took about the stupidest possible way they could think of to do it.'

'Still, you didn't have Bascom,' reiterated Starbuck.

'No; but he was the man who had been signing the requisitions for the big purchases of acid, and I was far enough along to chance a jump at him. I knew that if he were the man who was poisoning the locomotives, he wasn't trusting anybody else; he was doing it himself, often and by littles. I wasn't at all sure of catching him tonight, of course; but we saw him down here at the fire, and I thought there was an even chance that he might stay and do a little more devilment.'

Maxwell stood up and shook himself into his coat.

'I'm on to you now, Sprague,' he chuckled, in a brave attempt to jolly himself out of the depressive nightmare which had been weighing him down for weeks. 'You're a guesser –

a bold, bad four-flusher, with a perfectly miraculous knack of drawing the other card you need when you reach for it. Now, if you could only guess me out some way in which I can straighten up these poor fellows of mine who have been pulled neck and heels off of the water-wagon—'

'Pshaw! That's a cinch,' said the big man, yawning sleepily again. 'We'll just put our heads together and get out a little circular letter, talking to the boys just as you'd talk to a bunch of them in your office. Tell 'em it's all off, and the bar is closed and padlocked, and you'll have 'em all eating out of your hand again, same as they used to. You don't believe it can be done? You let me write the letter and I'll show you. All you have to do is to apply the scientific principle; surround the whole subject and look at it calmly and dispassionately, and – ye-ow! Say, I'm going to chance another guess – the last in the box. If you don't head me over to the hotel and my room, you'll have to carry me over and put me to bed. And that's no joke, with a man of my size. Let's go.'

THE KNIGHT'S CROSS SIGNAL PROBLEM

ERNEST BRAMAH

'Louis,' exclaimed Mr Carrados, with the air of genial gaiety that Carlyle had found so incongruous to his conception of a blind man, 'you have a mystery somewhere about you! I know it by your step.'

Nearly a month had passed since the incident of the false Dionysius had led to the two men meeting. It was now December. Whatever Mr Carlyle's step might indicate to the inner eye it betokened to the casual observer the manner of a crisp, alert, self-possessed man of business. Carlyle, in truth, betrayed nothing of the pessimism and despondency that had marked him on the earlier occasion.

'You have only yourself to thank that it is a very poor one,' he retorted. 'If you hadn't held me to a hasty promise—'

'To give me an option on the next case that baffled you, no matter what it was—'

'Just so. The consequence is that you get a very unsatisfactory affair that has no special interest to an amateur and is only baffling because it is – well—'

'Well, baffling?'

'Exactly, Max. Your would-be jest has discovered the proverbial truth. I need hardly tell you that it is only the insoluble that is finally baffling and this is very probably insoluble. You remember the awful smash on the Central and Suburban at Knight's Cross station a few weeks ago?'

'Yes,' replied Carrados, with interest. 'I read the whole ghastly details at the time.'

'You read?' exclaimed his friend suspiciously.

'I still use the familiar phrases,' explained Carrados, with a smile. 'As a matter of fact, my secretary reads to me. I mark what I want to hear and when he comes at ten o'clock we clear off the morning papers in no time.'

'And how do you know what to mark?' demanded Mr Carlyle cunningly.

Carrados's right hand, lying idly on the table, moved to a newspaper near. He ran his finger along a column heading, his eyes still turned towards his visitor.

' "The Money Market. Continued from page two. British Railways",' he announced.

'Extraordinary,' murmured Carlyle.

'Not very,' said Carrados. 'If someone dipped a stick in treacle and wrote "Rats" across a marble slab you would probably be able to distinguish what was there, blindfold.'

'Probably,' admitted Mr Carlyle. 'At all events we will not test the experiment.'

'The difference to you of treacle on a marble background is scarcely greater than that of printers' ink on newspaper to me. But anything smaller than pica I do not read with comfort, and below long primer I cannot read at all. Hence the secretary. Now the accident, Louis.'

'The accident: well, you remember all about that. An ordinary Central and Suburban passenger train, non-stop at Knight's Cross, ran past the signal and crashed into a crowded electric train that was just beginning to move out. It was like sending a garden roller down a row of handlights. Two carriages of the electric train were flattened out of existence; the next two were broken up. For the first time on an English railway there was a good stand-up smash between a heavy steam engine and a train of light cars, and it was "bad for the coo".'

'Twenty-seven killed, forty something injured, eight died since,' commented Carrados.

'That was bad for the Co.,' said Carlyle. 'Well, the main fact was plain enough. The heavy train was in the wrong. But was the engine-driver responsible? He claimed, and he claimed vehemently from the first and he never varied one iota, that he had a "clear" signal – that is to say, the green light, it being dark. The signalman concerned was equally dogged that he never pulled off the signal – that it was at "danger" when the accident happened and that it had been for five minutes before. Obviously, they could not both be right.'

'Why, Louis?' asked Mr Carrados smoothly.

'The signal must either have been up or down – red or green.'

'Did you ever notice the signals on the Great Northern Railway, Louis?'

'Not particularly. Why?'

'One wintery day, about the year when you and I were concerned in being born, the engine driver of a Scotch express received the "clear" from a signal near a little Huntingdon station called Abbots Ripton. He went on and crashed into a goods train and into the thick of the smash a down express mowed its way. Thirteen killed and the usual tale of injured. He was positive that the signal gave him a "clear"; the signalman was equally confident that he had never pulled it off the "danger". Both were right, and yet the signal was in working order. As I said, it was a wintery day; it had been snowing hard and the snow froze and accumulated on the upper edge of the signal arm until its weight bore it down. That is a fact that no fiction writer dare have invented, but to this day every signal on the Great Northern pivots from the centre of the arm instead of from the end, in memory of that snowstorm.'

'That came out at the inquest, I presume?' said Mr Carlyle. 'We have had the Board of Trade inquiry and the inquest here and no explanation is forthcoming. Everything was in perfect order. It rests between the word of the signalman and the word of the engine driver – not a jot of direct evidence either way. Which is right?'

'That is what you are going to find out, Louis?' suggested Carrados.

'It is what I am being paid for finding out,' admitted Mr Carlyle frankly. 'But so far we are just where the inquest left it, and, between ourselves, I candidly can't see an inch in front of my face in the matter.'

'Nor can I,' said the blind man, with a rather wry smile. 'Never mind. The engine driver is your client, of course?'

'Yes,' admitted Carlyle. 'But how the deuce did you know?'

'Let us say that your sympathies are enlisted on his behalf. The jury were inclined to exonerate the signalman, weren't they? What has the company done with your man?'

'Both are suspended. Hutchins, the driver, hears that he may probably be given charge of a lavatory at one of the stations. He is a decent, bluff, short-spoken old chap, with his heart in his work. Just now you'll find him at his worst

– bitter and suspicious. The thought of swabbing down a lavatory and taking pennies all day is poisoning him.'

'Naturally. Well, there we have honest Hutchins: taciturn, a little touchy perhaps, grown grey in the service of the company, and manifesting quite a bulldog-like devotion to his favourite 538.'

'Why, that actually was the number of his engine – how do you know it?' demanded Carlyle sharply.

'It was mentioned two or three times at the inquest, Louis,' replied Carrados mildly.

'And you remembered – with no reason to?'

'You can generally trust a blind man's memory; especially if he has taken the trouble to develop it.'

'Then you will remember that Hutchins did not make a very good impression at the time. He was surly and irritable under the ordeal. I want you to see the case from all sides.'

'He called the signalman – Mead – a "lying young dog", across the room, I believe. Now, Mead, what is he like? You have seen him, of course?'

'Yes. He does not impress me favourably. He is glib, ingratiating, and distinctly "greasy". He has a ready answer for everything almost before the question is out of your mouth. He has thought of everything.'

'And now you are going to tell me something, Louis,' said Carrados encouragingly.

Mr Carlyle laughed a little to cover an involuntary movement of surprise.

'There is a suggestive line that was not touched at the inquiries,' he admitted. 'Hutchins has been a saving man all his life, and he has received good wages. Among his class he is regarded as wealthy. I daresay that he has five hundred pounds in the bank. He is a widower with one daughter, a very nice-mannered girl of about twenty. Mead is a young man, and he and the girl are sweethearts – have been informally engaged for some time. But old Hutchins would not hear of it; he seems to have taken a dislike to the signalman from the first and latterly he had forbidden him to come to his house or his daughter to speak to him.'

'Excellent, Louis,' cried Carrados in great delight. 'We shall clear your man in a, blaze of red and green lights yet and hang the glib, "greasy" signalman from his own signal-post.'

'It is a significant fact, seriously?'

'It is absolutely convincing.'

'It may have been a slip, a mental lapse on Mead's part which he discovered the moment it was too late, and then, being too cowardly to admit his fault, and having so much at stake, he took care to make detection impossible. It may have been that, but my idea is rather that probably it was neither quite pure accident nor pure design. I can imagine

Mead meanly pluming himself over the fact that the life of this man who stands in his way, and whom he must cordially dislike, lies in his power. I can imagine the idea becoming an obsession as he dwells on it. A dozen times with his hand on the lever he lets his mind explore the possibilities of a moment's defection. Then one day he puts the signal off in sheer bravado – and hastily puts it at danger again. He may have done it once or he may have done it oftener before he was caught in a fatal moment of irresolution. The chances are about even that the engine driver would be killed. In any case he would be disgraced, for it is easier on the face of it to believe that a man might run past a danger signal in absentmindedness, without noticing it, than that a man should pull off a signal and replace it without being conscious of his actions.'

'The fireman was killed. Does your theory involve the certainty of the fireman being killed, Louis?'

'No,' said Carlyle. 'The fireman is a difficulty; but looking at it from Mead's point of view – whether he has been guilty of an error or a crime – it resolves itself into this: First, the fireman may be killed. Second, he may not notice the signal at all. Third, in any case he will loyally corroborate his driver and the good old jury will discount that.'

Carrados smoked thoughtfully, his open, sightless eyes merely appearing to be set in a tranquil gaze across the room.

'It would not be an improbable explanation,' he said presently. 'Ninety-nine men out of a hundred would say: "People do not do these things." But you and I, who have in our different ways studied criminology, know that they sometimes do, or else there would be no curious crimes. What have you done on that line?'

To anyone who could see, Mr Carlyle's expression conveyed an answer.

'You are behind the scenes, Max. What was there for me to do? Still I must do something for my money. Well, I have had a very close inquiry made confidentially among the men. There might be a whisper of one of them knowing more than had come out – a man restrained by friendship, or enmity, or even grade jealousy. Nothing came of that. Then there was the remote chance that some private person had noticed the signal without attaching any importance to it then, one who would be able to identify it still by something associated with the time. I went over the line myself. Opposite the signal the line on one side is shut in by a high blank wall; on the other side are houses, but coming below the butt-end of a scullery the signal does not happen to be visible from any road or from any window.'

'My poor Louis!' said Carrados, in friendly ridicule. 'You were at the end of your tether?'

'I was,' admitted Carlyle. 'And now that you know the sort of job it is I don't suppose that you are keen on wasting your time over it.'

'That would hardly be fair, would it?' said Carrados reasonably. 'No, Louis, I will take over your honest old driver and your greasy young signalman and your fatal signal that cannot be seen from anywhere.'

'But it is an important point for you to remember, Max, that although the signal cannot be seen from the box, if the mechanism had gone wrong, or anyone tampered with the arm, the automatic indicator would at once have told Mead that the green light was showing. Oh, I have gone very thoroughly into the technical points, I assure you.'

'I must do so too,' commented Mr Carrados gravely.

'For that matter, if there is anything you want to know, I dare say that I can tell you,' suggested his visitor. 'It might save your time.'

'True,' acquiesced Carrados. 'I should like to know whether anyone belonging to the houses that bound the line there came of age or got married on the twenty-sixth of November.'

Mr Carlyle looked across curiously at his host.

'I really do not know, Max,' he replied, in his crisp, precise way. 'What on earth has that got to do with it, may I enquire?'

'The only explanation of the Pont St Lin swing-bridge disaster of '75 was the reflection of a green Bengal light on a cottage window.'

Mr Carlyle smiled his indulgence privately.

'My dear chap, you mustn't let your retentive memory of obscure happenings run away with you,' he remarked wisely. 'In nine cases out of ten the obvious explanation is the true one. The difficulty, as here, lies in proving it. Now, you would like to see these men?'

'I expect so; in any case, I will see Hutchins first.'

'Both live in Holloway. Shall I ask Hutchins to come here to see you – say tomorrow? He is doing nothing.'

'No,' replied Carrados. 'Tomorrow I must call on my brokers and my time may be filled up.'

'Quite right; you mustn't neglect your own affairs for this – experiment,' assented Carlyle.

'Besides, I should prefer to drop in on Hutchins at his own home. Now, Louis, enough of the honest old man for one night. I have a lovely thing by Eumenes that I want to show you. Today is – Tuesday. Come to dinner on Sunday and pour the vials of your ridicule on my want of success.'

'That's an amiable way of putting it,' replied Carlyle. 'All right, I will.'

Two hours later Carrados was again in his study, apparently, for a wonder, sitting idle. Sometimes he smiled to himself, and once or twice he laughed a little, but for the most part his pleasant, impassive face reflected no emotion and he sat with his useless eyes tranquilly fixed on an unseen distance. It was a fantastic caprice of the man to mock his sightlessness by a parade of light, and under the soft brilliance of a dozen electric brackets the room was as bright as day. At length he stood up and rang the bell.

'I suppose Mr Greatorex isn't still here by any chance, Parkinson?' he asked, referring to his secretary.

'I think not, sir, but I will ascertain,' replied the man.

'Never mind. Go to his room and bring me the last two files of *The Times*. Now' – when he returned – 'turn to the earliest you have there. The date?'

'November the second.'

'That will do. Find the Money Market; it will be in the Supplement. Now look down the columns until you come to British Railways.'

'I have it, sir.'

'Central and Suburban. Read the closing price and the change.'

'Central and Suburban Ordinary, 66 1/2–67 1/2, fall of an eighth. Preferred Ordinary, 81–81 1/2, no change. Deferred Ordinary 27 1/2–27 3/4, fall of a quarter. That is all, sir.'

'Now take a paper about a week on. Read the Deferred only.'

'27–27 1/4, no change.'

'Another week.'

'29 1/2–30, rise of five-eighths.'

'Another.'

'31 1/2–32 1/2, rise of one.'

'Very good. Now on Tuesday the twenty-seventh November.'

'31 7/8–32 3/4, rise of a half.'

'Yes. The next day.'

'24 1/2–23 1/2, fall of nine.'

'Quite so, Parkinson. There had been an accident, you see.'

'Yes, sir. Very unpleasant accident. Jane knows a person whose sister's young man has a cousin who had his arm torn off in it – torn off at the socket, she says, sir. It seems to bring it home to one, sir.'

'That is all. Stay – in the paper you have, look down the first money column and see if there is any reference to the Central and Suburban.'

'Yes, sir. "City and Suburbans, which after their late depression on the projected extension of the motor bus service, had been steadily creeping up on the abandonment of the scheme, and as a result of their own excellent traffic returns, suffered a heavy slump through the lamentable accident of Thursday night. The Deferred in particular at one time fell eleven points as it was felt that the possible dividend, with which rumour has of late been busy, was now out of the question." '

'Yes; that is all. Now you can take the papers back. And let it be a warning to you, Parkinson, not to invest your savings in speculative railway deferreds.'

'Yes, sir. Thank you, sir, I will endeavour to remember.' He lingered for a moment as he shook the file of papers level. 'I may say, sir, that I have my eye on a small block of cottage property at Acton. But even cottage property scarcely seems safe from legislative depredation now, sir.'

The next day Mr Carrados called on his brokers in the city. It is to be presumed that he got through his private business quicker than he expected, for after leaving Austin Friars he continued his journey to Holloway, where he found Hutchins at home and sitting morosely before his kitchen fire. Rightly assuming that his luxuriant car would involve him in a certain amount of public attention in Klondyke Street, the blind man dismissed it some distance from the house, and walked the rest of the way, guided by the almost imperceptible touch of Parkinson's arm.

'Here is a gentleman to see you, father,' explained Miss Hutchins, who had come to the door. She divined the relative positions of the two visitors at a glance.

'Then why don't you take him into the parlour?' grumbled

the ex-driver. His face was a testimonial of hard work and general sobriety but at the moment one might hazard from his voice and manner that he had been drinking earlier in the day.

'I don't think that the gentleman would be impressed by the difference between our parlour and our kitchen,' replied the girl quaintly, 'and it is warmer here.'

'What's the matter with the parlour now?' demanded her father sourly. 'It was good enough for your mother and me. It used to be good enough for you.'

'There is nothing the matter with it, nor with the kitchen either.' She turned impassively to the two who had followed her along the narrow passage. 'Will you go in, sir?'

'I don't want to see no gentleman,' cried Hutchins noisily. 'Unless' – his manner suddenly changed to one of pitiable anxiety – 'unless you're from the Company, sir, to – to—'

'No; I have come on Mr Carlyle's behalf,' replied Carrados, walking to a chair as though he moved by a kind of instinct.

Hutchins laughed his wry contempt.

'Mr Carlyle!' he reiterated; 'Mr Carlyle! Fat lot of good he's been. Why don't he *do* something for his money?'

'He has,' replied Carrados, with imperturbable good humour; 'he has sent me. Now, I want to ask you a few questions.'

'A few questions!' roared the irate man. 'Why, blast it, I have done nothing else but answer questions for a month. I didn't pay Mr Carlyle to ask me questions; I can get enough of that for nixes. Why don't you go and ask Mr Herbert Ananias Mead your few questions – then you might find out something.'

There was a slight movement by the door and Carrados knew that the girl had quietly left the room.

'You saw that, sir?' demanded the father, diverted to a new line of bitterness. 'You saw that girl – my own daughter, that I've worked for all her life?'

'No,' replied Carrados.

'The girl that's just gone out – she's my daughter,' explained Hutchins.

'I know, but I did not see her. I see nothing. I am blind.'

'Blind!' exclaimed the old fellow, sitting up in startled wonderment. 'You mean it, sir? You walk all right and you look at me as if you saw me. You're kidding surely.'

'No,' smiled Carrados. 'It's quite right.'

'Then it's a funny business, sir – you what are blind expecting to find something that those with their eyes couldn't,' ruminated Hutchins sagely.

'There are things that you can't see with your eyes, Hutchins.'

'Perhaps you are right, sir. Well, what is it you want

153

to know?'

'Light a cigar first,' said the blind man, holding out his case and waiting until the various sounds told him that his host was smoking contentedly. 'The train you were driving at the time of the accident was the six-twenty-seven from Notcliff. It stopped everywhere until it reached Lambeth Bridge, the chief London station of your line. There it became something of an express, and leaving Lambeth Bridge at seven-eleven, should not stop again until it fetched Swanstead on Thames, eleven miles out, at seven-thirty-four. Then it stopped on and off from Swanstead to Ingerfield, the terminus of that branch, which it reached at eight-five.'

Hutchins nodded, and then, remembering, said: 'That's right, sir.'

'That was your business all day – running between Notcliff and Ingerfield?'

'Yes, sir. Three journeys up and three down mostly.'

'With the same stops on all the down journeys?'

'No. The seven-eleven is the only one that does a run from the Bridge to Swanstead. You see, it is just on the close of the evening rush, as they call it. A good many late business gentlemen living at Swanstead use the seven-eleven regular. The other journeys we stop at every station to Lambeth Bridge, and then here and there beyond.'

'There are, of course, other trains doing exactly the same

journey – a service, in fact?'

'Yes, sir. About six.'

'And do any of those – say, during the rush – do any of those run non-stop from Lambeth to Swanstead?'

Hutchins reflected a moment. All the choler and restlessness had melted out of the man's face. He was again the excellent artisan, slow but capable and self-reliant.

'That I couldn't definitely say, sir. Very few short-distance trains pass the junction, but some of those may. A guide would show us in a minute but I haven't got one.'

'Never mind. You said at the inquest that it was no uncommon thing for you to be pulled up at the "stop" signal east of Knight's Cross station. How often would that happen – only with the seven-eleven, mind.'

'Perhaps three times a week; perhaps twice.'

'The accident was on a Thursday. Have you noticed that you were pulled up oftener on a Thursday than on any other day?'

A smile crossed the driver's face at the question.

'You don't happen to live at Swanstead yourself, sir?' he asked in reply.

'No,' admitted Carrados. 'Why?'

'Well, sir, we were *always* pulled up on Thursday; practically always, you may say. It got to be quite a saying among those who used the train regular; they used to look out for it.'

Carrados's sightless eyes had the one quality of concealing emotion supremely. 'Oh,' he commented softly, 'always; and it was quite a saying, was it? And *why* was it always so on Thursday?'

'It had to do with the early closing, I'm told. The suburban traffic was a bit different. By rights we ought to have been set back two minutes for that day, but I suppose it wasn't thought worth while to alter us in the timetable, so we most always had to wait outside Three Deep tunnel for a westbound electric to make good.'

'You were prepared for it then?'

'Yes, sir, I was,' said Hutchins, reddening at some recollection, 'and very down about it was one of the jury over that. But, mayhap once in three months, I did get through even on a Thursday, and it's not for me to question whether things are right or wrong just because they are not what I may expect. The signals are my orders, sir – stop! go on! and it's for me to obey, as you would a general on the field of battle. What would happen otherwise! It was nonsense what they said about going cautious; and the man who started it was a barber who didn't know the difference between a "distance" and a "stop" signal down to the minute they gave their verdict. My orders, sir, given me by that signal, was "Go right ahead and keep to your running time!" '

Carrados nodded a soothing assent. 'That is all, I think,'

he remarked.

'All!' exclaimed Hutchins in surprise. 'Why, sir, you can't have got much idea of it yet.'

'Quite enough. And I know it isn't pleasant for you to be taken along the same ground over and over again.'

The man moved awkwardly in his chair and pulled nervously at his grizzled beard.

'You mustn't take any notice of what I said just now, sir,' he apologised. 'You somehow make me feel that something may come of it; but I've been badgered about and accused and cross-examined from one to another of them these weeks till it's fairly made me bitter against everything. And now they talk of putting me in a lavatory – me that has been with the company for five and forty years and on the footplate thirty-two – a man suspected of running past a danger signal.'

'You have had a rough time, Hutchins; you will have to exercise your patience a little longer yet,' said Carrados sympathetically.

'You think something may come of it, sir? You think you will be able to clear me? Believe me, sir, if you could give me something to look forward to it might save me from—' He pulled himself up and shook his head sorrowfully. 'I've been near it,' he added simply.

Carrados reflected and took his resolution.

'Today is Wednesday. I think you may hope to hear

something from your general manager towards the middle of next week.'

'Good God, sir! You really mean that?'

'In the interval show your good sense by behaving reasonably. Keep civilly to yourself and don't talk. Above all' – he nodded towards a quart jug that stood on the table between them, an incident that filled the simple-minded engineer with boundless wonder when he recalled it afterwards – 'above all, leave that alone.'

Hutchins snatched up the vessel and brought it crashing down on the hearthstone, his face shining with a set resolution.

'I've done with it, sir. It was the bitterness and despair that drove me to that. Now I can do without it.'

The door was hastily opened and Miss Hutchins looked anxiously from her father to the visitors and back again.

'Oh, whatever is the matter?' she exclaimed. 'I heard a great crash.'

'This gentleman is going to clear me, Meg, my dear,' blurted out the old man irrepressibly. 'And I've done with the drink for ever.'

'Hutchins! Hutchins!' said Carrados warningly.

'My daughter, sir; you wouldn't have her not know?' pleaded Hutchins, rather crestfallen. 'It won't go any further.'

Carrados laughed quietly to himself as he felt Margaret

Hutchins's startled and questioning eyes attempting to read his mind. He shook hands with the engine driver without further comment, however, and walked out into the commonplace little street under Parkinson's unobtrusive guidance.

'Very nice of Miss Hutchins to go into half-mourning, Parkinson,' he remarked as they went along. 'Thoughtful, and yet not ostentatious.'

'Yes, sir,' agreed Parkinson, who had long ceased to wonder at his master's perceptions.

'The Romans, Parkinson, had a saying to the effect that gold carries no smell. That is a pity sometimes. What jewellery did Miss Hutchins wear?'

'Very little, sir. A plain gold brooch representing a merry-thought – the merry-thought of a sparrow, I should say, sir. The only other article was a smooth-backed gun-metal watch, suspended from a gun-metal bow.'

'Nothing showy or expensive, eh?'

'Oh dear no, sir. Quite appropriate for a young person of her position.'

'Just what I should have expected.' He slackened his pace. 'We are passing a hoarding, are we not?'

'Yes, sir.'

'We will stand here a moment. Read me the letter-press of the poster before us.'

'This "Oxo" one, sir?'

'Yes.'

' "Oxo", sir.'

Carrados was convulsed with silent laughter. Parkinson had infinitely more dignity and conceded merely a tolerant recognition of the ludicrous.

'That was a bad shot, Parkinson,' remarked his master when he could speak. 'We will try another.'

For three minutes, with scrupulous conscientiousness on the part of the reader and every appearance of keen interest on the part of the hearer, there were set forth the particulars of a sale by auction of superfluous timber and builders' material.

'That will do,' said Carrados, when the last detail had been reached. 'We can be seen from the door of No. 107 still?'

'Yes, sir.'

'No indication of anyone coming to us from there?'

'No, sir.'

Carrados walked thoughtfully on again. In the Holloway Road they rejoined the waiting motor car. 'Lambeth Bridge station,' was the order the driver received.

From the station the car was sent on home and Parkinson was instructed to take two first-class singles for Richmond, which could be reached by changing at Stafford Road. The 'evening rush' had not yet commenced and they had no difficulty in finding an empty carriage when the train came in.

Parkinson was kept busy that journey describing what he saw at various points between Lambeth Bridge and Knight's Cross. For a quarter of a mile Carrados's demands on the eyes and the memory of his remarkable servant were wide and incessant. Then his questions ceased. They had passed the 'stop' signal, east of Knight's Cross station.

The following afternoon they made the return journey as far as Knight's Cross. This time, however, the surroundings failed to interest Carrados. 'We are going to look at some rooms,' was the information he offered on the subject, and an imperturbable 'Yes, sir' had been the extent of Parkinson's comment on the unusual proceeding. After leaving the station they turned sharply along a road that ran parallel with the line, a dull thoroughfare of substantial, elderly houses that were beginning to sink into decrepitude. Here and there a corner residence displayed the brass plate of a professional occupant, but for the most part they were given up to the various branches of second-rate apartment letting.

'The third house after the one with the flagstaff,' said Carrados.

Parkinson rang the bell, which was answered by a young servant, who took an early opportunity of assuring them that she was not tidy as it was rather early in the afternoon.

She informed Carrados, in reply to his enquiry, that Miss Chubb was at home, and showed them into a melancholy little sitting-room to await her appearance.

'I shall be "almost" blind here, Parkinson,' remarked Carrados, walking about the room. 'It saves explanation.'

'Very good, sir,' replied Parkinson.

Five minutes later, an interval suggesting that Miss Chubb also found it rather early in the afternoon, Carrados was arranging to take rooms for his attendant and himself for the short time that he would be in London, seeing an oculist.

'One bedroom, mine, must face north,' he stipulated. 'It has to do with the light.'

Miss Chubb replied that she quite understood. Some gentlemen, she added, had their requirements, others their fancies. She endeavoured to suit all. The bedroom she had in view from the first *did* face north. She would not have known, only the last gentleman, curiously enough, had made the same request.

'A sufferer like myself?' enquired Carrados affably.

Miss Chubb did not think so. In his case she regarded it merely as a fancy. She had had to turn out of her own room to accommodate him, but if one kept an apartment-house one had to be adaptable; and Mr Ghoosh was certainly very liberal in his ideas.

'Ghoosh? An Indian gentleman, I presume?'

hazarded Carrados.

It appeared that Mr Ghoosh was an Indian. Miss Chubb confided that at first she had been rather perturbed at the idea of taking in 'a black man', as she confessed to regarding him. She reiterated, however, that Mr Ghoosh proved to be 'quite the gentleman'. Five minutes of affability put Carrados in full possession of Mr Ghoosh's manner of life and movements – the dates of his arrival and departure, his solitariness and his daily habits.

'This would be the best bedroom,' said Miss Chubb.

It was a fair-sized room on the first floor. The window looked out on to the roof of an outbuilding; beyond, the deep cutting of the railway line. Opposite stood the dead wall that Mr Carlyle had spoken of.

Carrados 'looked' round the room with the discriminating glance that sometimes proved so embarrassing to those who knew him.

'I have to take a little daily exercise,' he remarked, walking to the window and running his hand up the woodwork. 'You will not mind my fixing a "developer" here, Miss Chubb – a few small screws?'

Miss Chubb thought not. Then she was sure not. Finally she ridiculed the idea of minding with scorn.

'If there is width enough,' mused Carrados, spanning the upright critically. 'Do you happen to have a wooden foot-rule convenient?'

'Well, to be sure!' exclaimed Miss Chubb, opening a rapid succession of drawers until she produced the required article. 'When we did out this room after Mr Ghoosh, there was this very ruler among the things that he hadn't thought worth taking. This is what you require, sir?'

'Yes,' replied Carrados, accepting it, 'I think this is exactly what I require.' It was a common new whitewood rule, such as one might buy at any small stationer's for a penny. He carelessly took off the width of the upright, reading the figures with a touch; and then continued to run a finger-tip delicately up and down the edges of the instrument.

'Four and seven-eighths,' was his unspoken conclusion.

'I hope it will do, sir.'

'Admirably,' replied Carrados. 'But I haven't reached the end of my requirements yet, Miss Chubb.'

'No, sir?' said the landlady, feeling that it would be a pleasure to oblige so agreeable a gentleman. 'What else might there be?'

'Although I can see very little I like to have a light, but not any kind of light. Gas I cannot do with. Do you think that you would be able to find me an oil lamp?'

'Certainly, sir. I got out a very nice brass lamp that I have specially for Mr Ghoosh. He read a good deal of an evening and he preferred a lamp.'

'That is very convenient. I suppose it is large enough to burn for a whole evening?'

'Yes, indeed. And very particular he was always to have it filled every day.'

'A lamp without oil is not very useful,' smiled Carrados, following her towards another room, and absentmindedly slipping the foot-rule into his pocket.

Whatever Parkinson thought of the arrangement of going into second-rate apartments in an obscure street it is to be inferred that his devotion to his master was sufficient to overcome his private emotions as a self-respecting 'man'. At all events, as they were approaching the station he asked, and without a trace of feeling, whether there were any orders for him with reference to the proposed migration.

'None, Parkinson,' replied his master. 'We must be satisfied with our present quarters.'

'I beg your pardon, sir,' said Parkinson, with some constraint. 'I understood that you had taken the rooms for a week certain.'

'I am afraid that Miss Chubb will be under the same impression. Unforeseen circumstances will prevent our going, however. Mr Greatorex must write tomorrow, enclosing a cheque, with my regrets, and adding a penny for this ruler which I seem to have brought away with me. It, at least, is something for the money.'

Parkinson may be excused for not attempting to understand the course of events.

'Here is your train coming in, sir,' he merely said.

'We will let it go and wait for another. Is there a signal at either end of the platform?'

'Yes, sir; at the further end.'

'Let us walk towards it. Are there any of the porters or officials about here?'

'No, sir; none.'

'Take this ruler. I want you to go up the steps – there are steps up the signal, by the way?'

'Yes, sir.'

'I want you to measure the glass of the lamp. Do not go up any higher than is necessary, but if you have to stretch be careful not to mark off the measurement with your nail, although the impulse is a natural one. That has been done already.'

Parkinson looked apprehensively around and about. Fortunately the part was a dark and unfrequented spot and everyone else was moving towards the exit at the other end of the platform. Fortunately, also, the signal was not a high one.

'As near as I can judge on the rounded surface, the glass is four and seven-eighths across,' reported Parkinson.

'Thank you,' replied Carrados, returning the measure to

his pocket, 'four and seven-eighths is quite near enough. Now we will take the next train back.'

Sunday evening came, and with it Mr Carlyle to The Turrets at the appointed hour. He brought to the situation a mind poised for any eventuality and a trenchant eye. As the time went on and the impenetrable Carrados made no allusion to the case, Carlyle's manner inclined to a waggish commiseration of his host's position. Actually, he said little, but the crisp precision of his voice when the path lay open to a remark of any significance left little to be said.

It was not until they had finished dinner and returned to the library that Carrados gave the slightest hint of anything unusual being in the air. His first indication of coming events was to remove the key from the outside to the inside of the door.

'What are you doing, Max?' demanded Mr Carlyle, his curiosity overcoming the indirect attitude.

'You have been very entertaining, Louis,' replied his friend, 'but Parkinson should be back very soon now and it is as well to be prepared. Do you happen to carry a revolver?'

'Not when I come to dine with you, Max,' replied Carlyle, with all the aplomb he could muster. 'Is it unusual?'

Carrados smiled affectionately at his guest's agile recovery and touched the secret spring of a drawer in an antique bureau by his side. The little hidden receptacle shot smoothly out, disclosing a pair of dull-blued pistols.

'Tonight, at all events, it might be prudent,' he replied, handing one to Carlyle and putting the other into his own pocket. 'Our man may be here at any minute, and we do not know in what temper he will come.'

'Our man!' exclaimed Carlyle, craning forward in excitement. 'Max! you don't mean to say that you have got Mead to admit it?'

'No one has admitted it,' said Carrados. 'And it is not Mead.'

'Not Mead . . . Do you mean that Hutchins—?'

'Neither Mead nor Hutchins. The man who tampered with the signal – for Hutchins was right and a green light *was* exhibited – is a young Indian from Bengal. His name is Drishna and he lives at Swanstead.'

Mr Carlyle stared at his friend between sheer surprise and blank incredulity.

'You really mean this, Carrados?' he said.

'My fatal reputation for humour!' smiled Carrados. 'If I am wrong, Louis, the next hour will expose it.'

'But why – why – why? The colossal villainy, the unparalleled audacity!' Mr Carlyle lost himself among incredulous superlatives and could only stare.

'Chiefly to get himself out of a disastrous speculation,' replied Carrados, answering the question. 'If there was another motive – or at least an incentive – which I suspect, doubtless we shall hear of it.'

'All the same, Max, I don't think that you have treated me quite fairly,' protested Carlyle, getting over his first surprise and passing to a sense of injury. 'Here we are and I know nothing, absolutely nothing, of the whole affair.'

'We both have our ideas of pleasantry, Louis,' replied Carrados genially. 'But I dare say you are right and perhaps there is still time to atone.' In the fewest possible words he outlined the course of his investigations. 'And now you know all that is to be known until Drishna arrives.'

'But will he come?' questioned Carlyle doubtfully. 'He may be suspicious.'

'Yes, he will be suspicious.'

'Then he will not come.'

'On the contrary, Louis, he will come because my letter will make him suspicious. He *is* coming; otherwise Parkinson would have telephoned me at once and we should have had to take other measures.'

'What did you say, Max?' asked Carlyle curiously.

'I wrote that I was anxious to discuss an Indo-Scythian inscription with him, and sent my car in the hope that he would be able to oblige me.'

'But is he interested in Indo-Scythian inscriptions?'

'I haven't the faintest idea,' admitted Carrados, and Mr

Carlyle was throwing up his hands in despair when the sound of motor-car wheels softly kissing the gravel surface of the drive outside brought him to his feet.

'By gad, you are right, Max!' he exclaimed, peeping through the curtains. 'There is a man inside.'

'Mr Drishna,' announced Parkinson, a minute later.

The visitor came into the room with leisurely self-possession that might have been real or a desperate assumption. He was a slightly built young man of about twenty-five, with black hair and eyes, a small, carefully trained moustache, and a dark olive skin. His physiognomy was not displeasing, but his expression had a harsh and supercilious tinge. In attire he erred towards the immaculately spruce.

'Mr Carrados?' he said enquiringly.

Carrados, who had risen, bowed slightly without offering his hand.

'This gentleman,' he said, indicating his friend, 'is Mr Carlyle, the celebrated private detective.'

The Indian shot a very sharp glance at the object of this description. Then he sat down.

'You wrote me a letter, Mr Carrados,' he remarked, in English that scarcely betrayed any foreign origin, 'a rather curious letter, I may say. You asked me about an ancient inscription. I know nothing of antiquities; but I thought, as you had sent, that it would be more courteous if I came and explained this to you.'

'That was the object of my letter,' replied Carrados.

'You wished to see me?' said Drishna, unable to stand the ordeal of the silence that Carrados imposed after his remark.

'When you left Miss Chubb's house you left a ruler behind.' One lay on the desk by Carrados and he took it up as he spoke.

'I don't understand what you are talking about,' said Drishna guardedly. 'You are making some mistake.'

'The ruler was marked at four and seven-eighths inches – the measure of the glass of the signal lamp outside.'

The unfortunate young man was unable to repress a start. His face lost its healthy tone. Then, with a sudden impulse, he made a step forward and snatched the object from Carrados's hand.

'If it is mine I have a right to it,' he exclaimed, snapping the ruler in two and throwing it on to the back of the blazing fire. 'It is nothing.'

'Pardon me, I did not say that the one you have so impetuously disposed of was yours. As a matter of fact, it was mine. Yours is – elsewhere.'

'Wherever it is you have no right to it if it is mine,' panted Drishna, with rising excitement. 'You are a thief, Mr Carrados. I will not stay any longer here.'

He jumped up and turned towards the door. Carlyle made a step forward, but the precaution was unnecessary.

'One moment, Mr Drishna,' interposed Carrados, in his smoothest tones. 'It is a pity, after you have come so far, to leave without hearing of my investigations in the neighbourhood of Shaftesbury Avenue.'

Drishna sat down again.

'As you like,' he muttered. 'It does not interest me.'

'I wanted to obtain a lamp of a certain pattern,' continued Carrados. 'It seemed to me that the simplest explanation would be to say that I wanted it for a motorcar. Naturally I went to Long Acre. At the first shop I said: "Wasn't it here that a friend of mine, an Indian gentleman, recently had a lamp made with a green glass that was nearly five inches across?" No, it was not there but they could make me one. At the next shop the same; at the third, and fourth, and so on. Finally my persistence was rewarded. I found the place where the lamp had been made, and at the cost of ordering another I obtained all the details I wanted. It was news to them, the shopman informed me, that in some parts of India green was the danger colour and therefore tail lamps had to show a green light. The incident made some impression on him and he would be able to identify their customer – who paid in advance and gave no address – among a thousand of his countrymen. Do I succeed in interesting you, Mr Drishna?'

'Do you?' replied Drishna, with a languid yawn. 'Do I look interested?'

'You must make allowance for my unfortunate blindness,' apologised Carrados, with grim irony.

'Blindness!' exclaimed Drishna, dropping his affectation of unconcern as though electrified by the word. 'Do you mean – really blind – that you do not see me?'

'Alas, no,' admitted Carrados.

The Indian withdrew his right hand from his coat pocket and with a tragic gesture flung a heavy revolver down on the table between them.

'I have had you covered all the time, Mr Carrados, and if I had wished to go and you or your friend had raised a hand to stop me, it would have been at the peril of your lives,' he said, in a voice of melancholy triumph. 'But what is the use of defying fate, and who successfully evades his destiny? A month ago I went to see one of our people who reads the future and sought to know the course of certain events. "You need fear no human eye," was the message given to me. Then she added: "But when the sightless sees the unseen, make your peace with Yama." And I thought she spoke of the Great Hereafter!'

'This amounts to an admission of your guilt,' exclaimed Mr Carlvle practically.

'I bow to the decree of fate,' replied Drishna. 'And it is

fitting to the universal irony of existence that a blind man should be the instrument. I don't imagine, Mr Carlyle,' he added maliciously, 'that you, with your eyes, would ever have brought that result about.'

'You are a very cold-blooded young scoundrel, sir!' retorted Mr Carlyle. 'Good heavens! Do you realise that you are responsible for the death of scores of innocent men and women?'

'Do *you* realise, Mr Carlyle, that you and your government and your soldiers are responsible for the death of thousands of innocent men and women in my country every day? If England was occupied by the Germans who quartered an army and an administration with their wives and their families and all their expensive paraphernalia on the unfortunate country until the whole nation was reduced to the verge of famine, and the appointment of every new official meant the callous death sentence on a thousand men and women to pay his salary, then if you went to Berlin and wrecked a train you would be hailed a patriot. What Boadicea did and – and Samson, so have I. If they were heroes, so am I.'

'Well, upon my word!' cried the highly scandalised Carlyle, 'what next! Boadicea was a – er – semi-legendary person, whom we may possibly admire at a distance. Personally, I do not profess to express an opinion. But Samson, I would remind you, is a biblical character. Samson was mocked as an enemy. You, I do not doubt, have been entertained as a friend.'

'And haven't I been mocked and despised and sneered at every day of my life here by your supercilious, superior, empty-headed men?' flashed back Drishna, his eyes leaping into malignity and his voice trembling with sudden passion. 'Oh! how I hated them as I passed them in the street and recognised by a thousand petty insults their lordly English contempt for me as an inferior being – a nigger. How I longed with Caligula that a nation had a single neck that I might destroy it at one blow. I loathe you in your complacent hypocrisy, Mr Carlyle, despise and utterly abominate you from an eminence of superiority that you can never even understand.'

'I think we are getting rather away from the point, Mr Drishna,' interposed Carrados, with the impartiality of a judge. 'Unless I am misinformed, you are not so ungallant as to include everyone you have met here in your execration?'

'Ah, no,' admitted Drishna, descending into a quite ingenuous frankness. 'Much as I hate your men I love your women. How is it possible that a nation should be so divided – its men so dull-witted and offensive, its women so quick, sympathetic and capable of appreciating?'

'But a little expensive, too, at times?' suggested Carrados. Drishna sighed heavily.

'Yes; it is incredible. It is the generosity of their large nature. My allowance, though what most of you would call noble, has proved quite inadequate. I was compelled to borrow money and the interest became overwhelming. Bankruptcy was impracticable because I should have then been recalled by my people, and much as I detest England a certain reason made the thought of leaving it unbearable.'

'Connected with the Arcady Theatre?'

'You know? Well, do not let us introduce the lady's name. In order to restore myself I speculated on the Stock Exchange. My credit was good through my father's position and the standing of the firm to which I am attached. I heard on reliable authority, and very early, that the Central and Suburban, and the Deferred especially, was safe to fall heavily, through a motor bus amalgamation that was then a secret. I opened a bear account and sold largely. The shares fell, but only fractionally, and I waited. Then, unfortunately, they began to go up. Adverse forces were at work and rumours were put about. I could not stand the settlement, and in order to carry over an account I was literally compelled to deal temporarily with some securities that were not technically my own property.'

'Embezzlement, sir,' commented Mr Carlyle icily. 'But what is embezzlement on the top of wholesale murder!'

'That is what it is called. In my case, however, it was only to be temporary. Unfortunately, the rise continued. Then, at the height of my despair, I chanced to be returning to Swanstead rather earlier than usual one evening, and the train was stopped at a certain signal to let another pass. There was conversation in the carriage and I learned certain details. One said that there would be an accident some day, and so forth. In a flash – as by an inspiration – I saw how the circumstance might be turned to account. A bad accident and the shares would certainly fall and my position would be retrieved. I think Mr Carrados has somehow learned the rest.'

'Max,' said Mr Carlyle, with emotion, 'is there any reason why you should not send your man for a police officer and have this monster arrested on his own confession without further delay?'

'Pray do so, Mr Carrados,' acquiesced Drishna. 'I shall certainly be hanged, but the speech I shall prepare will ring from one end of India to the other; my memory will be venerated as that of a martyr; and the emancipation of my motherland will be hastened by my sacrifice.'

'In other words,' commented Carrados, 'there will be disturbances at half-a-dozen disaffected places, a few unfortunate police will be clubbed to death, and possibly worse things may happen. That does not suit us, Mr Drishna.'

'And how do you propose to prevent it?' asked Drishna, with cool assurance.

'It is very unpleasant being hanged on a dark winter morning; very cold, very friendless, very inhuman. The long trial, the solitude and the confinement, the thoughts of the long sleepless night before, the hangman and the pinioning and the noosing of the rope, are apt to prey on the imagination. Only a very stupid man can take hanging easily.'

'What do you want me to do instead, Mr Carrados?' asked Drishna shrewdly.

Carrados's hand closed on the weapon that still lay on the table between them. Without a word he pushed it across.

'I see,' commented Drishna, with a short laugh and a gleaming eye. 'Shoot myself and hush it up to suit your purpose. Withhold my message to save the exposures of a trial, and keep the flame from the torch of insurrectionary freedom.'

'Also,' interposed Carrados mildly, 'to save your worthy people a good deal of shame, and to save the lady who is nameless the unpleasant necessity of relinquishing the house and the income which you have just settled on her. She certainly would not then venerate your memory.'

'What is that?'

'The transaction which you carried through was based on

a felony and could not be upheld. The firm you dealt with will go to the courts, and the money, being directly traceable, will be held forfeit as no good consideration passed.'

'Max!' cried Mr Carlyle hotly, 'you are not going to let this scoundrel cheat the gallows after all?'

'The best use you can make of the gallows is to cheat it, Louis,' replied Carrados. 'Have you ever reflected what human beings will think of us a hundred years hence?'

'Oh, of course I'm not really in favour of hanging,' admitted Mr Carlyle.

'Nobody really is. But we go on hanging. Mr Drishna is a dangerous animal who for the sake of pacific animals must cease to exist. Let his barbarous exploit pass into oblivion with him. The disadvantages of spreading it broadcast immeasurably outweigh the benefits.'

'I have considered,' announced Drishna. 'I will do as you wish.'

'Very well,' said Carrados. 'Here is some plain note-paper. You had better write a letter to someone saying that the financial difficulties in which you are involved make life unbearable.'

'But there are no financial difficulties – now.'

'That does not matter in the least. It will be put down to an hallucination and taken as showing the state of your mind.'

'But what guarantee have we that he will not escape?' whispered Mr Carlyle.

'He cannot escape,' replied Carrados tranquilly. 'His identity is too clear.'

'I have no intention of trying to escape,' put in Drishna, as he wrote. 'You hardly imagine that I have not considered this eventuality, do you?'

'All the same,' murmured the ex-lawyer, 'I should like to have a jury behind me. It is one thing to execute a man morally; it is another to do it almost literally.'

'Is that all right?' asked Drishna, passing across the letter he had written.

Carrados smiled at this tribute to his perception.

'Quite excellent,' he replied courteously. 'There is a train at nine-forty. Will that suit you?'

Drishna nodded and stood up. Mr Carlyle had a very uneasy feeling that he ought to do something but could not suggest to himself what.

The next moment he heard his friend heartily thanking the visitor for the assistance he had been in the matter of the Indo-Scythian inscription, as they walked across the hall together. Then a door closed.

'I believe that there is something positively uncanny about Max at times,' murmured the perturbed gentleman to himself.

ONCE UPON A TRAIN

CRAIG RICE AND STUART PALMER

'It was nothing, really,' said John J. Malone with weary modesty. 'After all, I never lost a client yet.'

The party in Chicago's famed Pump Room was being held to celebrate the miraculous acquittal of Stephen Larsen, a machine politician accused of dipping some thirty thousand dollars out of the municipal till. Malone had proved to the jury and to himself that his client was innocent – at least, innocent of that particular charge.

It was going to be a nice party, the little lawyer kept telling himself. By the way Larsen's so-called friends were bending their elbows, the tab would be colossal. Malone hoped fervently that his fee for services rendered would be taken care of today, before Larsen's guests bankrupted him. Because there was the matter of two months' back office rent . . .

'Thank you, I will,' Malone said, as the waiter picked up his empty glass. He wondered how he could meet the redhead at the next table, who looked sultry and bored in the midst of a dull family party. As soon as he got his money from Larsen he would start a rescue operation. The quickest way to make friends, he always said, was to break a hundred-dollar bill in a bar, and that applied even to curvaceous redheads in Fath models.

But where *was* Steve Larsen? Lolly was here, wearing her most angelic expression and a slinky gown which she overflowed considerably at the top. She was hinting that the party also celebrated a reconciliation between herself and Stevie; that the divorce was off. She had hocked her bracelet again, and Malone remembered hearing that her last show had closed after six performances. If she got her hand back into Steve's pocket, Malone reflected, goodbye to his fee of three grand.

He'd made elaborate plans for that money. They not only included the trip to Bermuda which he'd been promising himself for twenty years, but also the redhead he'd been promising himself for twenty minutes.

Others at the table were worrying too. 'Steve is late, even for him!' spoke up Allen Roth suddenly.

Malone glanced at the porcine paving-contractor who was rumoured to be Larsen's secret partner, and murmured, 'Maybe he got his dates mixed.'

'He'd *better* show,' Roth said, in a voice as cold as a gravedigger's shovel.

The little lawyer shivered, and realised that he wasn't the only guest who had come here to make a collection. But he simply had to have that money. $3,000 – $30,000. He wondered, half-musing, if he shouldn't have made his contingent fee, say, $2,995. This way it almost looked like . . .

'What did you say about ten per cent, counsellor?' Bert Glick spoke up wisely.

Malone recovered himself. 'You misunderstood me. I merely said, "When on pleasure bent, never muzzle the ox when he treadeth out the corn." I mean rye.' He turned to look for the waiter, not solely from thirst. The little lawyer would often have been very glad to buy back his introduction to Bert Glick.

True, the city-hall hanger-on had been helpful during the trial. In fact, it had been his testimony as a prosecution witness that cinched the acquittal, for he had made a surprise switch on several moot points of the indictment. Glick was a private detective turned bail-bondsman, clever at tapping wires and dipping his spoon into any gravy that was being passed.

Glick slapped Malone on the back and said, 'If you knew what I know, you wouldn't be looking at your watch all the time. Because this ain't a coming-out party, it's a surprise party. And the surprise is that the host ain't gonna be here!'

Malone went cold – as cold as Allen Roth's grey eyes across the table. 'Keep talking,' he said, adding in a whisper a few facts which Glick might not care to have brought to the attention of the district attorney.

'You don't need to be so nasty,' Glick said. He rose suddenly to his feet, lifting his glass. 'A toast! A toast to good ol' Stevie, our pal, who's taking the Super-Century for New York tonight, next stop Paris or Rio. And with him, my fine feathered friends, he's taking the dough he owes most of us, and a lot more too. Bon voyage!' The man absorbed the contents of his glass and slowly collapsed in his chair.

There was a sudden hullaballoo around the table. Malone closed his eyes for just five seconds, resigning himself to the certainty that his worst suspicions were true. When he opened his eyes again, the redhead was gone. He looked at his watch. There was still a chance of catching that New York train, with a quick stop at Joe the Angel's bar to borrow the price of a ticket. Malone rushed out of the place, wasting no time in farewells. Everybody else was leaving too. Finally, Bert Glick was alone, alone with the waiter and with the check.

As Malone had expected, Joe the Angel took a very dim view of the project, pointing out that it was probably only throwing good money after bad. But he handed over enough for a round trip, plus Pullman. By the time his cab had dumped him at the IC station, Malone had decided to settle for one-way. He needed spending money for the trip. There were poker games on trains.

Suddenly he saw the redhead! She was jammed in a crowd at the gate, crushed between old ladies, noisy sailors, and a bearded patriarch in the robes of the Greek Orthodox Church. She struggled with a mink coat, a yowling cat in a travelling case, and a caged parrot.

Malone leapt gallantly to her rescue, and for a brief moment was allowed to hold the menagerie, before a Redcap took over. The moment was just long enough for the lawyer to have his hand clawed by the irate cat, and for him and the parrot to develop a lifelong dislike. But he did hear the girl say, 'Compartment B in Car Ten, please.' And her warm grateful smile sent him racing off in search of the Pullman conductor.

Considerable eloquence, some trifling liberties with the truth, and a ten-dollar bill got him possession of the drawing-room next to a certain compartment. That settled, he paused to make a quick deal with a roving Western Union boy, and more money changed hands. When he finally swung aboard the already-moving train, he felt fairly confident that the trip would be pleasant and eventful. And lucrative, of course. The minute he got his hands on Steve Larsen . . .

Once established in the drawing-room, Malone studied himself in the mirror, whistling a few bars of 'On the Wabash Cannonball'. For the moment the primary target could wait. He was glad he was wearing his favourite Finchley suit, and his new green and lavender Sulka tie.

'A man of distinction,' he thought. True, his hair was slightly mussed, a few cigar ashes peppered his vest, and the Sulka tie was beginning to creep toward one ear, but the total effect was good. Inspired, he sat down to compose a note to Operation Redhead, in the next compartment. He knew it was the right compartment, for the parrot was already giving out with imitations of a boiler factory, assisted by the cat.

He wrote: *Lovely lady, let's not fight Fate. We were destined to have dinner together. I am holding my breath for your eyes. Your unknown admirer, JJM.* He poked the note under the connecting door, rapped lightly, and waited.

After a long moment the note came back, with an addition in a surprisingly precise hand. *Sir, you have picked the wrong girl. Besides, I had dinner in the Pump Room over an hour ago, and so I believe did you.*

Undaunted, Malone whistled another bar of the song. Just getting any answer at all was half the battle. So she'd noticed him in the Pump Room! He sat down and wrote swiftly, *Please, an after-dinner liqueur with me, then?*

This time the answer was: *My dear sir: MY DEAR SIR!*

But the little lawyer thought he heard sounds of feminine laughter, though of course it might have been the parrot. He sat back, lit a fresh cigar, and waited. They were almost to Gary now, and if the telegram had got through . . .

It had, and a messenger finally came aboard with an armful of luscious *Gruss von Teplitz* roses. Malone intercepted him long enough to add a note which really should be the clincher. *To the Rose of Tralee, who makes all other women look like withered dandelions. I'll be waiting in the club car. Faithfully, John J. Malone.* That was the way, he told himself happily. Don't give her a chance to say No again.

After a long and somewhat bruising trip through lurching Pullman cars, made longer still because he first headed fore instead of aft, Malone finally sank into a chair in the club-car lounge, facing the door. Of course, she would take time to arrange the roses, make a corsage out of a couple of buds, and probably shift into an even more startling gown. It might be quite a wait. He waved at the bar steward and say, 'Rye, please, with a rye chaser.'

'You mean rye with a beer chaser, Mista Malone?'

'If you know my name, you know enough not to confuse me. I mean beer with a rye chaser!' When the drink arrived Malone put it where it would do the most good, and then for lack of anything better to do fell to staring in awed fascination at the lady who had just settled down across the aisle.

She was a tall, angular person who somehow suggested a fairly well-dressed scarecrow. Her face seemed faintly familiar, and Malone wondered if they'd met before. Then he decided that she reminded him of a three-year-old who had winked at him in the paddock at Washington Park one Saturday and then run out of the money.

Topping the face – as if anything could – was an incredible headpiece consisting of a grass-green crown surrounded by a brim of nodding flowers, wreaths, and ivy. All it seemed to need was a nice marble tombstone.

She looked up suddenly from her magazine. 'Pardon me, but did you say something about a well-kept grave?' Her voice reminded Malone of a certain Miss Hackett who had talked him out of quitting second-year high school. Somehow he found himself strangely unable to lie to her.

'Madam, do you read minds?'

'Not minds, Mr Malone. *Lips*, sometimes.' She smiled. 'Are you really *the* John J. Malone?'

He blinked. 'How in the – oh, of course! The *magazine*! Those fact detective sheets *will* keep writing up my old cases. Are you a crime-story fan, Mrs—?'

'Miss Hildegarde Withers, schoolteacher by profession and meddlesome old snoop by avocation, at least according to the police. Yes, I've read about you. You solve crimes and right wrongs, but usually by pure accident while chasing through saloons after some young woman who is no better than she should be. Are you on a case now?'

'Working my way through the second bottle,' he muttered, suddenly desperate. It would never do for the redhead to come in and find him tied up with this character.

'I didn't mean that kind of a case,' Miss Withers explained. 'I gather that even though you've never lost a client, you have mislaid one at the moment?'

Malone shivered. The woman had second sight, at least. He decided that it would be better if he went back through the train and met the Rose of Tralee, who must certainly be on her way here by this time. He could also keep an eye open for Steve Larsen. With a hasty apology he got out of the club car, pausing only to purchase a handy pint of rye from the bar steward, and started on a long slow prowl of mile after mile of wobbling, jerking cars. The rye, blending not unpleasantly with the champagne he had taken on earlier, made everything a little hazy and unreal. He kept getting turned around and blundering into the long-deserted diner. Two or three times he bumped into the Greek Orthodox priest with the whiskers, and similarly kept interrupting four sailors shooting craps in a men's lounge.

But – no redhead. And no Larsen. Finally the train stopped – could it be Toledo already? Malone dashed to the vestibule and hung over the step, to make sure that Steve didn't disembark. When they were moving again he resumed his pilgrimage, though by this time he had resigned himself to the fact that he was being stood up by the Rose of Tralee. At last, he turned mournfully back toward where his own lonesome cubicle ought to be – and then suddenly found himself back in the club car!

No redheaded Rose. Even The Hat had departed, taking her copy of *Official Fact Detective Stories* with her. The car was deserted except for a bridge game going on in one corner and a sailor – obviously half-seas over – who was drowsing in a big chair with a newspaper over his face.

The pint was empty. Malone told the steward to have it buried with full military honours, and to fetch him a cheese on rye. 'On second thought, skip the cheese and make it just straight rye, please.'

The drink arrived, and with it a whispered message. There was a lady waiting down the corridor.

Malone emptied his glass and followed the steward, trying to slip him five dollars. It slipped right back. 'Thanks, Mister Malone, but I can't take money from an old classmate. Remember, we went through the last two years of Kent College of Law together?'

Malone gasped. 'Class of '25. And you're Homer – no *Horace* Lee Randolph. But—'

'What am I doing here? The old story. Didn't know my place, and got into Chicago southside politics. Bumped up against the machine, and got disbarred on a phoney charge of subornation of perjury. It could have been squared by handing a grand to a certain sharper at City Hall, but I didn't have the money.' Horace shrugged. 'This pays better than law, anyway. For instance, that lady handed me five dollars just to unlock the private lounge and tell you she's waiting to see you there.'

The little lawyer winced. 'She – was she a queer old maid in a hat that looked like she'd made it herself?'

'Oh, no. No hat.'

Malone breathed easier. 'Was she young and lovely?'

'My weakness is the Numbers game, but I should say the description is accurate.'

Humming 'But 'twas not her beauty alone that won me, oh, no, 'twas the truth', Malone straightened his tie and opened the door.

Lolly Larsen exploded in his face with all the power of a firecracker under a tin can. She grabbed his lapels and yelped: 'Well, where is the dirty—'

'Be more specific. Which dirty—?' Malone said, pulling himself loose.

'*Steve*, of course!'

'I don't know, but I still hope he's somewhere on this train.

191

You joining me in the search? Nice to have your pretty face among us.'

Lolly had the face of a homesick angel. Her hair was exactly the colour of a twist of lemon peel in a glass of champagne brut, her mouth was an overripe strawberry, and her figure might have inspired the french bathing-suit, but her eyes were cold and strange as a mermaid's. 'Are you in this with Steve?' she demanded.

Malone said: 'In simple, one-syllable words that even you can understand – No!'

Lolly suddenly relaxed, swaying against him so that he got a good whiff of brandy, nail polish, and Chanel Number Five. 'I'm sorry. I guess I'm just upset. I feel so terribly helpless.' For Malone's money, she was as helpless as an eight-button rattlesnake. 'You see,' Lolly murmured, 'I'm partly to blame for Steve's running away. I should have stood by him at the trial, but I hadn't the courage. Even afterward – I didn't actually promise to come back to him, I just said I'd come to his party. I meant to tell him – in the Pump Room. So, please, please help me find him – so I can make him see how much we really *need* each other!'

Malone said, 'Try it again, and flick the eyelashes a little bit more when you come to "need each other".'

Lolly jerked away and called him a number of things, of which 'dirty little shyster' was the most complimentary.

'All right,' she finally said in a matter-of-fact tone. 'Steve's carrying a hundred grand, and you can guess how he got it. I happen to know – Glick isn't the *only* one who's been spying on him since he got out of jail yesterday. I don't want Steve back, but I do want a fat slice for keeping my mouth shut. One word from me to the DA or the papers, and not even you can get him off.'

'Go on,' Malone said wearily. 'But you interest me in less ways than one.'

'Find Steve!' she told him. 'Make a deal and I'll give you ten per cent of the take. But work fast, because we're not the only ones looking for him. Steve doublecrossed everybody who was at that party this afternoon. He's somewhere on this train, but he's probably shaved off his moustache, or put on a fright-wig, or—'

Malone yawned and said, 'Where can I get in touch with you?'

'I couldn't get a reservation of any kind.' Her strange eyes warmed hopefully. 'But I hear you have a drawing-room?'

'Don't look at me in that tone of voice,' Malone said hastily. 'Besides, I snore. Maybe there'll be something available for you at the next stop.'

He was out of there and back in the club car before Lolly could turn on any more of the charm. He decided to have one for the road – the New York Central Road, and one for the Pennsy too. The sensible thing was to find Steve Larsen, collect his own hard-earned fee, and let Lolly alone. Her offer of ten per cent of the blackmail take touched on a sore spot.

Malone began to work his way through the train again, this time desperately questioning porters. The worst of it was, there was nothing remarkable about Larsen's appearance except curly hair, which he'd probably had straightened and dyed, a moustache that could have been shaved off, and a briefcase full of money, which he'd probably hidden. In fact, the man was undoubtedly laughing at everybody from behind a false set of whiskers.

Such were Malone's thoughts as he suddenly came face to face again with the Greek Orthodox priest, who stared past him through thick, tinted spectacles. The little lawyer hesitated and was lost. Throwing caution to the winds, he yanked vigorously at the beard. But it was an orthodox beard, attached in the orthodox manner. Its owner let loose a blast which just possibly might have been an orthodox Greek blessing. Malone didn't wait to find out.

His ears were still burning when he stepped into a vestibule and ran head on into Miss Hildegarde Withers. He nodded coldly and started past her.

'Ah, go soak your fat head!'

Malone gasped.

'It's the parrot,' Miss Withers explained, holding up the caged monstrosity. 'It's been making such a racket that I'm taking it to the baggage car for the night.'

'Where – where did you get that – bird?' Malone asked weakly.

'Why, Sinbad is a legacy from the aunt whose funeral I just went back to attend. I'm taking him back to New York with me.'

'New York!' Malone moaned. 'We'll be there before I find that—'

'You mean that Mr Larsen?' As he stood speechless, she went briskly on. 'You see, I happened to be at a family farewell party at the table next to yours in the Pump Room, and my hearing is very acute. So, for that matter, is my eyesight. Has it occurred to you that Larsen may be wearing a disguise of some sort?'

'That it has,' admitted Malone sadly, thinking of the Greek priest.

The schoolteacher lowered her voice. 'You remember that when we had our little chat in the club car some time ago, there was an obviously inebriated sailor dozing behind a newspaper?'

'There's one on every train,' Malone said. 'One or more.'

'Exactly. Like Chesterton's postman, you never notice them. But somehow that particular sailor managed to stay intoxicated without ordering a single drink or nipping at a private bottle. More than that, when you suddenly left he poked his head out from behind the paper and stared after you with a very odd expression, rather as if he suspected you had leprosy. I couldn't help noticing—'

'Madam, I love you,' the lawyer said fervently. 'I love you because you remind me of Miss Hackett back in Dorchester High, and because of your hat, and because you are sharper than a tack.'

Miss Withers sniffed, but it was a mollified sniff. 'Sorry to interrupt, but that same sailor entered our car just as I left it with the parrot. I just happened to look back, and I rather think he was trying the door of your drawing-room.'

Malone clasped her hand fondly. Unfortunately it was the hand that held the cage, and the parrot took advantage of the long-awaited opportunity to nip viciously at his thumb. 'Thank you so very much – some day I'll wring your silly neck,' was Malone's sincere but somewhat garbled exit-line.

'Go boil your head in lard,' the bird screamed after him.

The maiden schoolteacher sighed. 'Come on, Sinbad, you're going into durance vile. And I'm going to retire to my lonely couch, drat it all.' She looked wistfully over her shoulder. 'Some people have all the fun!'

But twelve cars, ten minutes, and four drinks later, Malone was lost again. A worried porter was saying, 'If you could only remember your car number, sah?' A much-harassed Pullman conductor added, 'If you'd just show us your ticket stub, we'd locate you.'

'You don't need to locate *me*,' Malone insisted. 'I'm right here.'

'Maybe you haven't got a stub.'

'I have so a stub. It's in my hatband.' Crafty as an Indian guide, Malone backtracked them unerringly to his drawing-room. 'Here's the stub – now where am I?'

The porter looked out the window and said, 'Just coming into Altoona, sah.'

'They lay in the wreck when they found them, they had died when the engine had fell . . .' sang Malone happily. But the conductor winced and said they'd be going.

'You might as well,' Malone told him. 'If neither of you can sing baritone.'

The door closed behind them, and a moment later a soft voice called, 'Mr Malone?'

He stared at the connecting door. The Rose of Tralee, Malone told himself happily. He adjusted his tie, and tried the door. Miraculously, it opened. Then he saw that it was Miss Hildegarde Withers, looking very worried, who stared back at him.

Malone said, 'What have you done with my redhead?'

'If you refer to my niece Joannie,' the schoolteacher

said sharply, 'she only helped me get my stuff aboard and rode as far as Englewood. But never mind that now. I'm in trouble.'

'I knew there couldn't be two parrots like that on one train,' Malone groaned. 'Or even in one world.'

'There's worse than parrots on this train,' snapped Miss Withers. 'This man Larsen you were looking for—'

The little lawyer's eyes narrowed. 'Just what is your interest in Larsen?'

'None whatever, except that he's here in my compartment. It's very embarrassing, because he's not only dead, he's *undressed*!'

'Holy St Vitus!' gulped Malone. 'Quiet! Keep *calm*. Lock your door and *don't* talk!'

'My door is locked, and who's talking?' the schoolteacher stepped aside and Malone peered gingerly past her. The speed with which he was sobering up probably established a new record. It was Larsen, all right. He was face down on the floor, dressed only in black shoes, blue socks, and a suit of long underwear. There was also a moderate amount of blood.

At last Malone said hoarsely, 'I suspect foul play!'

'Knife job,' said Miss Withers with professional coolness. 'From the back, through the *latissimus dorsi*. Within the last twenty minutes, I'd say. If I hadn't had some difficulty in convincing the baggage men that Sinbad should be theirs for the night, I might have walked in on the murderer at work.' She gave Malone a searching glance. 'It wasn't *you*, by any chance?'

'Do you think I'd murder a man who owed me $3,000?' Malone demanded indignantly. He scowled. 'But a lot of people are going to jump to that conclusion. Nice of you not to raise an alarm.'

She sniffed. 'You didn't think I'd care to have a man – even a dead man – found in my room in this state of undress? Obviously, he hasn't your money on his person. So – what is to be done about it?'

'I'll defend you for nothing,' John J. Malone promised. 'Justifiable homicide. Besides, you were framed. He burst in upon you and you stabbed him in defence of your honour . . .'

'*Just* a minute! The corpse was *your* client. You've been publicly asking for him all through the train. I'm only an innocent bystander.' She paused. 'In my opinion, Larsen was lured to your room purposely by someone who had penetrated his disguise. He was stabbed, and dumped here. Very clever, because if the body had been left in your room, you could have got rid of it or claimed that you were framed. But this way, to the police mind at least, it would be obvious that you did the job and then tried to palm it off on the nearest neighbour.'

Malone sagged weakly against the berth. His hand brushed against the leather case, and something slashed viciously at his fingers. 'But I thought you got rid of that parrot!' he cried.

'I did,' Miss Withers assured him. 'That's Precious in his case. A twenty-pound Siamese, also part of my recent legacy. Don't get too close, the creature dislikes train travel and is in a foul temper.'

Malone stared through the wire window and said, 'It's father must have been either a bobcat or a buzz saw.'

'My aunt left me her mink coat, on condition that I take both her pets,' Miss Withers explained wearily. 'But I'm beginning to think it would be better to shiver through these cold winters. And speaking of cold – I'm a patient woman, but not very. You have one minute, Mr Malone, to get your dead friend out of here!'

'He's no friend of mine, dead or alive,' Malone began. 'And I suggest—'

There was a heavy knocking on the corridor door. 'Open up in there!'

'Say something!' whispered Malone. 'Say you're undressed!'

'You're undressed – I mean, I'm undressed,' she cried obediently.

'Sorry, ma'am,' a masculine voice said on the other side of the door. 'But we're searching this train for a fugitive from justice. Hurry, please.'

'Just a minute,' sang out the schoolteacher, making frantic gestures at Malone.

The little lawyer shuddered, then grabbed the late Steve Larsen and tugged him through the connecting door into his drawing-room. Meanwhile, Miss Withers cast aside maidenly modesty and tore pins from her hair, the dress from her shoulders. Clutching a robe around her, she opened the door a crack and announced, This is an *outrage!*'

The train conductor, a Pullman conductor, and two Altoona police detectives crowded in, ignoring her protest. They pawed through the wardrobe, peered into every nook and cranny.

Miss Withers stood rooted to the spot, in more ways than one. There was a damp brownish-red spot on the carpet, and she had one foot firmly holding it down. At last the delegation backed out, with apologies. Then she heard a feeble, imploring tapping on the connecting door, and John J. Malone's voice whispering, 'Help!'

The maiden schoolteacher stuck her head out into the corridor again, where the search-party was already waiting for Malone to open up. 'Oh, officer!' she cried tremulously, 'is there any danger?'

'No, ma'am.'

'Was the man you're looking for a burly, dark-complexioned cut-throat with dark glasses and a pronounced limp in the left leg?'

'No, lady. Get lost, please, lady.'

'Because on my way back from the diner I saw a man like that. He leered, and then followed me through three cars.'

The man we're looking for is an embezzler, not a mental case.' They hammered on Malone's door again. 'Open up in there!'

Over her shoulder Miss Withers could see the pale, perspiring face of John J. Malone as he dragged Steve Larsen back into her compartment again.

'But, officer,' she improvised desperately, 'I'm sure that the awful dark man who followed me was a distinct criminal type—' There was a reassuring whisper of 'Okay' from behind her, and the sound of a softly closing door. Miss Withers backed into her compartment, closed and locked the connecting door, and then sank down on the edge of her berth, trying to avoid the blankly staring eyes of the dead man.

Next door there was a rumble of voices, and then suddenly Malone's high tenor doing rough justice to 'Did Your Mother Come from Ireland?' The schoolteacher heard no more than the first line of the chorus before the jello in her knees melted completely. When she opened her eyes again, she saw Malone holding a dagger before her, and she very nearly fainted again.

'You were so right,' the little lawyer told her admiringly. 'It was a frame-up all right – but meant for me. *This* was tucked into the upholstery of my room. I sat on it while they were searching, and had to burst into song to cover my howl of anguish.'

'Oh, dear!' said Miss Withers.

He sat down beside her, patted her comfortingly on the shoulder, and said, 'Maybe I can shove the body out the window!'

'We're still in the station,' she reminded him crisply. 'And from what experience I've had with train windows, it would be easier to solve the murder than open one. Why don't we start searching for clues?'

Malone stood up so quickly that he rapped his head on the bottom of the upper berth. 'Never mind *clues*. Let's just find the murderer!'

'Just as easy as that?'

'Look,' he said. 'This train was searched at the request of the Chicago police because somebody – probably Bert Glick – tipped them off that Larsen and a lot of stolen money are on board. The word has got around. Obviously, somebody else knew – somebody who caught the train and did the dirty work. It's reasonable to assume that whoever has the money is the killer.'

There was a new glint in Miss Withers' blue-grey eyes. 'Go on.'

'Also, Larsen's ex-wife – or do I mean ex-widow? – is aboard. I saw her. She is a lovely girl whose many friends agree that she would eat her young or sell her old mother down the river into slavery for a fast buck.' He took out a cigar. 'I'll go next door and have a smoke while you change, and then we'll go look for Lolly Larsen.'

'I'm practically ready now,' the schoolteacher agreed. 'But take *that* with you!'

Malone hesitated, and then with a deep sigh reached down and took a firm grasp of all that was mortal of his late client. 'Here we go again!'

A few minutes later Miss Hildegarde Withers was following Malone through the now-darkened train. The fact that this was somebody else's problem never occurred to her. Murder, according to her tenets, was everybody's business.

Malone touched her arm as they came at last to the door of the club car. 'Here is where I saw Lolly last,' he whispered. 'She only got aboard at the last minute, and didn't have a reservation.' He pointed down the corridor. 'See that door, just this side of the pantry? It's a private lounge, used only for railroad officials or big-shots like governors or senators.

Lolly bribed the steward to let her use it when she wanted to have a private talk with me. It just occurred to me that she might have talked him into letting her have it for the rest of the night. If she's still there—'

'Say no more,' Miss Withers cut in. 'I am a fellow-passenger, also without a berth, seeking only a place to rest my weary head After all, I have as much right in there as she has. But you will be within call, won't you?'

'If you need help, just holler,' he promised. Malone watched as the schoolteacher marched down the corridor, tried the lounge door gently, and then knocked. The door opened and she vanished inside.

The little lawyer had an argument with his conscience. It wasn't just that she reminded him of Miss Hackett, it was that she had become a sort of partner. Besides, he was getting almost fond of that equine face.

Oh, well, he'd be within earshot. And if there was anything in the inspiration which had just come to him, she wasn't in any real danger anyway. He went on into the bar. It was half-dark and empty now, except for a little group of men in Navy uniforms at the far end, who were sleeping sprawled and entangled like a litter of puppies.

'Sorry, Mister Malone, but the bar is closed,' a voice spoke up behind him. It was Horace Lee Randoph, looking drawn and exhausted. He caught Malone's glance toward the sleeping sailors and added, 'Against the rules, but the conductor said don't bother 'em.'

Malone nodded, and then said, 'Horace, we're old friends and classmates. You know me of old, and you know you can trust me. *Where did you hide it?*'

'Where did I hide what?'

'You know what!' Malone fixed the man with the cold and baleful eye he used on prosecution witnesses. 'Let me have it before it's too late, and I'll do my best for you.'

The eyes rolled. 'Oh, Lawdy! I knew I shouldn't a done it, Mista Malone! I'll show you!' Horace hurried on down through the car and unlocked a small closet filled with mops and brooms. From a box labelled Soap Flakes he came up with a paper sack. It was a very small sack to hold a hundred thousand dollars, Malone thought, even if the money was in big bills. Horace fumbled inside the sack.

'What's *that?*' Malone demanded.

'What would it be but the bottle of gin I sneaked from the bar? Join me?'

The breath went out of John J. Malone like air out of a busted balloon. He caught the doorknob for support, swaying like an aspen in the wind. It was just at that moment that they both heard the screams.

The rush of self-confidence with which Miss Hildegarde Withers had pushed her way into the lounge ebbed somewhat as she came face to face with Lolly Larsen. Appeals to sympathy, as from one supposedly stranded fellow passenger to another, failed utterly. It was not until the schoolteacher played her last card, reminding Lolly sharply that if there was any commotion the Pullman conductor would undoubtedly have them both evicted, that she succeeded in getting a toe-hold.

'Oh, *all right!*' snarled Lolly ungraciously. 'Only shut up and go to sleep.'

During the few minutes before the room went dark again, Miss Withers made a mental snapshot of everything in it. No toilet, no wardrobe, no closet. A small suitcase, a coat, and a handbag were on the only chair. The money must be somewhere in this room, the schoolteacher thought. There was a way to find out.

As the train flashed through the moonlit night, Miss Withers busily wriggled out of her petticoat and ripped it into shreds. Using a bit of paper from her handbag for tinder – and inwardly praying it wasn't a ten-dollar bill — she did what had to be done. A few minutes later she burst out into the corridor, holding her handkerchief to her mouth.

She almost bumped into one of the sailors who came lurching toward her along the narrow passage, and gasped, 'What do you want?'

He stared at her with heavy eyes, 'If it's any of your

business, I'm looking for the latrine,' he said dryly.

When he was out of sight, Miss Withers turned and peeked back into the lounge. A burst of acrid smoke struck her in the face. Now was the time. '*Fire!*' she shrieked.

Thick billows of greasy smoke flooded out through the half-open door. Inside, little tongues of red flame ran greedily along the edge of the seat where Miss Withers had tucked the burning rags and paper.

Down the corridor came Malone and Horace Lee Randolph, and a couple of startled bluejackets appeared from the other direction. Somebody tore an extinguisher from the wall.

Miss Winters grabbed Malone's arm. 'Watch her! She'll go for the money—'

The fire extinguisher sent a stream of foaming chemicals into the doorway just as Lolly Larsen burst out. Her mascara streaked down her face, already blackened by smoke, and her yellow hair was plastered unflatteringly to her skull. But she clutched a small leather case.

Somehow she tripped over Miss Withers' outstretched foot. The leather case flew across the corridor to smash against the wall, where it flew open, disclosing a multitude of creams, oils, and tiny bottles – a portable beauty parlour.

'She must have gone to sleep smoking a cigarette!' put in Miss Withers in loud clear tones. 'A lucky thing I was there to smell the smoke and give the alarm—'

But John J. Malone seized her firmly by the arm and propelled her back through the train. 'It was a good try, but you can stop acting now. She doesn't have the money.' Back in her own compartment he confessed about Horace. 'I had a wonderful idea, but it didn't pay off. The poor guy's career as a lawyer was busted by a City Hall chiseller. If Larsen was the one, Horace might have spotted him on the train and decided to get even.'

'You were holding out on me,' said Miss Withers, slightly miffed.

Malone unwrapped a cigar and said, 'If anybody finds that money, I want it to be me. Because I've got to get my fee out of it or I can't even get back to Chicago.'

'Perhaps you'll learn to like Manhattan,' she told him brightly.

Malone said grimly, 'If something isn't done soon, I'm going to see Manhattan through those cold iron bars.'

'We're in the same boat. Except,' she added honestly, 'that I don't think the inspector would go so far as to lock me up. But he does take a dim view of anybody who finds a body and doesn't report it.' She sighed. 'Do you think we *could* get one of these windows open?'

Malone smothered a yawn and said, 'Not in my present condition of exhaustion.'

'Let's begin at the beginning,' the schoolteacher said. 'Larsen invited a number of people to a party he didn't plan to attend. He sneaked on this train, presumably disguised in a Navy enlisted man's uniform. How he got hold of it—'

'He was in the Service for a while,' said the little lawyer.

'The murderer made a date to meet his victim in your drawing-room, hoping to set *you* up as the goat. He stuck a knife in him and then stripped him, looking for a money-belt or something.'

'You don't have to undress a man to find a money-belt,' Malone murmured.

'Really? I wouldn't know.' Miss Withers sniffed. 'The knife was then hidden in your room, but the body was moved in here. The money—' She paused and studied him searchingly. 'Mr Malone, are you sure you didn't—?'

'We plead not guilty and not guilty by reason of insanity,' Malone muttered. He closed his eyes for just five seconds' much-needed rest, and when he opened them a dirty-looking dawn was glaring in at him through the window.

'Good morning,' Miss Withers greeted him, entirely too cheerfully. 'Did you get any ideas while you were in dreamland?' She put away her toothbrush and added, 'You know, I've sometimes found that if a problem seems insoluble, you can sleep on it and sometimes your subconscious comes up with the answer. Sometimes it's even happened to me in a dream.'

'It does? It *has*?' Malone sat up suddenly. 'Okay. Burglars can't be choosers. Sleep and the world sleeps – I mean, I'll just stand watch for a while and you try taking a nap. Maybe you can dream up an answer out of your subconscious. But dream fast, lady, because we get in about two hours from now.'

But when Miss Withers had finally been comfortably settled against the pillows, she found that her eyelids stubbornly refused to stay shut.

'Try once more,' John J. Malone said soothingly. She closed her eyes obediently, and his high, whispering tenor filled the little compartment, singing a fine old song. It was probably the first time in history, Miss Withers thought, that anyone had tried to use 'Throw Him Down, McCluskey' as a lullaby, but she found herself drifting off . . .

Malone passed the time by trying to imagine what he would do with a Jiundred grand if he were the murderer. There must have been a desperate need for haste – at any moment, someone might come back to the murder room. The money would have to be put somewhere handy – some obvious place where nobody would ever think of looking, and where it could be quickly and easily retrieved when all was clear.

There was an angry growl from Precious in his cage.

'If you could only say something besides "Meeerow" and "Fssst"!' Malone murmured wistfully. 'Because you're the only witness. Now if it had been the parrot . . .'

At last he touched Miss Withers apologetically on the shoulder. 'Wake up, ma'am, we're coming into New York. Quick, what did you dream?'

She blinked, sniffed, and came wide awake. 'My dream? Why – I was buying a hat, a darling little sailor hat, only it had to be exchanged because the ribbon was yellow. But first I wore it out to dinner with Inspector Piper, who took me to a Greek restaurant and the proprietor was so glad to see us that he said dinner was on the house. But naturally we didn't eat anything because you have to beware of the Greeks when they come bearing gifts. His name was Mr Roberts. That's all I remember.'

'Oh, *brother*!' said John J. Malone.

'And there wasn't anyone named Roberts mixed up in this case, or anyone of Greek extraction, was there?' She sighed. 'Pure nonsense. I guess a watched subconscious never boils.'

The train was crawling laboriously up an elevated platform. 'A drowning man will grasp at a strawberry,' Malone said suddenly. 'I've got a sort of an idea. Greeks bearing gifts – that means look out for somebody who wants to give you something for nothing. And that something could include gratuitous information.'

She nodded. 'Perhaps someone planned to murder Larsen aboard this train and wanted you aboard to be the obvious suspect.'

The train shuddered to a stop. Malone leapt up, startled, but the schoolteacher told him it was only 125th Street. 'Perhaps we should check and see who gets off.' She glanced out the window and said, 'On second thought, let's not. The platform is swarming with police.'

They were interrupted by the porter, who brushed off Miss Withers, accepted a dollar from the gallant Malone, and then lugged her suitcases and the pet container down to the vestibule. 'He'll be in your room next,' she whispered to Malone. 'What do we do now?'

'We think fast,' Malone said. 'The rest of your dream! The sailor hat with the wrong ribbon! And Mr Roberts—'

The door burst open and suddenly they were surrounded by detectives, led by a grizzled sergeant in plain clothes. Lolly Larsen was with them. She had removed most of the traces of the holocaust, her face was lovely and her hair was gleaming, but her mood was that of a dyspeptic cobra. She breathlessly accused Miss Withers of assaulting her and trying to burn her alive, and Malone of engineering Steve Larsen's successful disappearance.

'So,' said Malone. 'You wired ahead from Albany,

crying copper?'

'Maybe she did,' said the sergeant. 'But we'd already been contacted by the Chicago police. Somebody out there swore a warrant for Steve Larsen's arrest . . .'

'Glick, maybe?'

'A Mr Allen Roth, according to the teletype. Now, folks—'

But Malone was trying to pretend that Lolly, the sergeant, and the whole police department didn't exist. He faced Miss Withers and said, 'About that dream! It must mèan a sailor under false colours. We already know that Larsen was disguised in Navy uniform . . .'

'Shaddap!' said the sergeant. 'Maybe you don't know, mister, that helping an embezzler to escape makes you an assessory after the fact.'

'*Acce*ssory,' corrected Miss Withers firmly.

'If you want Larsen,' Malone said easily, 'he's next door in my drawing-room, wrapped up in the blankets.'

'Sure, sure,' said the sergeant, mopping his face. 'Wise guy, eh?'

'Somebody helped Larsen escape – escape out of this world, with a shiv through the – through the—?' Malone looked hopefully at Miss Withers.

'The *latissimus dorsi*,' she prompted.

The sergeant barked, 'Never mind the double-talk. Where

is this Larsen?'

Then Lolly, who had pushed open the connecting door, let out a thin scream like tearing silk. 'It *is* Steve!' she cried. 'It's Steve, and he's dead!'

Momentarily the attention of the Law was drawn elsewhere. 'Now or never,' said Miss Withers coolly. 'About the Mr Roberts thing – I just remembered that there was a play by that name a while back. All about sailors in the last war. I saw it, and was somewhat shocked at certain scenes. Their language – but anyway, I ran into a sailor just after I started that fire, and he said he was looking for the *latrine*. Sailors don't use Army talk – in "Mr Roberts" they called it *the head*!'

Suddenly the Law was back, very direct and grim about everything. Miss Withers gasped with indignation as she found herself suddenly handcuffed to John J. Malone. But stone walls do not a prison make, as she pointed out to her companion-in-crime. 'And don't you see? It means—'

'Madam, I am ahead of you. There was a *wrong* sailor aboard this train even after Larsen got his. The murderer must have taken a plane from Chicago and caught this train at Toledo. I was watching to see who got off, not who got on. The man penetrated Larsen's disguise—'

'In more ways than one,' the schoolteacher put in grimly.

'And then after he'd murdered his victim, he took Larsen's

sailor suit and got rid of his own clothes, realising that nobody notices a sailor on a train! Madam, I salute your subconscious!' Malone waved his hand, magnificent even in chains. 'The defence rests! Officer, call a cop!'

The train was crawling into one of the tunnels beneath Grand Central station, and the harried sergeant was beside himself. 'You listen to Mr Malone,' Miss Withers told their captor firmly, 'or I'll hint to my old friend Inspector Oscar Piper that you would look well on a bicycle beat way out in Brooklyn!'

'Oh, no!' the unhappy officer moaned. 'Not *that* Miss Withers!'

'That Miss Withers,' she snapped. 'My good man, all we ask is that you find the real murderer, who must still be on this train. He's wearing a Navy uniform . . .'

'Lady,' the sergeant said sincerely, 'you ask the impossible. The train is full of sailors. Grand Central is full of sailors.'

'But this particular sailor,' Malone put in, 'is wearing the uniform of the man he killed. *There will be a slit in the back of the jumper* – just under the shoulder blade!'

'When the knife went in' Miss Withers added. 'Hurry, man! The train is stopping.'

It might still have been a lost cause had not Lolly put in her five cents. 'Don't listen to that old witch!' she cried. 'Officer, you do your duty!'

The sergeant disliked being yelled at, even by blondes. 'Hold all of 'em – her too,' he ordered, and leapt out on the platform. He seized upon a railroad dick, who listened and then grabbed a telephone attached to a nearby pillar. Somewhere far off an alarm began to ring, and an emotionless voice spoke over the public address system. . .

In less than two minutes the vast labyrinth of Grand Central was alerted, and men in Navy uniforms were suddenly intercepted by polite but firm railroad detectives who sprang up out of nowhere. Only one of the sailors, a somewhat older man who was lugging a pet container that wasn't his, had any real difficulty. He alone had a narrow slit in the back of his jumper.

Bert Glick flung the leather case down the track and tried vainly to run, but there was no place to go. The container flew open, and Precious scooted. Only a dumb Siamese cat, as Malone commented later, would have abandoned a lair that had a hundred grand tucked under its carpet of old newspapers.

'And to think that I spent the night within reach of that dough, and didn't grab my fee!' said Malone.

But it developed that there was a comfortable reward for the apprehension of Steve Larson, alive or dead. Before John J. Malone took off for Chicago, he accepted an invitation for dinner at Miss Withers' modest little apartment on West

74th Street, arriving with four dozen roses. It was a good dinner, and Malone cheerfully put up with the screamed insults of Sinbad and the well-meant attentions of Talley, the apricot poodle. 'Just as long as the cat stays lost!' he said.

'Yes, isn't it odd that nobody has seen hide nor hair of Precious! It's my idea that he's waxing fat in the caverns beneath Grand Central, preying on the rats who are rumoured to flourish there. Would you care for another piece of pie, Mr Malone?'

'All I really want,' said the little lawyer hopefully, 'is an introduction to your redheaded niece.'

'Oh, yes, Joannie. Her husband played guard for Southern California, and he even made all-American,' Miss Withers tactfully explained.

'On second thought, I'll settle for coffee,' said John J. Malone.

Miss Withers sniffed, not unsympathetically.

A MYSTERY OF THE UNDERGROUND

JOHN OXENHAM

The underground station at Charing Cross was the scene of considerable excitement on the night of Tuesday, the fourth of November. As the 9.17 London and North-Western train rumbled up the platform, a lady was seen standing at the door of one of the first-class carriages, frantically endeavouring to get out, and screaming wildly.

The station inspector ran up to the carriage, and pulled open the door, when the lady literally sprang into his arms. She was in a state of violent hysterics, and it was with difficulty that he assisted her across the platform to a seat.

Meanwhile, a small crowd gathered round the open carriage door. The guard of the train had come up, elbowed his way through, and entered the carriage. The spectators could see a man sitting in the further corner, apparently asleep, his hat over his eyes, his head sunk forward.

'Drunken brute! he's frightened the lydy!'

'Pitch him out, guard, and we'll jump on 'im!'

The guard shook the man roughly, his hat rolled off, and the crowd jeered.

Then, suddenly, the guard came back to the door, waved his flag to a porter, and said hurriedly:

'Block the line behind – quick – and send the inspector.'

The porter hurried off, shouted to the inspector, and ran down the train to the signal-box.

The inspector left his charge in care of some ladies, and pushed his way into the carriage. The guard said a word to him, and they bent over the man in the corner. Then, with startled faces and compressed lips, after a momentary hesitation, they stopped and lifted him out of the carriage. The head fell back as they carried him awkwardly across the platform, and the crowd shrank away, silent and scared, at sight of the ghastly limpness and the stains of blood.

'Where to?' said the guard.

'Upstairs, I suppose,' said the inspector; and then added: 'Best thing would be to take him right on to Westminster. It's a Scotland Yard job, is this!'

'That's so!' said the guard. 'And her, too?' nodding towards the hysterical lady on the seat.

'Yes. Put him in again, and lock the door. I'll see to her. Tell Bob to keep the line blocked till they get the word from Westminster.'

They put the body back into the carriage, locked the door,

and the guard went off to the signal-box, while the inspector took in hand the more difficult task of getting the lady, still in a state of hysterics, back into a carriage.

Finally, he had to have her carried in; he stepped in himself, and the train rolled off through the fog, past the line of scared faces on the platform, into the darkness which led towards Westminster; and the red stern light blinked ghoulishly back at the crowd, and tremulously disappeared up the tunnel like a great clot of blood.

Within seven minutes of the arrival of the train at Westminster, Scotland Yard was in possession of the facts, and of the chief factors in the case – the body – and the lady – by this time in a state of extreme nervous prostration. A couple of detectives were minutely examining the carriage as it sped on its journey, and the traffic on the Underground resumed its normal course.

The morning papers contained a brief announcement of the discovery. The evening papers imaginatively worked up all the details they had been able to obtain, and promoted the item to a prominent position among the day's news, in large type, well spaced out. But with the inquest, held next day, the excitement increased. Briefly, all that was learned was this:

From letters and papers found upon the deceased, the body was identified as that of Conrad Grosheim, a financier and speculator in the City. The identification was confirmed by Grosheim's clerk, and by the landlady of the room he occupied in King's Road, Chelsea.

The station inspector at Charing Cross and the guard of the train spoke to the finding of the body.

Maud Jones stated that she had had a race to catch the train at Temple station. She was running up towards the second-class carriages when the train started and the inspector flung open the door of a first-class and assisted her in, telling her to change at the next station. She had not noticed anything wrong with the gentleman in the corner – thought he was asleep – remembered his cigarette had slipped from his fingers, and was still smoking on the floor, when suddenly her eyes caught sight of blood dripping from his coat, and it flashed upon her that he was dead. She was so horrified that she nearly lost her senses. Was positive the cigarette on the floor was smoking when she got in. No, she did not smell anything like powder – nothing but the cigarette. The window next to the dead man was up. She touched nothing in the carriage, and got out of it as soon as she could. She was a waitress at Belloni's Restaurant, in the Strand. She had never seen the gentleman before, and was only sorry she had ever set eyes on him at all.

The inspector at Temple station confirmed Miss Jones's story as to her being put into the carriage.

The ticket porter at Temple station swore positively that no one whatever got out of the train. He had watched the young lady helped into the first-class carriage by the inspector, and there was not a single person on the platform when the train went out, except the inspector. Nobody could possibly have got up the stairs while he was watching. He had snapped the ingress gate as the lady passed through, and had not opened the egress one.

Dr Mortimer stated that he had examined the body, and was of the opinion that death had taken place not more than fifteen minutes, certainly not more than half an hour, before his examination. Cause of death was a bullet through the heart. It had entered the body level and straight, passed through the heart, causing instant death, and was found inside the ribs on the right side of the body. Bullet produced. It was of an unusually conical shape, and by impact with the ribs had been slightly flattened. In its natural shape it would be sharper, almost pointed. There were no signs of singeing or burning on deceased's clothing. The bullet made a clean cut through coat and vest, and did its work. If, as he understood, deceased was sitting in the corner of the carriage facing slightly towards the corner which Miss Jones occupied, the shot must have been fired from the seat exactly opposite where deceased sat.

'Or through the window?' queried the coroner.

'Or through the window,' granted the doctor. 'The exact spot from which the shot was fired would depend upon the angle at which deceased was sitting, but I understood the window was found closed.'

'Could the wound have been self-inflicted?'

'It could, of course, but not without singeing the clothing.'

'Could deceased have shot himself, thrown the revolver out of the window, and raised the window?'

'Absolutely impossible; death was instantaneous.'

Miss Jones, recalled, stated that the window was up when she entered the carriage. She was quite certain of that. It was a close, muggy night, and she felt half-suffocated. The window nearest her was jammed, and she could not let it down. She had looked across at the other, and thought of trying to open it. Then she saw the cigarette smoking on the floor, and then she saw the blood, and then she remembered screaming.

Detective-Sergeant Doane, of Scotland Yard, stated that the case had been placed in his hands; that he had taken possession of the carriage within a few minutes of the discovery of the body. It had been examined most minutely by himself and a colleague, both inside and out. Beyond the cigarette, trampled flat, probably in the removal of the body, and a few drops of blood on the floor, nothing whatever had been found. There was no weapon, no sign of a struggle. The contents of deceased's pockets, including a valuable watch and chain, had not been touched. He had questioned the passengers in the next compartments, but no one had heard a shot, or any sound whatever, except the screams of Miss Jones. Further stated that if Miss Jones was correct in stating that the cigarette was still burning on the floor when she entered, and he had no reason to doubt it, he judged that the deed was committed in the tunnel between Mansion House and Blackfriars, and he arrived at it thus. A cigarette of that brand would burn on the floor for five minutes; the train took one and a half minutes to travel from Temple to Charing Cross, half a minute's stoppage at Temple; two minutes from Blackfriars to Temple, half a minute's stoppage at Blackfriars took them into the tunnel between Mansion House and Blackfriars, and there the shot must have been fired. That tunnel had been searched inch by inch, so had the others, but nothing whatever had been found. He had his own ideas on the subject, but declined at present to make them public. Deceased's ticket was from Mansion House to Sloane Square.

The jury returned a verdict of wilful murder against some person or persons unknown; and so one more was added to the long list of undiscovered crimes of the Metropolis.

(From the *Link*, 12 November 1894)
ANOTHER MURDER ON THE UNDERGROUND
THE *LINK* MAN ON THE SPOT, AS USUAL

At 9.21 exactly, last night, as the weary *Link* man, having finished his appointed tasks, was patiently travelling in an Underground train to his humble abode at Chelsea, a piece of great good fortune befell him. Great good fortune to one man generally means corresponding bad fortune to some other man, and so it was in this case. Without desiring to appear over-presumptuous, it does seem providential, that is, to the readers of the *Link*, that the *Link* man was right on the spot, and is therefore able to give an eye-witness's account of the very strange occurrence which took place at St James's Park station on the Underground railway last night.

Our contemporaries have published more or less garbled versions of the matter. They have done their best. The *Link*, however, was the only paper actually represented, and able, therefore, to give an absolutely exact account of what happened.

The *Link* man entered the train at Blackfriars, travelling third-class, as usual. He always travels third – not, as you might imagine, from necessity, but from choice. He thereby sees and feels, and, in every sense of the word, comes so much more in contact with his fellows, than is possible in the cold, refined, varnish-and-saddlebag atmosphere of the first-class. After standing patiently past three stations, the *Link* man had just managed to gently insinuate his person into the sixth place on a seat intended for five, and was jocularly remarking to his scowling neighbours, upon portions of whom he was sitting, that the tighter you sat the less you joggled, when a series of piercing screams from the next carriage forward rent the darkness of the tunnel, and heated all the *Link* man's professional instincts to boiling point. He sprang to the door. Something was happening – something untoward and out of the common. Such screams – off the stage – were an outrage, or implied one.

His first intention was to climb along the footboard till he arrived at the screams. But thoughts of Mrs *Link*-man and all the little *Link* men and women deterred him, and he decided not to risk his precious life, but to be first on the scene, all the same.

The screams had ceased. The silence seemed even more pregnant. While the screams continued something was happening. With their cessation, it–whatever it was – had happened. As the train slowed up at St James's Park, the *Link* man dashed forward to the next carriage – the rearmost first-class – and this is what he saw on opening the door – a lady lying apparently lifeless in the corner seat nearest the platform, and on the floor face downwards, the body of a man.

A crowd rushed to the door almost as soon as the *Link* man, but his were the first eyes that witnessed the scene. The station inspector came up, and was for ordering the *Link* man away, but, upon the latter disclosing his identity, became the courteous official the *Link* man has always found him, except upon that one unfortunate occasion when he (the inspector) found him (the *Link* man) riding first with a third-class ticket, and only let him off imprisonment for life with a reprimand, which still tingles in the *Link* man's ears, on the *Link* man's proving to him by ocular demonstration that every third-class carriage was carrying thirty per cent more humanity than it had any right to do.

The guard came up, too, and *ex officio*, the *Link* man was privileged to share the labours and cogitations of these officials.

By virtue of her sex, the lady claimed their first attention. She was in a dead faint, and was carefully carried through a double line of curious faces by the *Link* man and the guard to one of the station seats.

The *Link* man left the guard in charge, and hurried back to the carriage.

The inspector was stooping over the prostrate man, and as the *Link* man stepped in, he looked up with scared face, and said, 'It's another murder!'

'Good God!' said the *Link* man, involuntarily, for this was getting exciting. Then he saw blood on the inspector's hands.

'Better block the line behind, and wire to Scotland Yard, hadn't you?' he suggested.

'It blocks itself,' said the inspector; 'but we'll make doubly sure. Stop here in charge, will you, and I'll wire Scotland Yard at same time.' And he went off at a run, leaving the *Link* man in full charge.

Notebook and pencil came out of their own accord, with the following results: 'First-class carriage No. 32. London and North-Western train, St James's Park; time 9.25 p.m. Body dressed in dark grey overcoat with velvet collar – dark trousers – black diagonal coat and vest – patent leather shoes – Lincoln and Bennet hat, bruised from a fall. Face, so far as visible, dark and pale – age about forty-five – four-coil snake ring, with ruby and diamond in head, on third finger of left hand. In vest, exactly over heart, small, clean-cut hole, no singeing or burning, no smell of powder – no signs of struggle – window furthest from platform closed. Note – Exactly a week, to the minute almost, since discovery of the murder at Charing Cross last week. Is this accident or horrible intention?'

Link man acknowledges to creepy feeling. Door opens. Inspector returns, and a few minutes later, Scotland Yard, in the person of quiet, stern-faced Detective-Sergeant Doane, who has the previous case in hand, arrives with a colleague. They examine carriage minutely, inside and out, rear-side and off-side, under and over. They say little, but make many notes.

Carriage is locked up, and train sent on. *Link* man notices that most carriages are about half as full as when train came in, as though many had conceived sudden distaste for underground travel – that no single travellers are to be seen – general mistrustful gregariousness observable. *Link* man feels himself that sooner than travel in a carriage alone, or with only one other person, he would stop on the platform all night, and sleep on Smith's bookstall.

Body is carried to ambulance. Lady, now reviving, is placed in cab, and all drive off to Scotland Yard.

The unfortunate victim of this second outrage has since been identified as George Villars, commercial traveller, residing at West Kensington. The lady is Mrs Corbett, manageress of the ABC shop in Albert Street, Westminster.

Her account is simply that she entered the train at Westminster, and had barely got seated when the gentleman opposite lurched forward in his seat, presumably with the shaking of the carriage, and then fell prone on the floor. She saw blood on the floor, and screamed, and then fainted.

What may be the meaning of this exact repetition of the

murder at Charing Cross exactly a week ago it is impossible to say. The time, the manner, the general conditions, are as nearly as possible identical.

Are both murders the act of the same hand; or is Number Two but one more proof of the epidemic nature of abnormal crimes – the result, in fact, of the action of Crime Number One on some weak intellect, with a morbid craving for notoriety?

One thing is certain: travel on the Underground is less attractive than of yore, and the homely 'bus is rising in public estimation.

(From the *Daily Telephone*, 19 November 1894)
A THIRD MURDER ON THE UNDERGROUND

The appalling discovery last night at Ealing Broadway station, on the District Railway, places beyond possibility of doubt the fact that a cold-blooded murderer is at large in our midst, and that travellers on that at all times depressing line are completely at his mercy. The police, we are willing to believe, are doing their best in the matter, but so far their efforts have apparently been fruitless. Every Tuesday night for the last three weeks, at, as near as can be told, exactly the same time to the minute, the mysterious death-dealer has chosen his victim, fired his fatal shot, and vanished.

Whatever his motive and whatever his method, he has succeeded in instilling such a sense of dread into the public mind that the District Railway is beginning to be shunned by all persons of nervous temperament.

This curious state of things recalls to mind a similar series of crimes perpetrated on the Ceinture Railway, in Paris, about seven years ago. There, too, the victims were smitten down by an undiscoverable hand, and it was only when the seventh had fallen that the slaughter stopped. If it had not, the traffic on that line would have ceased, for the excitement was indescribable, and travellers shunned the Ceinture Railway as they would a pesthouse.

Much the same feeling is growing in the minds of travellers by the District Railway, and especially so on Tuesday nights, which is the time fixed by the mysterious one for his horrible work. Last Tuesday night the trains ran nearly empty. Numbers of people, so curious is the hankering of the morbid mind after sensation, gathered in the stations most likely to afford the chance of a thrill. The platforms at Charing Cross, Westminster, St James's Park and Victoria were crowded with sensation-seekers, who had taken tickets which they had no intentions of using, but simply with the idea of being on the spot in case anything happened. And a very curious study those platforms were.

Throngs of people, waiting silently, in a damp fog, peering

into carriage after carriage as the almost empty trains rolled slowly, like processions of funeral cars, in and out of the stations. In one carriage a party of young roughs had ensconced themselves, and endeavoured to make things lively by chaffing and jeering the silent crowds on the platforms as they passed through. They met with no encouragement, however, and had things all their own way. We wonder how those lively youths feel now when they know that, beyond a doubt, the mysterious murderer looked in on them, and could, had he so chosen, have launched his deadly bullet into their midst. But, as usual, his fatal choice fell upon a solitary wayfarer occupying a corner seat in a carriage by himself, and within three compartments of one occupied by the rowdy gang referred to.

Many of the crowd on the stations remarked on the temerity of the occupant of that corner seat. He might well sit so quiet. The fatal bullet was in his heart before he reached Victoria, at all events. But he journeyed peacefully on until he reached Ealing Broadway station, the terminus of the line. There, one of the principal duties of the porters is to arouse all the passengers who have succumbed to the monotony of the journey from the City and there John Small, the Ealing porter, tried in vain to arouse Carl Groeb, the occupant of the corner seat in the rear compartment of one of the first-class carriages, and found him dead – murdered, in the same way, and, beyond all doubt, by the same hand which struck down Conrad Grosheim, at, or about, 9.15 on the evening of Tuesday, the fourth inst., at Charing Cross, and which struck down George Villars, at 9.15 on the evening of Tuesday, the eleventh inst., at St James's Park.

The crowds at the stations up the line had dispersed with a sigh of disappointment, or let us take a charitable view, and say of relief. But the tragedy was there all the same, and the victim had passed beneath their eyes, though the public had to wait till Wednesday morning to get its thrill.

It is a terrible fact, but one that has to be faced that, in the greatest city in the world, in this year of grace 1894, such an appalling series of crimes can be perpetrated with impunity.

The police seem powerless. We give them credit for doing their utmost, but, up to now, nothing, so far as they let it be known, has resulted from their efforts.

One thing is certain, if the criminal cannot be brought to justice the directors of the District Railway can close up their line. It would pay them to run the electric light through every tunnel, and to line the route and sprinkle the carriages with detectives, in the style of an Imperial progress in Russia. The matter is really too gruesome for a jest, but *Punch* certainly hit the case off admirably in Bernard Partidge's clever sketch of the young City man attracting all the attentions of all the beauties in the drawing-room by the simple assertion that he had travelled from town by the District Railway, in a first-class carriage, *all by himself*, while the season's lions scowl at him from a distance, and twirl their moustaches, and growl in their neglected corners.

While, in another portion of the same journal, Mr Anstey's 'Voces Populi', describing the scene at Victoria station on Tuesday night, while the crowds waited for what they feared, and made simple bets on the basis of murder or no murder, and more complicated ones as to the age and nationality of the expected victim, the station where the discovery would be made, and so on, is immensely clever, but grim in the extreme. It proves the identity of one of the crowd at all events, and it will afford matter for much wondering comment on the part of readers of this year's *Punch* twenty years hence.

To return to the facts which confront us, however. Murder, grim, cold, calculating, glides unchecked in our midst. No man's life is safe. You yourself, reading this, may be the next victim – that is, if you are so unwise as to trust yourself alone in a carriage on the District Railway. And this in London, AD 1894! What a satire on our boasted civilisation!

The official report of this latest crime is, with the necessary alterations of names, places, and dates, a mere duplication of the previous ones.

Carl Groeb took ticket at Mansion House for Victoria on

the evening of Tuesday, the twenty-fifth inst., at 9.20. Before he reached Victoria he was dead – shot through the heart, in identically the same manner as the previous victims, and not a trace of the murderer is discoverable.

It is beyond belief, and yet it is horrible fact.

(From the *Daily Telephone*, 23 November 1894)

More light has been thrown on the dark comers of the Underground railway during the last few days than at any period of its existence, and yet the mystery remains unsolved. Travellers between 9 and 10.30 p.m. have been few and far between. Indeed, between those hours the service has been almost suspended, not more than one train in ten being run, and that running practically empty. But such hardy voyagers as have ventured, at risk of their lives, to run the passage from the City to Earl's Court, have travelled through a torchlight procession. Every tunnel has been filled with men with flare-lights, and the grotesque effects of the continuous blaze and the weird gigantic shadows are things to be remembered for a lifetime.

Not only is traffic on the Underground disorganised – business and pleasure alike are interrupted in their regular courses. Never, during the last twenty years, has London worked itself up into such a state of excitement as it has done over these mysterious crimes on the Underground. Suburban residents find words even of the most cerulean hue quite inadequate to express the annoyance and inconvenience they are being put to.

Scotland Yard has had a detective patrolling the footboard of every train. This, however, is to be stopped. The sensation of suddenly finding a strange face peering in at your ear as you sit harmlessly reading your evening paper in your favourite corner seat, is enough to startle any man. It has given rise to some most ludicrous scenes. Going home in a Richmond train last night, the writer sat opposite to a quiet, nervous-looking old gentleman. He happened to raise his eyes from his paper just as the patrol on the footboard passed the window. The old gentleman made up his mind at once that he had been selected as the murderer's next victim, and that the deadly bullet was just about to be launched. He instinctively sheltered his head behind his newspaper, and sank suddenly off his seat, and remained flat on the floor, nor could he be induced to rise till the next station was reached. Many ladies have been driven into hysterics in the same way, and the patrols are to be abolished.

In connection with the murder of Carl Groeb, it is now proved beyond doubt that the murderer has added to his other crime the meaner one of robbery. Groeb's pockets were empty when he was discovered – money, watch, chain, all were gone, though the evidence is conclusive that, when he left his office in Houndsditch, he carried a good round sum, and wore a good gold watch and chain. There is more hope of catching the murderer if he is driven by the exigencies of want, or the desire for gain, to unite the functions of footpad with those of self-constituted executioner. At all events, he descends from the sphere of the supernatural, into which popular credulity has been inclined to elevate him, and becomes a mere murderous thief.

(From the *Daily Telephone*, 25 November, 1894)

We have received the following letter:
To the Editor of the *Daily Telephone*.

Sir, – You are wrong. I never touched the money or effects of Carl Groeb, or any other of my victims. I kill; I do not rob. – Yours truly,

The Underground Murderer.

The letter is post-marked 'London, SE, 24 November, 1894'. Is it a grim jest, or is it a genuine document? We give it for what it is worth.

(From the *Daily Telephone*, 26 November, 1894)

To the Editor of the *Daily Telephone*.

SIR, – The Underground Murderer has enough on his conscience. He did *not* rob Carl Groeb of his watch, chain and money. I did. I entered the carriage at Sloane Square. The attitude of the figure in the corner startled me. When we had passed South Kensington I spoke to him. He did not answer. I touched him. He did not move. I saw he was dead. I was stone-broke myself. I had bilked the ticket-man at Sloane Square, and intended doing the same at Earl's Court. The opportunity was too good to be missed. The man in the corner had no further use for his money. I had. I relieved him of it, and also of his watch and chain. The latter I pawned in Liverpool, and I enclose you the ticket. I am a bad lot, but, thank Heaven, lam

(Signed) Not the Underground Murderer.

The above letter was received by us two days ago, post-marked 'Liverpool'. We sent the pawn-ticket on to Liverpool. The watch and chain, recovered from the pawnbroker, have been sent to London, and have been identified beyond all doubt as Carl Groeb's!

Both letters are in possession of the police.

(From the *Daily Telephone*, 27 November 1894)

What, in Heaven's name, is this monstrous thing that is waging cruel, remorseless and indiscriminate warfare with that section of London that travels by the Underground? Is it against the Underground railway itself, as a system or as a corporation, that this foul fiend is fighting? Or is it some lunatic registering in this gruesome fashion his protest against the influx of foreigners into English business life? – for it is a noticeable fact that three out of the four victims have been foreigners.

Last night was 'Murder Night', as Tuesday night has come to be grimly dubbed on the Underground, and two more victims fell to the assassin's bullet-one in the usual neat and finished style to which we are becoming accustomed, but with a change of locality, necessitated, no doubt, by the close and incessant watch kept on every corner of the murderer's old haunts; the other was a gratuitous slap in the face – or, to be precise, bullet in the leg – of one of the guardians of the public safety in charge of the tunnel between Victoria and Sloane Square.

As the train which left Mansion House at 9.16, and left Victoria at 9.31, was running through the tunnel between

Victoria and Sloane Square, it passed an up-line train proceeding to Mansion House.

The flare-light men are mostly concentrated between Victoria and Mansion House, in the tunnels of which section all the murders have hitherto been committed. As a precautionary measure, however, half a dozen men have been told off for duty each night in the tunnel between Victoria and Sloane Square. As the two trains passed, one of the flare-men standing in the six-foot fell to the ground, shot through the leg. No report was heard. Nothing but the rattle of the passing trains, which drowned the man's groans as he sank to the ground. His mate down the line saw a blaze of light as his flare fell over, and the oil caught fire and spread along the ground. Running up, he dragged the wounded man away from the flames, and yelled to the other men further down the tunnel.

Among them they carried this latest victim up to Victoria station, where their arrival caused a stampede of all except the officials.

The men's accounts of the matter are confused.

The bullet, of course, came from one of the passing trains, but which they cannot say. Even the wounded man is not certain how he was standing when the bullet struck him, but in any case only the very promptest action could have thrown any light on the matter. Had the men promptly wired to the next stations, both up and down the line, at which both trains would stop, strict search, might have led to some discovery. But their wounded mate absorbed all their attention, and the chance, such as it was, was lost. We may, however, conclude, without doubt, that the shot came from the down train. That train reached Baker Street at 9.58, and four minutes later the murderer's fifth victim was discovered in a first-class carriage at Gower Street, in the person of John Stern, merchant, of Jewin Street, who was discovered shot through the heart, in exactly the same way as all the previous victims of the Underground fiend.

How much longer this state of matters is to continue depends, apparently, entirely on the will of the mysterious and bloodthirsty perpetrator of these atrocious crimes. The arm of the law seems powerless. It only remains now for the Underground fiend to shoot down an engine driver and his mate to bring about a catastrophe too horrible to contemplate. The bare possibility of an Underground train deprived of its natural controllers, and crashing madly along at its own sweet will, is enough to make one forswear for ever the delights of travel on that much-maligned line.

(From the *Link*, 4 December 1894)
ANOTHER OUTRAGE ON THE UNDERGROUND
THE *LINK* MAN THE SIXTH VICTIM

To all intents and purposes, I am a dead man.

To all intents and purposes, I am victim No. Six of the Underground Demon.

That I am here alive to tell the tale is no fault of his, but is due to a little precautionary measure of my own.

I have passed through a very strange experience.

I have done what no other man has done. I have looked Death in the face – the Death of the Underground. I have looked down the barrel of the weapon with which the Underground Death-dealer slaughters his victims.

I myself was the victim.

I am free to confess that I am shaken in nerves and sorely bruised in body.

After the detailed account given below of my experiences last 'Murder Night' I have done with the matter. I have had enough of it. My constitution cannot stand the exigencies of up-to-date travel on the Underground. The facts I am about to relate are so passing strange, that I may state at once that they are vouched for by the one man who has had more to do with the Underground Murders (except, of course, the chief actor of all) than anyone else – Detective-Sergeant Doane, of Scotland Yard. Sergeant Doane, into whose hands, from the first, has been entrusted the discovery of the mysterious murderer, has been greatly exercised by the failure of all the ingenious plans laid for his capture, and the apparent impossibility of coming to grips with the invisible one.

It is obviously impossible to have a detective on the step of every carriage of every train on the Underground railway. It is impossible to line the whole length of the system with flare-light men, even on 'Murder Night'. As a matter of fact, since the shooting of John Cran, the flare-man, in Sloane Square tunnel, it is not easy to induce the men to undertake the duty at all, for every one of them feels that he takes his life in his hand when he picks up his lamp. Every man of them knows that, as like as not, he may be the next victim.

I came into contact with Sergeant Doane over the second murder, the one at St James's Park, as readers of the *Link* will remember. I have met him many times since, and we have discussed the matter from many points of view.

On Saturday last I laid before him a scheme which seemed to me to offer at least the chance of a solution of the mystery.

My proposition was this: I offered to take my place, alone, in a first-class compartment in the train leaving Mansion House at 9.12 on 'Murder Night,' and to afford the Underground Fiend every facility for selecting me as his next victim. As a precaution, I was to wear inside my waistcoat a breastplate of solid steel; I was to have the company of an armed detective beneath the opposite seat within reach of a kick, and on top of the carriage, lying flat on the roof, directly over each window of my compartment, were to be two other detectives.

Sergeant Doane turned this idea over in his mind before cautiously venturing the remark that it might do – might do for me, in any case, he grimly added.

The idea was carried out precisely as given above, and 9.13 last Tuesday night found me comfortably ensconced, steel breastplate and all, in the rear first-class compartment of the London and North-Western train from Mansion House to Willesden, gliding through brilliant tunnel after tunnel into the comparative obscurity of the stations, and patiently waiting to be shot at. Beneath the opposite seat, within easy reach of my toe, was one of Doane's trusty followers, armed with a revolver. Flat On the roof, feet to engine, and head over my window, with the cold night wind ploughing up his back hair, was Sergeant Doane himself and over the opposite window another of his men, both armed with revolvers. A slight iron framework had been fixed to the top of the carriage to prevent their rolling off.

Now, a scheme of this kind – I speak from experience – is all very well in the heat of inception and preliminary discussion, but, in the carrying out of it, one's temperature is apt to fall.

I must confess to feeling distinctly nervous as I took my seat in the carriage, and, as the train rumbled along through the weird, irregular illumination of the flare-light men, an odd idea grew upon me that the compartment I was sitting in was somehow unpleasantly familiar to me.

The sensation grew, and the feelings of discomfort increased in proportion. It was likely enough I had ridden in that same carriage dozens of times, for I use the Underground freely, and occasionally go 'first' when, in my opinion, the 'thirds' are full. I was arguing myself into the idea that it was just the natural nervousness incidental to the job I had in hand, when my eye, roving around, caught the number of the carriage – No. 3 2 – on the small enamelled plate above the door, and I experienced all the sensation of a cold douche down the spine.

'Nonsense!' said I to myself. 'Don't be an idiot!'

But I sat and stared at that small enamelled plate till it began to hypnotise me.

To prove myself a tool, and disperse the blue devils, I hauled out my notebook, and turned over the pages till I came to what was in my mind. And then – I had a strong inclination to get out of the carriage, and have done with the business.

I was sitting in the exact spot of the very compartment of the very carriage in which George Villars was shot exactly five weeks ago to the day, and almost to the minute. As readers of the *Link* will remember, I was the first to discover his body at St James's Park station. It was distinctly unpleasant, but it could not be helped.

For companionship's sake, I landed a kick on a tender portion of the recumbent detective under the seat opposite, and he grunted wakefully. Then, feeling deucedly uncomfortable, I sank my head down into the pose of a tired man, drew my hat down over my brow, and turned my eyes almost upside down in the endeavour to keep a bright lookout from under the brim of it.

Blackfriars, Temple, Charing Cross, Westminster, St James's, Victoria, Sloane Square: I heaved a sigh of relief. We were through the original murder zone, and looked like drawing blank this time. Still, as the murderer had broken fresh ground at Baker Street last week, there was no knowing where he might strike this time. And so the train rumbled on.

Earl's Court, and tickets; Addison Road, Uxbridge Road, Shepherd's Bush, and we were rushing across the wilds of Wormwood Scrubs, when my eyes, wearied almost to blindness with the unnatural strain, closed for a moment's rest.

When I opened them, to my amazement, the window on my left, which I had carefully closed, was down, and wind and rain were pouring in. It sank to the bottom. Every drop of blood in me was tingling with excitement. My heart was going like a sledge-hammer. I wanted to kick the man under the seat, but could not move a toe.

As I glanced at the window, along the polished framework of the part that slides down, there came gently and silently into view a shining steel barrel, pointing straight for my heart. I caught just one vague glimpse of a face beyond it, then – without any report, or any warning, an awful shock – and – blank.

They tell me that I was lifted out at Willesden, and that I was unconscious for upwards of four hours.

I take their word for it; at present I will take anybody's word for anything. As far as I am personally concerned, I have done with the Underground Murders. I hold a season ticket on that abnormal line from Blackfriars to Sloane Square. Anyone who wants it, and will take it with all risks, including its non-transferability, is welcome to it. I would suggest that whoever takes it, should also take out a £10,000 Life Policy for the benefit of his widow and children.

For myself, as I said at the beginning. Underground travel is not adapted to my peculiar constitution. I now go home by 'bus.

As this story is passing strange, and may, in some quarters, be received with incredulity, Sergeant Doane has very kindly offered to add a few words concerning his experiences on Tuesday night.

If any of my fellow-journalists desire ocular demonstration of the truth of my story, and will call at St Bartholomew's Hospital, they can see for themselves the documents in the case, viz.: one steel shield, and one journalist, with a bruise, of the dimensions of a soup-plate, round about the spot where his heart is supposed to be.

Sergeant Doane's account is as follows:—

'I have read the foregoing statement, and endorse it in every particular which came under my own knowledge. Journeying on one's stomach, stern foremost, on top of the Underground train, is not a mode of locomotion that I can recommend. The motion of the train, much more violent up there than in the body of the carriage, the peculiar position, and the horrible atmosphere, produced a feeling of nausea to such an extent that my colleague, on the other side of the roof, when he descended at Willesden, was white as a sheet, and was practically in the throes of sea-sickness.

'Nothing happened on our journey till we reached Wormwood Scrubs. It was blowing half a gale. The heavy rain stung like pellets, and, combined with the rattle of the train, drowned every other sound.

'Half-way between Wormwood Scrubs station and Willesden Junction, the gale seemed to seize the train and shake it, and it was all we could do to hang on by main force. It was at that moment that I heard a shout in the carriage below; then my colleague, Detective Trevor, who had been hidden under the seat, put his head through the window, shouting, "Doane, Doane, he is shot." Half a minute more, and we ran into Willesden station. Mr Lester was insensible from the impact of the bullet, which was flattened on the shield like a shilling. I heard no report, and feel sure there was none. Trevor confirms this fact. Beyond the "ping" of the bullet on the shield, he heard nothing. On hearing that, however, he crawled out, found Mr Lester with all the breath knocked out of him, and yelled for me.'

(From the *Daily Telephone*, 10 December 1894)

We feel like accessories before the fact – like partners in the horrible work of the Underground Murderer.

Ten days ago we hinted in these columns at the appalling catastrophe which might result from the massacre of an Underground engine driver and his mate by the Underground Murderer.

Last night, William Johnson, driver of the 9.1 Outer Circle train, was shot at and wounded, fortunately not fatally, as the train ran through the tunnel beyond South Kensington station.

When the train steamed into Gloucester Road station, it was seen at once that something was wrong. Charles Jones, the fireman, was hanging on to the brake lever, white as a sheet, shouting for help. As the train came to a stand, and the inspectors and guard ran up, Driver Johnson was found lying in a heap on the floor of the cab.

Jones explained hurriedly that, as they ran through the tunnel Johnson suddenly clapped his hand to his side, and cried, 'My God! I'm shot!' and fell all of a heap.

'I'm off,' said Jones, when he had finished his story. 'I'll have no more o' this – a man's life isn't safe.' Neither threats nor persuasion availed to induce him to resume his place on the engine. Another driver and fireman were eventually procured from Mansion House, and traffic was resumed.

Matters, however, have come to a pretty pass when such an occurrence is possible, and something has got to be done, and at once, to put an end to this unheard-of state of affairs.

The following proclamation has been posted broadcast over the Metropolis. May it have some effect:—

£1,000 REWARD

WHEREAS, on the night of Tuesday, 4 November 1894, Conrad Grosheim was murdered in a first-class carriage on the Underground railway between Mansion House and Charing Cross stations; and

WHEREAS on the night of Tuesday, 11 November 1894, George Villars was murdered in a first-class carriage on the Underground railway between Mansion House and Westminster Stations; and

WHEREAS, on the night of Tuesday, 18 November Carl Groeb was murdered in a first-class carriage on the Underground railway between Mansion House and Victoria stations; and

WHEREAS, on the night of Tuesday, 25 November John Cran was shot in the leg in the tunnel between Victoria and Sloane Square stations on the Underground railway; and, on the same night, John Stern was found murdered, in a first-class carriage at Baker Street station; and

WHEREAS, on the night of Tuesday, 2 December Charles Lester was shot at and wounded, with intent to murder, while travelling in a first-class carriage between Wormwood Scrubs and Willesden; and

WHEREAS, on the night of Tuesday, 9 December William Johnson, engine-driver, was shot at and wounded, with intent to murder, while travelling on his engine, between South Kensington and Gloucester Road station on the Underground railway:

The sum of ONE THOUSAND POUNDS (£1,000) will be paid to any person or persons (not being the actual murderer or murderers) who shall give such information as shall lead to the detection of the perpetrator of the above deeds.

The above emanated from Scotland Yard. The chairman of the District Railway Company authorises us to state that his company will double the government reward for information.

(From the *Link*. Third Edition. Wednesday, 12 December 1894)

The £1,000 reward seems to have had its effect. Last night was 'Murder Night' on the Underground, and, for the first time in six weeks, we have no murder to chronicle.

Is the Underground Fiend sated with blood – or, having accomplished the magical number 'Seven', has he retired, satisfied with his work?

Time will show. The terrible chain, however, is broken, and from this we may draw some slight hope that the reign of terror on the Underground is over – until such time as the Death-dealer chooses to resume his self-imposed duties.

Receiving a tip-off that a man believed to be the Underground Murderer is about to flee the country on a boat sailing for Australia, the Link *man Charles Lester joins the vessel, the* Bendigo. *During the following weeks at sea two more murders are committed before Lester finally narrows down the suspects to the most unlikely passenger on board: an old man named Hood who is travelling with his pretty young grand-daughter. When the murderer strikes a third time, however, and tries to kill the ship's doctor, Shannon, who has also become increasingly suspicious of the old fellow, the medical man defends himself with an iron bar and causes his adversary to fall down a stairway to his death. As soon as the news of the old man's death is conveyed to his grand-daughter she is overwhelmed with relief, having apparently been an unwitting accomplice to the reign of terror on the London subway and at sea. After Hood's body has been committed to the ocean, Charles Lester is summoned by Miss Hood to the cabin that had been occupied by her grandfather and there he finally learns the secret of the Underground mystery . . .*

The girl was kneeling on the floor, amid piles of books, papers, clothing, etc., which she had taken from his boxes.

She beckoned me inside, and bade me close the door.

'You have a right to see some of these things, Mr Lester,' she said. 'When you have seen all you care to, will you help me to get rid of them? I only learned this morning from

Captain Joram that you were the Mr Lester who—' She faltered, and the large eyes, turned pathetically up to mine, were swimming with tears.

'Try and forget all about it,' I said, 'and let me help you.'

She stooped hurriedly, and picked up a bundle of papers.

'Read those – and those – and look at these,' putting into my hand some strange steel instruments, quite unlike anything I had ever seen before. One had a horse-shoe clutch at the end, and, at the other extremity, it was pinned on to another long, thin steel rod, one end of which terminated in four fine sharp teeth, like the prongs of a fork.

I turned it over in my hand, but could make nothing of it, so proceeded to look over the papers. And, reading them, I arrived at old Hood's story.

A mechanical engineer, of quite unique powers, he had patented a number of inventions, and offered them to the District Railway Company, in whose employment he had spent the best part of his life. Nothing had come of them, however, and I gathered from some of the company's letters in reply that the old man had accused them of using his ideas, but giving him no benefit of them. Then he left the company's service, with his brain bursting with grievances, and it was easy to conceive that he determined to strike at them in a way that was as horribly effective as it was, for him, easy of accomplishment.

I was puzzling over the strange implements, and trying to get at their use. In thought, I went back to one of the murderer's journeys along the swinging footboards, and suddenly it all flashed upon me. A long steel rod, with curved top – that hitched on to the edge of the carriage roof, and had enabled him to pass rapidly along, without troubling to grasp each handle. That spidery implement, with the curved horse-shoe clutch and the pronged lever – I could see the sharp teeth inserted quietly into the window sash, the clutch fitted to the bottom outside frame, the pressing of the lever – and my closed window was sliding quietly down, the wind and rain of Wormwood Scrubs were beating in on me again, and my paralysed eyes were looking once more down the deadly death-tube. I could see myself lying bruised and stunned in the corner, and, in imagination, could follow the murderer as he rapidly made his way back to the carriage he had issued from, and, perhaps, concealed himself under the seat, or, riding between two carriages, dropped quietly off as the train began to slow up to the station.

There were other curious contrivances, whose meaning I could not fathom, but had no doubt they all tended to the same end – the boarding of, or hanging on to, trains in motion.

I looked up at the girl.

'What do you want me to do with all these things?'

'Throw them all overboard – clothes – books – papers – everything. I have kept the only papers I need. Please get rid of them all for me.'

I did. Shannon, however, claimed the air-gun, and certainly no one who wanted it had a better right to it.

It was a wonderful weapon, the only remaining monument to the old engineer's skill. With two twists it came into three pieces, and was easily stowed in one's ordinary pockets. The first day Shannon appeared on deck, Miss Hood being below, he tried that demon air-gun on the main-mast with a bullet of his own making. It buried itself out of sight, and a three-inch probe failed to reach it.

'No wonder it knocked the wind out of you, old man,' he said; 'if you hadn't had that breastplate on, you wouldn't be here now.'

We cleaned our memories of Old Man Hood as far as we could, as we had cleaned the ship of himself and his belongings, and Mary Hood grew brighter every day. Her burden lay behind her at the bottom of the Indian Ocean, and her sweet face was set bravely and hopefully towards the new life that awaited her in the unknown land that lay beneath the rising sun.

THE MYSTERIOUS DEATH ON THE UNDERGROUND RAILWAY

BARONESS EMMUSKA ORCZY

It was all very well for Mr Richard Frobisher (of the *London Mail*) to cut up rough about it. Polly did not altogether blame him.

She liked him all the better for that frank outburst of manlike ill-temper which, after all said and done, was only a very flattering form of masculine jealousy.

Moreover, Polly distinctly felt guilty about the whole thing. She had promised to meet Dickie – that is Mr Richard Frobisher – at two o'clock sharp outside the Palace Theatre, because she wanted to go to a Maud Allan matinée, and because he naturally wished to go with her.

But at two o'clock sharp she was still in Norfolk Street, Strand, inside an ABC shop, sipping cold coffee opposite a grotesque old man who was fiddling with a bit of string.

How could she be expected to remember Maud Allan or

the Palace Theatre, or Dickie himself for a matter of that? The man in the corner had begun to talk of that mysterious death on the Underground railway, and Polly had lost count of time, of place, and circumstance.

She had gone to lunch quite early, for she was looking forward to the matinée at the Palace. The old scarecrow was sitting in his accustomed place when she came into the ABC shop, but he had made no remark all the time that the young girl was munching her scone and butter. She was just busy thinking how rude he was not even to have said 'Good morning', when an abrupt remark from him caused her to look up.

'Will you be good enough,' he said suddenly, 'to give me a description of the man who sat next to you just now, while you were having your cup of coffee and scone.'

Involuntarily Polly turned her head towards the distant door, through which a man in a light overcoat was even now quickly passing. That man had certainly sat at the next table to hers, when she first sat down to her coffee and scone: he had finished his luncheon – whatever it was – a moment ago, had paid at the desk and gone out. The incident did not appear to Polly as being of the slightest consequence.

Therefore she did not reply to the rude old man, but shrugged her shoulders, and called to the waitress to bring her bill.

'Do you know if he was tall or short, dark or fair?' continued the man in the corner, seemingly not the least disconcerted by the young girl's indifference. 'Can you tell me at all what he was like?'

'Of course I can,' rejoined Polly impatiently, 'but I don't see that my description of one of the customers of an ABC shop can have the slightest importance.'

He was silent for a minute, while his nervous fingers fumbled about in his capacious pockets in search of the inevitable piece of string. When he had found this necessary 'adjunct to thought', he viewed the young girl again through his half-closed lids, and added maliciously:

'But supposing it were of paramount importance that you should give an accurate description of a man who sat next to you for half an hour today, how would you proceed?'

'I should say that he was of medium height—'

'Five foot eight, nine, or ten?' he interrupted quietly.

'How can one tell to an inch or two?' rejoined Polly crossly. 'He was between colours.'

'What's that?' he enquired blandly.

'Neither fair nor dark – his nose—'

'Well, what was his nose like? Will you sketch it?'

'I am not an artist. His nose was fairly straight – his eyes—'

'Were neither dark nor light – his hair had the same striking peculiarity – he was neither short nor tall – his nose was neither aquiline nor snub—' he recapitulated sarcastically.

'No,' she retorted; 'he was just ordinary-looking.'

'Would you know him again – say tomorrow, and among a number of other men who were "neither tall nor short, dark nor fair, aquiline nor snub-nosed", etc.?'

'I don't know – I might – he was certainly not striking enough to be specially remembered.'

'Exactly,' he said, while he leant forward excitedly, for all the world like a Jack-in-the-box let loose. 'Precisely; and you are a journalist – call yourself one, at least – and it should be part of your business to notice and describe people. I don't mean only the wonderful personage with the clear Saxon features, the fine blue eyes, the noble brow and classic face, but the ordinary person – the person who represents ninety out of every hundred of his own kind — the average Englishman, say, of the middle classes, who is neither very tall nor very short, who wears a moustache which is neither fair nor dark, but which masks his mouth, and a top hat which hides the shape of his head and brow, a man, in fact, who dresses like hundreds of his fellow-creatures, moves like them, speaks like them, has no peculiarity.

'Try to describe *him*, to recognise him, say a week hence, among his other eighty-nine doubles; worse still, to swear his life away, if he happened to be implicated in some crime, wherein *your* recognition of him would place the halter round his neck.

'Try that, I say, and having utterly failed you will more readily understand how one of the greatest scoundrels unhung is still at large, and why the mystery on the Underground railway was never cleared up.

'I think it was the only time in my life that I was seriously tempted to give the police the benefit of my own views upon the matter. You see, though I admire the brute for his cleverness, I did not see that his being unpunished could possibly benefit anyone.

'In these days of tubes and motor traction of all kinds, the old-fashioned "best, cheapest, and quickest route to City and West End" is often deserted, and the good old Metropolitan railway carriages cannot at any time be said to be overcrowded. Anyway, when that particular train steamed into Aldgate at about four p.m. on March eighteenth last, the first-class carriages were all but empty.

'The guard marched up and down the platform looking into all the carriages to see if anyone had left a halfpenny evening paper behind for him, and opening the door of one of the first-class compartments, he noticed a lady sitting in the further corner, with her head turned away towards the window, evidently oblivious of the fact that on this line Aldgate is the terminal station.

' "Where are you for, lady?" he said.

'The lady did not move, and the guard stepped into the carriage, thinking that perhaps the lady was asleep. He touched her arm lightly and looked into her face. In his own poetic language, he was "struck all of a 'eap". In the glassy eyes, the ashen colour of the cheeks, the rigidity of the head, there was the unmistakable look of death.

'Hastily the guard, having carefully locked the carriage door, summoned a couple of porters, and sent one of them off to the police station, and the other in search of the stationmaster.

'Fortunately at this time of day the up platform is not very crowded, all the traffic tending westward in the afternoon. It was only when an inspector and two police constables, accompanied by a detective in plain clothes and a medical officer, appeared upon the scene, and stood round a first-class railway compartment, that a few idlers realised that something unusual had occurred, and crowded round, eager and curious.

'Thus it was that the later editions of the evening papers, under the sensational heading, "Mysterious Suicide on the Underground Railway", had already an account of the extraordinary event. The medical officer had very soon come to the decision that the guard had not been mistaken, and that life was indeed extinct.

'The lady was young, and must have been very pretty before the look of fright and horror had so terribly distorted her features. She was very elegantly dressed, and the more frivolous papers were able to give their feminine readers a detailed account of the unfortunate woman's gown, her shoes, hat, and gloves.

'It appears that one of the latter, the one on the right hand, was partly off, leaving the thumb and wrist bare. That hand held a small satchel, which the police opened, with a view to the possible identification of the deceased, but which was found to contain only a little loose silver, some smelling-salts, and a small empty bottle, which was handed over to the medical officer for purposes of analysis.

'It was the presence of that small bottle which had caused the report to circulate freely that the mysterious case on the Underground railway was one of suicide. Certain it was that neither about the lady's person, nor in the appearance of the railway carriage, was there the slightest sign of struggle or even of resistance. Only the look in the poor woman's eyes spoke of sudden terror, of the rapid vision of an unexpected and violent death, which probably only lasted an infinitesimal fraction of a second, but which had left its indelible mark upon the face, otherwise so placid and so still.

'The body of the deceased was conveyed to the mortuary. So far, of course, not a soul had been able to identify her, or to throw the slightest light upon the mystery which hung around her death.

'Against that, quite a crowd of idlers – genuinely interested or not – obtained admission to view the body, on the pretext of having lost or mislaid a relative or a friend. At about eight-thirty p.m. a young man, very well dressed, drove up to the station in a hansom, and sent in his card to the superintendent. It was Mr Hazeldene, shipping agent, of II, Crown Lane, EC, and No. 19, Addison Row, Kensington.

'The young man looked in a pitiable state of mental distress; his hand clutched nervously a copy of the *St James's Gazette* which contained the fatal news. He said very little to the superintendent except that a person who was very dear to him had not returned home that evening.

'He had not felt really anxious until half an hour ago, when suddenly he thought of looking at his paper. The description of the deceased lady, though vague, had terribly alarmed him. He had jumped into a hansom, and now begged permission to view the body, in order that his worst fears might be allayed.

'You know what followed, of course,' continued the man in the corner, 'the grief of the young man was truly pitiable. In the woman lying there in a public mortuary before him, Mr Hazeldene had recognised his wife.

'I am waxing melodramatic,' said the man in the corner,

who looked up at Polly with a mild and gentle smile, while his nervous fingers vainly endeavoured to add another knot on the scrappy bit of string with which he was continually playing, 'and I fear that the whole story savours of the penny novelette, but you must admit, and no doubt you remember, that it was an intensely pathetic and truly dramatic moment.

'The unfortunate young husband of the deceased lady was not much worried with questions that night. As a matter of fact, he was not in a fit condition to make any coherent statement. It was at the coroner's inquest on the following day that certain facts came to light, which for the time being seemed to clear up the mystery surrounding Mrs Hazeldene's death, only to plunge that same mystery, later on, into denser gloom than before.

'The first witness at the inquest was, of course, Mr Hazeldene himself. I think everyone's sympathy went out to the young man as he stood before the coroner and tried to throw what light he could upon the mystery. He was well dressed, as he had been the day before, but he looked terribly ill and worried, and no doubt the fact that he had not shaved gave his face a careworn and neglected air.

'It appears that he and the deceased had been married some six years or so, and that they had always been happy in their married life. They had no children. Mrs Hazeldene seemed to enjoy the best of health till lately, when she had had a slight attack of influenza, in which Dr Arthur Jones had attended her. The doctor was present at this moment, and would no doubt explain to the coroner and the jury whether he thought that Mrs Hazeldene had the slightest tendency to heart disease, which might have had a sudden and fatal ending.

'The coroner was, of course, very considerate to the bereaved husband. He tried by circumlocution to get at the point he wanted, namely, Mrs Hazeldene's mental condition lately. Mr Hazeldene seemed loath to talk about this. No doubt he had been warned as to the existence of the small bottle found in his wife's satchel.

' "It certainly did seem to me at times," he at last reluctantly admitted, "that my wife did not seem quite herself. She used to be very gay and bright, and lately I often saw her in the evening sitting, as if brooding over some matters, which evidently she did not care to communicate to me."

'Still the coroner insisted, and suggested the small bottle.

' "I know, I know," replied the young man, with a short, heavy sigh. "You mean – the question of suicide – I cannot understand it at all – it seems so sudden and so terrible – she certainly had seemed listless and troubled lately – but only at times – and yesterday morning, when I went to business, she appeared quite herself again, and I suggested that we should go to the opera in the evening. She was delighted, I know, and told me she would do some shopping, and pay a few calls in the afternoon.

' "Do you know at all where she intended to go when she got into the Underground railway?"

' "Well, not with certainty. You see, she may have meant to get out at Baker Street, and go down to Bond Street to do her shopping. Then again, she sometimes goes to a shop in St Paul's Churchyard, in which case she would take a ticket to Aldersgate Street; but I cannot say."

' "Now, Mr Hazeldene," said the coroner at last very kindly, "will you try to tell me if there was anything in Mrs Hazeldene's life which you know of, and which might in some measure explain the cause of the distressed state of mind, which you yourself had noticed? Did there exist any financial difficulty which might have preyed upon Mrs Hazeldene's mind; was there any friend – to whose intercourse with Mrs Hazeldene – you – er – at any time took exception? In fact," added the coroner, as if thankful that he had got over an unpleasant moment, "can you give me the slightest indication which would tend to confirm the suspicion that the unfortunate lady, in a moment of mental anxiety or derangement, may have wished to take her own life?"

'There was silence in the court for a few moments. Mr Hazeldene seemed to everyone there present to be labouring under some terrible moral doubt. He looked very pale and wretched, and twice attempted to speak before he at last said in scarcely audible tones:

' "No; there were no financial difficulties of any sort. My wife had an independent fortune of her own – and she had no extravagant tastes—"

' "Nor any friend you at any time objected to?" insisted the coroner.

' "Nor any friend, I – at any time objected to," stammered the unfortunate young man, evidently speaking with an effort.

'I was present at the inquest,' resumed the man in the corner, after he had drunk a glass of milk and ordered another, 'and I can assure you that the most obtuse person there plainly realised that Mr Hazeldene was telling a lie. It was pretty plain to the meanest intelligence that the unfortunate lady had not fallen into a state of morbid dejection for nothing, and that perhaps there existed a third person who could throw more light on her strange and sudden death than the unhappy, bereaved young widower.

'That the death was more mysterious even than it had at first appeared became very soon apparent. You read the case at the time, no doubt, and must remember the excitement in the public mind caused by the evidence of the two doctors. Dr Arthur Jones, the lady's usual medical man, who had attended her in a last very slight illness, and who had seen her in a professional capacity fairly recently, declared most emphatically that Mrs Hazeldene suffered from no organic complaint which could possibly have been the cause of sudden death. Moreover, he had assisted Mr Andrew Thornton, the district medical officer, in making a post-mortem examination, and together they had come to the conclusion that death was due to the action of prussic acid, which had caused instantaneous failure of the heart, but how the drug had been administered neither he nor his colleague were at present able to state.

' "Do I understand, then, Dr Jones, that the deceased died, poisoned with prussic acid?"

' "Such is my opinion," replied the doctor.

' "Did the bottle found in her satchel contain prussic acid?"

' "It had contained some at one time, certainly."

' "In your opinion, then, the lady caused her own death by taking a dose of that drug?"

' "Pardon me, I never suggested such a thing; the lady died poisoned by the drug, but how the drug was administered we cannot say. By injection of some sort, certainly. The drug certainly was not swallowed; there was not a vestige of it in the stomach."

' "Yes," added the doctor in reply to another question from

the coroner, "death had probably followed the injection in this case almost immediately; say within a couple of minutes, or perhaps three. It was quite possible that the body would not have more than one quick and sudden convulsion, perhaps not that; death in such cases is absolutely sudden and crushing."

'I don't think that at the time anyone in the room realised how important the doctor's statement was, a statement which, by the way, was confirmed in all its details by the district medical officer, who had conducted the postmortem. Mrs Hazeldene had died suddenly from an injection of prussic acid, administered no one knew how or when. She had been travelling in a first-class railway carriage at a busy time of the day. That young and elegant woman must have had singular nerve and coolness to go through the process of a self-inflicted injection of a deadly poison in the presence of perhaps two or three other persons.

'Mind you, when I say that no one there realised the importance of the doctor's statement at that moment, I am wrong; there were three persons, who fully understood at once the gravity of the situation, and the astounding development which the case was beginning to assume.

'Of course, I should have put myself out of the question,' added the weird old man, with that inimitable self-conceit peculiar to himself. 'I guessed then and there in a moment where the police were going wrong, and where they would go on going wrong until the mysterious death on the Underground railway had sunk into oblivion, together with the other cases which they mismanage from time to time.

'I said there were three persons who understood the gravity of the two doctors' statements – the other two were, firstly, the detective who had originally examined the railway carriage, a young man of energy and plenty of misguided intelligence, the other was Mr Hazeldene.

'At this point the interesting element of the whole story was first introduced into the proceedings, and this was done through the humble channel of Emma Funnel, Mrs Hazeldene's maid, who, as far as was known then, was the last person who had seen the unfortunate lady alive and had spoken to her.

' "Mrs Hazeldene lunched at home," explained Emma, who was shy, and spoke almost in a whisper; "she seemed well and cheerful. She went out at about half-past three, and told me she was going to Spence's, in St Paul's Churchyard, to try on her new tailor-made gown. Mrs Hazeldene had meant to go there in the morning, but was prevented as Mr Errington called."

' "Mr Errington?" asked the coroner casually. "Who is Mr Errington?"

'But this Emma found difficult to explain. Mr Errington

was – Mr Errington, that's all.

' "Mr Errington was a friend of the family. He lived in a flat in the Albert Mansions. He very often came to Addison Row, and generally stayed late."

'Pressed still further with questions, Emma at last stated that latterly Mrs Hazeldene had been to the theatre several times with Mr Errington, and that on those nights the master looked very gloomy, and was very cross.

'Recalled, the young widower was strangely reticent. He gave forth his answers very grudgingly, and the coroner was evidently absolutely satisfied with himself at the marvellous way in which, after a quarter of an hour of firm yet very kind questionings, he had elicited from the witness what information he wanted.

'Mr Errington was a friend of his wife. He was a gentleman of means, and seemed to have a great deal of time at his command. He himself did not particularly care about Mr Errington, but he certainly had never made any observations to his wife on the subject.

' "But who is Mr Errington?" repeated the coroner once more. "What does he do? What is his business or profession?"

' "He has no business or profession."

' "What is his occupation, then?"

' "He has no special occupation. He has ample private

means. But he has a great and very absorbing hobby."

' "What is that?"

' "He spends all his time in chemical experiments, and is, I believe, as an amateur, a very distinguished toxicologist." '

'Did you ever see Mr Errington, the gentleman so closely connected with the mysterious death on the Underground railway?' asked the man in the corner as he placed one or two of his little snap-shot photos before Miss Polly Burton.

'There he is, to the very life. Fairly good-looking, a pleasant face enough, but ordinary, absolutely ordinary.

'It was this absence of any peculiarity which very nearly, but not quite, placed the halter round Mr Errington's neck.

'But I am going too fast, and you will lose the thread.

'The public, of course, never heard how it actually came about that Mr Errington, the wealthy bachelor of Albert Mansions, of the Grosvenor, and other young dandies' clubs, one fine day found himself before the magistrate at Bow Street, charged with being concerned in the death of Mary Beatrice Hazeldene, late of No. 19, Addison Row.

'I can assure you both press and public were literally flabbergasted. You see, Mr Errington was a well-known and very popular member of a certain smart section of London society. He was a constant visitor at the opera, the racecourse, the Park, and the Carlton, he had a great many friends, and there was consequently quite a large attendance at the police court that morning.

'What had transpired was this:

'After the very scrappy bits of evidence which came to light at the inquest, two gentlemen bethought themselves that perhaps they had some duty to perform towards the State and the public generally. Accordingly they had come forward, offering to throw what light they could upon the mysterious affair on the Underground railway.

'The police naturally felt that their information, such as it was, came rather late in the day, but as it proved of paramount importance, and the two gentlemen, moreover, were of undoubtedly good position in the world, they were thankful for what they could get, and acted accordingly; they accordingly brought Mr Errington up before the magistrate on a charge of murder.

'The accused looked pale and worried when I first caught sight of him in the court that day, which was not to be wondered at, considering the terrible position in which he found himself.

'He had been arrested at Marseilles, where he was preparing to start for Colombo. I don't think he realised how terrible his position really was until later in the proceedings, when all the evidence relating to the arrest had been heard, and Emma Funnel had repeated her statement as to Mr Errington's call at 19, Addison Row, in the morning, and Mrs Hazeldene starting off for St Paul's Churchyard at three-thirty in the afternoon.

'Mr Hazeldene had nothing to add to the statements he had made at the coroner's inquest. He had last seen his wife alive on the morning of the fatal day. She had seemed very well and cheerful.

'I think everyone present understood that he was trying to say as little as possible that could in any way couple his deceased wife's name with that of the accused.

'And yet, from the servant's evidence, it undoubtedly leaked out that Mrs Hazeldene, who was young, pretty, and evidently fond of admiration, had once or twice annoyed her husband by her somewhat open, yet perfectly innocent, flirtation with Mr Errington.

'I think everyone was most agreeably impressed by the widower's moderate and dignified attitude. You will see his photo there, among this bundle. That is just how he appeared in court. In deep black, of course, but without any sign of ostentation in his mourning. He had allowed his beard to grow lately, and wore it closely cut in a point.

'After his evidence, the sensation of the day occurred. A tall, dark-haired man, with the word "City" written metaphorically all over him, had kissed the book, and was waiting to tell the truth, and nothing but the truth.

'He gave his name as Andrew Campbell, head of the firm

of Campbell & Co., brokers, of Throgmorton Street.

'In the afternoon of March eighteenth Mr Campbell, travelling on the Underground railway, had noticed a very pretty woman in the same carriage as himself. She had asked him if she was in the right train for Aldersgate. Mr Campbell replied in the affirmative, and then buried himself in the Stock Exchange quotations of his evening paper.

'At Gower Street, a gentleman in a tweed suit and bowler hat got into the carriage, and took a seat opposite the lady. She seemed very much astonished at seeing him, but Mr Andrew Campbell did not recollect the exact words she said.

'The two talked to one another a good deal, and certainly the lady appeared animated and cheerful. Witness took no notice of them; he was very much engrossed in some calculations, and finally got out at Farringdon Street. He noticed that the man in the tweed suit also got out close behind him, having shaken hands with the lady, and said in a pleasant way: "Au revoir! Don't be late tonight." Mr Campbell did not hear the lady's reply, and soon lost sight of the man in the crowd.

'Everyone was on tenter-hooks, and eagerly waiting for the palpitating moment when witness would describe and identify the man who last had seen and spoken to the unfortunate woman, within five minutes probably of her strange and unaccountable death.

'Personally I knew what was coming before the Scots stockbroker spoke.

'I could have jotted down the graphic and lifelike description he would give of a probable murderer. It would have fitted equally well the man who sat and had luncheon at this table just now; it would certainly have described five out of every ten young Englishmen you know.

'The individual was of medium height, he wore a moustache which was not very fair nor yet very dark, his hair was between colours. He wore a bowler hat, and a tweed suit – and – and – that was all – Mr Campbell might perhaps know him again, but then again, he might not – he was not paying much attention – the gentleman was sitting on the same side of the carriage as himself – and he had his hat on all the time. He himself was busy with his newspaper – yes – he might know him again – but he really could not say.

'Mr Andrew Campbell's evidence was not worth very much, you will say. No, it was not in itself, and would not have justified any arrest were it not for the additional statements made by Mr James Verner, manager of Messrs Rodney & Co., colour printers.

'Mr Verner is a personal friend of Mr Andrew Campbell, and it appears that at Farringdon Street, where he was waiting for his train, he saw Mr Campbell get out of a first-class railway carriage. Mr Verner spoke to him for a second, and then, just as the train was moving off, he stepped into the same compartment which had just been vacated by the stockbroker and the man in the tweed suit. He vaguely recollects a lady sitting in the opposite corner to his own, with her face turned away from him, apparently asleep, but he paid no special attention to her. He was like nearly all businessmen when they are travelling – engrossed in his paper. Presently a special quotation interested him; he wished to make a note of it, took out a pencil from his waistcoat pocket, and seeing a clean piece of paste-board on the floor, he picked it up, and scribbled on it the memorandum, which he wished to keep. He then slipped the card into his pocket-book.

' "It was only two or three days later," added Mr Verner in the midst of breathless silence, "that I had occasion to refer to these same notes again.

' "In the meanwhile the papers had been full of the mysterious death on the Underground railway, and the names of those connected with it were pretty familiar to me. It was, therefore, with much astonishment that on looking at the paste-board which I had casually picked up in the railway carriage I saw the name on it, Frank Errington."

'There was no doubt that the sensation in court was almost unprecedented. Never since the days of the Fen-

279

church Street mystery, and the trial of Smethurst, had I seen so much excitement. Mind you, I was not excited – I knew by now every detail of that crime as if I had committed it myself. In fact, I could not have done it better, although I have been a student of crime for many years now. Many people there – his friends, mostly – believed that Errington was doomed. I think he thought so, too, for I could see that his face was terribly white, and he now and then passed his tongue over his lips, as if they were parched.

'You see he was in the awful dilemma – a perfectly natural one, by the way – of being absolutely incapable of *proving* an alibi. The crime – if crime there was – had been committed three weeks ago. A man about town like Mr Frank Errington might remember that he spent certain hours of a special afternoon at his club, or in the Park, but it is very doubtful in nine cases out of ten if he can find a friend who could positively swear as to having seem him there. No! no! Mr Errington was in a tight corner, and he knew it. You see, there were – besides the evidence – two or three circumstances which did not improve matters for him. His hobby in the direction of toxicology, to begin with. The police had found in his room every description of poisonous susbtances, including prussic acid.

'Then, again, that journey to Marseilles, the start for Colombo, was, though perfectly innocent, a very unfortunate one. Mr Errington had gone on an aimless voyage, but the public thought that he had fled, terrified at his own crime. Sir Arthur Inglewood, however, here again displayed his marvellous skill on behalf of his client by the masterly way in which he literally turned all the witnesses for the Crown inside out.

'Having first got Mr Andrew Campbell to state positively that in the accused he certainly did *not* recognise the man in the tweed suit, the eminent lawyer, after twenty minutes' cross-examination, had so completely upset the stockbroker's equanimity that it is very likely he would not have recognised his own office-boy.

'But through all his flurry and all his annoyance Mr Andrew Campbell remained very sure of one thing; namely, that the lady was alive and cheerful, and talking pleasantly with the man in the tweed suit up to the moment when the latter, having shaken hands with her, left her with a pleasant "Au revoir! Don't be late tonight." He had heard neither scream nor struggle, and in his opinion, if the individual in the tweed suit had administered a dose of poison to his companion, it must have been with her own knowledge and free will; and the lady in the train most emphatically neither looked nor spoke like a woman prepared for a sudden and violent death.

'Mr James Verner, against that, swore equally positively

that he had stood in full view of the carriage door from the moment that Mr Campbell got out until he himself stepped into the compartment, that there was no one else in that carriage between Farringdon Street and Aldgate, and that the lady, to the best of his belief, had made no movement during the whole of that journey.

'No; Frank Errington was *not* committed for trial on the capital charge,' said the man in the corner with one of his sardonic smiles, 'thanks to the cleverness of Sir Arthur Inglewood, his lawyer. He absolutely denied his identity with the man in the tweed suit, and swore he had not seen Mrs Hazeldene since eleven o'clock in the morning of that fatal day. There was no *proof* that he had; moreover, according to Mr Campbell's opinion, the man in the tweed suit was in all probability not the murderer. Common sense would not admit that a woman could have a deadly poison injected into her without her knowledge, while chatting pleasantly to her murderer.

'Mr Errington lives abroad now. He is about to marry. I don't think any of his real friends for a moment believed that he committed the dastardly crime. The police think they know better. They do know this much, that it could not have been a case of suicide, that if the man who undoubtedly travelled with Mrs Hazeldene on that fatal afternoon had no crime upon his conscience he would long ago have come forward and thrown what light he could upon the mystery.

'As to who that man was, the police in their blindness have not the faintest doubt. Under the unshakeable belief that Errington is guilty they have spent the last few months in unceasing labour to try and find further and stronger proofs of his guilt. But they won't find them, because there are none. There are no positive proofs against the actual murderer, for he was one of those clever blackguards who think of everything, foresee every eventuality, who know human nature well, and can foretell exactly what evidence will be brought against them, and act accordingly.

'This blackguard from the first kept the figure, the personality, of Frank Errington before his mind. Frank Errington was the dust which the scoundrel threw metaphorically in the eyes of the police, and you must admit that he succeeded in blinding them – to the extent even of making them entirely forget the one simple little sentence, overheard by Mr Andrew Campbell, and which was, of course, the clue to the whole thing – the only slip the cunning rogue made – "Au revoir! Don't be late tonight." Mrs Hazeldene was going that night to the opera with her husband—

'You are astonished?' he added with a shrug of the shoulders, 'you do not see the tragedy yet, as I have seen it before me all along. The frivolous young wife, the flirtation with the friend? – all a blind, all pretence. I took the trouble which the police should have taken immediately, of finding out something about the finances of the Hazeldene *ménage*. Money is in nine cases out of ten the keynote to a crime.

'I found that the will of Mary Beatrice Hazeldene had been proved by the husband, her sole executor, the estate being sworn at fifteen thousand pounds. I found out, moreover, that Mr Edward Sholto Hazeldene was a poor shipper's clerk when he married the daughter of a wealthy builder in Kensington – and then I made note of the fact that the disconsolate widower had allowed his beard to grow since the death of his wife.

'There's no doubt that he was a clever rogue,' added the strange creature, leaning excitedly over the table, and peering into Polly's face. 'Do you know how that deadly poison was injected into the poor woman's system? By the simplest of all means, one known to every scoundrel in southern Europe. A ring – yes! a ring, which has a tiny hollow needle capable of holding a sufficient quantity of prussic acid to have killed two persons instead of one. The man in the tweed suit shook hands with his fair companion – probably she hardly felt the prick, not sufficiently in any case to make her utter a scream. And, mind you, the scoundrel had every facility, through his friendship with Mr Errington, of procuring what poison he required, not to mention his friend's visiting card. We cannot gauge how many months ago he began to try and copy Frank Errington in his style of dress, the cut of his moustache, his general appearance, making the change probably so gradual, that no one in his own entourage would notice it. He selected for his model a man his own height and build, with the same coloured hair.'

'But there was the terrible risk of being identified by his fellow-traveller in the Underground,' suggested Polly.

'Yes, there certainly was that risk; he chose to take it, and he was wise. He reckoned that several days would in any case elapse before that person, who, by the way, was a businessman absorbed in his newspaper, would actually see him again. The great secret of successful crime is to study human nature,' added the man in the corner, as he began looking for his hat and coat. 'Edward Hazeldene knew it well.'

'But the ring?'

'He may have bought that when he was on his honeymoon,' he suggested with a grim chuckle; 'the tragedy was not planned in a week, it may have taken years to mature. But you will own that there goes a frightful scoundrel unhung. I have left you his photograph as he was a year ago, and as he is now. You will see he has shaved his beard again, but also his moustache. I fancy he is a friend now of Mr Andrew Campbell.'

He left Miss Polly Burton wondering, not knowing what to believe.

And that is why she missed her appointment with Mr Richard Frobisher (of the *London Mail*) to go and see Maud Allan dance at the Palace Theatre that afternoon.

THUBWAY THAME'S BOMB SCARE

JOHNSTON MCCULLEY

When Thubway Tham finally decided to make his life work a career as a pickpocket he found an expert tutor in Jack Burle. Jack's advice was a thing born of experience, and he coached Tham thoroughly, and not for money or a percentage of the take. He had known Tham from young boyhood, felt sorry for him, believed Tham had talent along certain lines – and as a genuine artist in any cultural pursuit, creative or interpretative, generally will do, Jack Burle decided to develop the dormant talent, and made the future Thubway Tham his protégé.

Into Tham's ears, Jack Burle poured a torrent of words whenever they met – systems, warnings, injunctions. He was a success in the business himself, so Tham listened intently to every word, stored knowledge in his brain cells, prepared for his life work. It was something like going to college and working up to graduation with a bachelor degree, and then working for a master's degree, and finally going after a doctorate. This, naturally, would take some time. Tham had to become educated.

Jack Burle explained how a cop could easily take a man in if he had no visible means of support, and so make him a vag. Burle himself was prepared for that; he was a husky product of a semi-slum district, as was Tham, and early had hung around gyms. He began fighting amateur bouts for small sums, offered his services as a human punching-bag when fighters with records were training. Policemen saw him frequently with a battered face, black eyes and patches over cuts on his face, and considered him nothing but a third-degree pug.

Tham had his alibi all ready. In the lodging house on a side street, he got room rent and a small amount of money for doing janitor work each evening from eight to eleven. The rest of the time was for him to do as he pleased.

Bit by bit, Jack Burle taught him things to avoid, dangerous situations, and began instructing Tham in the best manners in which to extract wallets without being detected.

'Never get tangled with a gun gang,' Burle warned. 'A gangster is nothin' but a coward with a gun in his hand. He's the lowest of the low. Can't work except with a gang around him. A good dip is high class. He's what you call a specialist.'

'Yeah, thpecialitht,' Tham agreed.

'A good dip can travel faster and safer when he travels alone. Remember that, Tham.'

'Yeth, thir.'

'A gangster is always tangled up with girls, gun molls. And they get into trouble that way. The girls get jealous or the boys start stealing one another's girls, or some guy tries to take over the gang, when they're fightin' among themselves, and they wind up in the jail house or the morgue. Stay away from girls, Tham. Never trust a skirt.'

'I underthtand,' Tham said. 'Never trutht a thkirt.'

'And never forget that, boy! Now we're ready to go out and watch you begin your work. I'll go with you at first. You catch, and I'll carry.'

'Thir?'

'We'll nail a victim. You'll go after his wallet and I'll stand right behind you, but we'll act like we never saw each other before. When you get the wallet, slip it back to me. If you're grabbed, you won't have the leather on you, and you'll howl to the sky that you're being mistreated. I'll get the folding money out of the wallet and drop the leather on the floor under the crowd's feet.'

'Yeth, thir. That ith clever.'

'You always lift a leather when a subway car door opens and people crowd to get in and out. I'm a tall, husky man, so I bully my way out, thrusting people aside, elbowing them like a roughneck, and get a leather as I plough my way through and get to the platform.'

'Yeth, thir.'

'But you, Tham, are a little man, and you'll have to use a different manner. You can duck and lurch and squeeze up against a man and touch him, and squirm through the crowd almost without being noticed except as a nuisance and a guy who isn't polite.'

'Who,' Tham asked, 'ith ever polite in the thubway?'

'I get your point,' Burle admitted. 'Now, you must wear dark clothes and a cap, and baggy suit that looks like you'd slept in it for a month, the kind of a guy who won't stick out in a crowd and be noticed. The less a dip is noticed, the better.'

'Yeth, thir. I'll remember everything you have thaid.'

So, Tham started his career, and rapidly grew expert in his work. And finally he attracted the attention of a certain Detective Craddock, who watched Tham as much as he could, and who told Tham he knew the latter was a dip, and that he'd catch him some day and send him up to the Big House. Tham obeyed Jack Burle's instructions to the letter, and prospered.

He always remembered one of Burle's warnings as he developed skill in his work: 'Never trutht a thkirt!'

And then Tham became involved with a woman.

She was a little lady who worked as head waitress in a small restaurant where Tham generally ate his breakfast a little before the noon hour, because his janitor work kept him up until late at night. She began her show of interest by smiling sweetly at Tham, and commencing to put a little more food on the table than he had ordered without increasing the amount on his tab. Perhaps she had read or heard of the old legend that the closest way to a man's heart was through his stomach.

It was Tham's habit to sit at a table in the rear of the restaurant, the restaurant generally being crowded at the time of his arrival. Directly behind his table was the exit from the kitchen, and near it a large table where the waitresses assorted their various orders before taking them forward to the main tables. The head waitress always smiled at him as she stopped there.

In front of Tham's table was a screen about five feet high. You couldn't see through it, but you could hear what was being said by anyone at the table on the opposite side. Often the little head waitress whispered before going on forward, as she left something a little extra for Tham's meal. Her interest in Tham grew swiftly, and he felt himself drawn to her by what a bard might call invisible gossamer threads holding with the strength of steel, or something like that.

This reciprocal attachment, however, had not been brought

about by the nude little rascal who is supposed to use a bow and arrow to shoot at hearts and make them palpitate until they get into a state where Hymen takes over the task and causes invisible gossamer threads to appear and show they really are steel.

The head waitress was a darling of a little lady with silvery hair. Tham had the appearance of a half-fed waif in a cast-off suit. Their attachment was that of a motherly woman making life a bit easier for an orphan with not a friend in the world. Jack Burle's injunction, 'Never trutht a thkirt,' did not apply in this case.

As far as Tham was concerned, the elderly waitress had a motherly fixation. She was known to everyone simply as Tillie. Her ancestors had come from Russia after the downfall of the Tsar's regime, and down through the years the family fortune had dwindled, also the family itself, until the last of them had reached America, there to continue dying off until Tillie was left alone. She told Tham all about herself. At intervals she encountered a Russian family and delighted in using the language again.

Before long, queried as to his source of eating money, he first told her he was a lowly janitor, then one day confessed that he was a pickpocket at times. He expected his confession to ruin his association with Tillie, that she would turn with abhorrence.

Her reaction to his confession was rather startling. 'Oh, that's wonderful!' Tillie declared. 'You are the one of those brave and dashing heroes who have passed through history. "Rob the rich and give to the poor! Balance the scales in the name of justice! Feed the hungry from the larders of those who have too much stored away!" Those have been their fighting songs.'

Tham felt a little abashed. It wasn't exactly like that, but he did not want to disillusion her when she seemed to be so happy about it.

Tham learned that Tillie had a little two-room apartment in a side street not far away, where another of the waitresses lived with her and shared the cost of upkeep. Tillie had good blood in her, and the ruination of her family had not soured her against the world. She loved her adopted country – she had become a citizen long before. She had educated herself in English while working for some years as a lady's maid in a Long Island mansion, had devoured books; and as she grew older she became unsuitable for maid's work, because she was not snappy enough to please the guests, not so fast in her actions as before, she did not consider it menial labour to work as the head waitress in a small restaurant, since she was the *head* waitress.

She and Tham continued their association, and a couple of times he strolled home with her on her day off. They talked of many things, and seemed to agree on most of the topics discussed. And they soon learned that both of them hated Communism and all it meant to the free world.

'Anybody who thtepth on the toeth of Uncle Tham ith in for thome thad trouble from me,' Tham declared to her with an amount of vehemence.

For that, Tillie squealed joyously a little and clasped Tham around the neck and gave him a motherly kiss. And only a few days later their joint hatred of what Tham called 'thoth thneaky red ratth' resulted in what a financial wizard could have called gigantic dividends.

Tham was busy with his breakfast when he heard two men at the table on the opposite side of the screen. One of the waitresses took their orders delivered in somewhat guttural tones. After they had been served, and the waitress was giving her attention to other customers, the two men began speaking in a language strange to Tham.

When Tillie emerged from the kitchen again and began arranging her trays, Tham had a mouth filled with food and was chewing it with the enthusiasm of a hungry man. He realised that Tillie was suddenly quiet, and glanced at her. She was listening to the men in front of the screen as they talked. She put a finger to her lips in an ancient gesture meaning Tham was not to speak. She bent closer to the screen, for the men were talking in lower tones.

Tham looked up at her. An expression of horror was in her face. She bent and whispered to Tham: 'Be very quiet. Come with me into the kitchen.'

Tham obeyed. The expression in her face startled him. Inside the kitchen, she clasped his hand and pulled him to a corner where there was a telephone booth for the use of the employees of the restaurant. Then she whispered to Tham again:

'Those men were Russians – Reds. They were talking about having placed two bombs in the big building across Madison Square, where the clock strikes. The bombs are set to explode, one on the second floor and another on the fifth floor, at exactly half past one. That's when all the secretaries and office girls will be going back into the building after eating lunch in the park or some place near. They'll be blown to pieces!'

'What you goin' to do?' Tham asked.

'We must act fast, Tham. I heard them talking about going out and watching from the Fifth Avenue side of the Square. They'll get a laugh out of it, the devils. And they were talking about going back to Washington to report, and about having plenty of Washington money in their pockets and more coming when they got back to their big Red boss there.'

'You got any ideath?' Tham asked, gulping as he began visualising what might happen.

'I know Mike Malone, the desk sergeant at the police precinct station down the street. He and his wife live right near me, and they've had me to dinner several times on my day off. He'll know I'm not fooling, knows I know Russian and how I hate the Reds. He will know what to do.'

She went into the phone booth and closed the door, and Tham watched her dialling a number. The terror grew on him, and he tried to fight it back. This was a time to be calm and act naturally, he knew. It was not a time for panic.

Tillie emerged from the phone booth. 'Mike Malone will attend to everything,' she told Tham. 'He knows I'm not fooling. Tham, you watch them after they go out. See where they go and what they do, and keep close to them so you can point them out. In a few minutes, I'll pretend I don't feel well and want to go home. One of the other girls can take my place. Then I'll get to you, and we both can watch them until we can turn them over. When I come out, I'll look for you on the Fifth Avenue side of the Square.'

Tham picked up his tab and wandered slowly towards the cashier's cage, fighting to keep from showing excitement. He paid his bill and exchanged salutations with the fat cashier, who knew him well from several years of loyalty to the restaurant. He went out upon the street, ignited a cigarette, crossed over the street and stood on a corner.

It was a soft, beautiful day. Many from the office buildings around the Square had chosen to eat luncheons in the park, food gathered mostly from nearby sandwich carts. There seemed to Tham to be at least a couple of thousand out there in the open. By half past one, they would be getting back into the office buildings, and if the bombs caught them there it would be wholesale slaughter, also possibly wrecked buildings and fires.

He glanced back across the street. The two men had not left the restaurant to come his way, and he did not see Tillie leave the restaurant and come towards him. Tham told himself to act in ordinary fashion, that he was not supposed to know anything unusual was transpiring. His job was only to get close to the two men so he could point them out later to Tillie. She was the one to put the finger on them. If Tham gave the alarm, anyone who knew him, especially Detective Craddock if he happened to be loitering in the Square hoping to have his usual repartee with him, would not believe anything Tham might say.

With horror, Tham noticed that many of those in the Square were strolling back towards the buildings where they worked. And just then, as he turned, he saw the two men come out of the restaurant and saunter towards him. Tillie was not in sight.

He glanced in the other direction, and saw Detective Craddock approaching slowly, puffing at a gigantic cigar, his battered old derby hat cocked over one ear in a nonchalant manner. 'He ith thinkin' of thomething thmart to thay to me,' Tham muttered to himself.

And then it happened!

From all directions they came, dashing along the streets. Police cars, fire department apparatus, ambulances, cars holding the police bomb squad – they all converged around Madison Square. Extra police reserves came, scattering around to control the gathering crowd. Men rushed to the buildings and ordered an immediate evacuation.

Something Tillie had said had informed Tham of a certain touchy situation. What she had heard the two men say in the Russian language could have been serious. This could be a genuine bomb affair, or it could be a hoax. So, officially, no hand could be put upon the two unless it developed it was a real attempt at bombing. They could only be watched until the outcome; and then, with Tillie's testimony, they possibly would be given a short sentence for causing the scare.

At that instant, Tham and Detective Craddock came into contact. Craddock did not know the cause of the sudden confusion, and Tham decided not to inform him.

'Well, well!' Tham exclaimed. 'If it ithn't my old college chum. What ith all thith noithe about? Don't tell me –

I know.'

'Oh, you do? Let me in on the secret,' Craddock said.

'Thertainly. It ith a great honour for me. All theth earth and thingth – copth and firemen and all – jutht to watch me and thee that I do not go down into the thubway and maybe attend to thome buthineth.'

'Don't flatter yourself,' Craddock growled. 'There's something big going on, and I'm cussed well going to learn what it is.' He whirled and headed for the police officer not far away, getting out his badge to identify himself and ask what was happening.

Tham glanced back again. The two men had come out of the restaurant and were sauntering towards him on the Fifth Avenue side of the Square. Tillie had not yet appeared, and Tham wondered what had happened to her. The two men stopped at the kerb within a few feet of Tham. A charge of policemen was coming towards them. 'Keep back by the kerb!' they were calling. 'Don't move forward into the park!'

Tham turned and glanced across the Square. The crowd was screaming, acting like cattle in a stampede, fighting to get as far away from the buildings as possible. The panic was on. Tham saw policemen threatening with their clubs, trying to herd the frantic men and women. Some of them had broken out of the mob and were racing down the side streets. Over near the scene of danger, Tham saw an important man he knew by sight – Inspector Allison, an official who generally appeared at scenes such as this, a man who gave command, who knew how to break up a riot or quell a panic to a certain extent.

Tham turned again, and found himself behind the two men who had caused all this. They were speaking in a guttural English. They looked ordinary, dressed a little like working men, their coats a little baggy. As Tham watched them, not seeming to do so, he saw one handling a roll of currency, and almost gulped when he saw the man thrust it into the left-hand hip pocket of his trousers.

The thilly ath,' Tham muttered to himself. 'Theth Redth are not very thmart. A hick from the thtickth would know better than that. Good Uncle Tham money in their filthy handth. Um.'

He glanced around again, and saw Tillie approaching with a man beside her. Tham backed away a few feet to meet her, standing so the two men who were watching something across the Square, would not see Tillie's approach and possibly get suspicious.

A glance told Tham that the space in front of the building where the bombs were supposed to be had been cleared of everyone. The hour the men had mentioned was at hand. In a moment, it would be known whether this was the real thing or a foolish hoax.

Suddenly Tham saw a man appear in a window on the second floor of the building and toss something down into the street. There was a terrific explosion, and the frantic crowd still in the Square began fighting to get back.

It was no hoax.

The crowd surged back towards the Fifth Avenue kerb. Tham looked towards Tillie again. Three men were with her now, and they were rushing forward. From a window on the fifth floor of the building, another bomb was tossed out to explode with terrific force to make a hole in the pavement.

Tham guessed the bombs had been located by the squad, and that the time was so short there was nothing to do except toss them out. Now firemen and ambulance men, as well as police, rushed into the building. More of the mob were fighting their way into the side streets.

Tillie and the men with her were coming on faster now. Tham turned towards the two men again. A surge of the crowd engulfed them for a moment, and he found himself jammed against them. Then the crowd broke again, and Tham was tossed aside.

He could see Tillie pointing. The three men beckoned plainclothes men who had been standing around, and the Reds found themselves grasped roughly, slammed together, found handcuffs on them behind their backs.

'Those are the men,' Tham heard Tillie say, by way of legal identification.

Tham slipped away; this was Tillie's own game. He felt proud for her as he began realising all she had done. But for her, people could have been slaughtered, buildings set aflame. He watched as a police car drew up to the kerb. The Reds were protesting in loud guttural voices and demanding to know the meaning of the assault on them. Though manacled, they tried to fight when they were thrust towards the police car. The three officers gave them a rather rough treatment and got them into the car without further trouble.

As Tham watched, he saw Tillie escorted to another police car, which followed the first. He knew her presence would be needed at Police Headquarters, where her statement would be recorded. And he realised she might be in danger afterward, when the men had been sent to prison for a long term. This was only one incident as far as the Reds were concerned. But Tham knew they had ways of dealing with any person who had obstructed their nefarious work.

Gradually, order was restored. Those who had worked in the building were told to go home for the remainder of the day and quiet their nerves. Places were roped off, and policemen stationed to restrain the mob of curious sightseers which undoubtedly would appear after the news got out. And trained plainclothes men undoubtedly would scatter through the crowd, eyes and ears open, listening for any hint of sympathy, any word that would identify them as persons to be watched.

Tham drifted away without meeting Craddock again. He strolled back to his lodging house, for he had some work to do there. He had been on the scene, but all he told anyone at the lodging house was that he had seen the mob and heard the crashing of the bombs.

He began thinking again of Tillie. 'What a thkirt!' he muttered.

In time, he got a telephone call, something he seldom received. It was from Tillie, asking him to come over to her place. It was only a short distance away, and Tham got there in record time. Tillie was alone, and she had prepared a luncheon for them after her ordeal at Police Headquarters.

'An officer told them at the restaurant to let me have the remainder of the day off,' she explained. 'I'm so glad I was able to help. I should be ashamed to say it, I suppose, but I'm a tiny bit proud of myself.' She giggled a little; she was still a little tense from what had happened.

'I thure am proud of you, too,' Tham told her. 'It wath a good day.' He reached in a pocket, and brought forth a wad of United States currency.

Tillie's eyes bulged. 'What's that, Tham?'

'It ith like thith – I thaw one of thoth men thtick all thith money in hith hip pocket. Tho I got it. It ith good Uncle Tham money, and thoth thneakin' apeth have no buthnith havin' it. Ain't I a nephew of my Uncle Tham? Thure I am! Tho I jutht took money. And I am goin' to give you an even thplit on it. You can buy yourthelf fanthy clotheth or thomethin'.'

Tillie giggled, and kissed him again on the cheek.

'Tomorrow for breakfast,' she told him, 'I'll have the chef build you the finest omelette you ever saw or tasted. As you said, Tham, it's been a good day.'

THE RIDDLE OF THE 5.28

THOMAS W. HANSHEW

It was exactly thirty-two minutes past five o'clock on the evening of Friday, 8 December when the stationmaster at Anerley – which, no doubt you know, lies but a gunshot from the Crystal Palace on the London, Brighton and South Coast railway – received the following communication by wire from the signal-box at Forest Hill: 'Five twenty-eight down from London Bridge just passed. One first-class compartment in total darkness. Investigate.'

As two stations – Sydenham and Penge – lie between Forest Hill and Anerley, in the ordinary course of events this signal-box message would have been dispatched to one or the other of these. But it so happens that the five twenty-eight from London Bridge to Croydon is a special train, which makes no stop short of Anerley station on the way down; consequently, the signalman had no choice but to act as he did.

Promptly at five forty-two – the scheduled time for its arrival – the train came pelting up the snow-covered metals from Penge, and made its first stop since starting. It was packed to the point of suffocation, as it always is, and in an instant the station was in a state of congestion. Far down the uncovered portion of the platform Webb, the porter, who had now joined the stationmaster, spied a gap in the long line of brightly lit windows, and the pair bore down upon it forthwith, each with a glowing lantern in his hand.

'Here she is – now then, let's see what's the difficulty,' said the stationmaster as they came abreast of the lightless compartment, where, much to his surprise, he found nobody leaning out and making a 'to do' over the matter. 'Looks as if the blessed thing was empty, though that's by no means likely in a packed train like the five twenty-eight. Hullo! door's locked. And here's an "Engaged" label on the window. What the dickens did I do with my key? Oh, here it is. Now, then, let's see what's amiss.'

A great deal was amiss, as he saw the instant he unlocked the door and pulled it open. For the first lifting of the lantern made the cause of the darkness startlingly plain. The shallow glass globe which should have been in the centre of the ceiling had been smashed – ragged fragments of it still clinging to their fastenings – and the three electric bulbs had been removed bodily. A downward glance showed him that both these and the fragments of the broken globe lay on one seat, partly wrapped in a wet cloth, and on the other . . . He gave a jump and a howl and retreated a step or two in a state of absolute panic. For there in a corner, with his face towards the engine, half sat, half leaned the figure of a dead man with a bullet hole between his eyes and a small nickel-plated revolver loosely clasped in the bent fingers of one limp and lifeless hand.

The body was that of a man whose age could not at the most have exceeded eight-and-thirty – a man who must, in life, have been more than ordinarily handsome. His hair and moustache were fair; his clothing was of extreme elegance in both material and fashioning. An evening paper lay between his feet – open, as though it had been read. The body was quite alone in the compartment, and there was not a scrap of luggage of any description.

'Suicide!' gulped the startled stationmaster, as soon as he could find strength to say anything; then he hastily slammed and relocked the door, set Webb on guard before it, and flew to notify the engine driver and to send word to the local police.

The news of the tragedy spread like wildfire, but the stationmaster, who had his wits about him, would allow nobody to leave the station until the authorities had arrived, and suffer no man or woman to come within a yard of the compartment where the dead man lay.

Someone has said that 'nothing comes by chance'; but whether that be true or not, it happened that Mr Maverick Narkom was among those who were standing on the opposite platform waiting for the train to Victoria, which train was to convey Cleek – whom he had promised to join at Anerley – returning from a day spent with Captain Morrison and his daughter in the beautiful home they had bought when the law decided that the captain was the legitimate heir of George Carboys and lawful successor to Abdul ben Meerza's money.

As soon as the news of the tragedy reached him, Mr Narkom crossed to the scene of action and made known his identity. He first looked to see if any name was attached, as is often the case, to the 'Engaged' label secured to the window of the compartment occupied by the dead man. There was. Written in pencil under the blue-printed 'Engaged' were the three words 'For Lord Stavornel'.

'By George!' he exclaimed as he read the name – which was one that half England had heard of at one time or another, and knew to belong to a man whose wild, dissipated life and violent temper had passed into a proverb. 'Come to the end at last, has he? Give me your lantern, porter, and open the door. Let's have a look and see if there's any mistake, or—' The whistle of the arriving train for Victoria cut in upon his words, and, putting the local police in charge, he ran for the tunnel, made for the up platform, and caught Cleek. They returned together.

'Mr George Headland, one of my best men,' he explained to the local inspector, who had just arrived. 'Let us have all the light you can, please. Mr Headland wishes to view the body. Crowd round, the rest of you, and keep the passengers back. Tell the engine driver he'll get his orders in a minute. Now, then, Cl— Headland: decide – it rests with you.'

Cleek opened the door of the compartment, stepped in, gave one glance at the dead man, and then spoke.

'Murder!' he said. 'Look how the pistol lies in his hand. Wait a moment, however, and let me make sure.' Then he took the revolver from the yielding fingers, smelt it, smiled, then 'broke' it and looked at the cylinder. 'Just as I supposed,' he added, turning to Narkom. 'One chamber has been fouled by a shot and one cartridge has been exploded. But not today – not even yesterday. That sour smell tells its own story, Mr Narkom. This revolver was discharged two or three days ago. The assassin had everything prepared for this little event. But he was a fool for all his cleverness, for you will observe that in his haste when he put the revolver in the dead hand to make it appear a case of suicide, he laid it down just as he himself took it from his pocket – with the butt towards the victim's body and the muzzle pointing outward between the thumb and forefinger – and with bottom of the cylinder instead of the top of the trigger touching the ball of the thumb! It is a clear case of murder, Mr Narkom.'

'But, sir,' interposed the stationmaster, overhearing this assertion and looking at Cleek with eyes of blank bewilderment, 'if somebody killed him, where has that "somebody" gone? Both doors were locked and both windows closed when we discovered the body.'

'Get your men to examine all tickets – both in the train and out of it – and if there's one that's not clipped as it passed the barrier at London Bridge, look out for it, and detain the holder,' answered Cleek. 'I'll take the gate here and examine all local tickets. Meantime, wire all up the road to every station from here to London Bridge and find out if any other signalman than the one at Forest Hill noticed this dark compartment when the train went past.'

Both suggestions were acted upon immediately. But every ticket, save, of course, the season tickets (and the holders of these were in every case identified), was found to be properly clipped; and, in the end, every signal-box from New Cross on wired back 'All compartments lighted when train passed here.'

'That narrows the search, Mr Narkom,' said Cleek, when he heard this. 'The lights were put out somewhere between Honor Oak Park and Forest Hill – and, somewhere between

Honor Oak Park and Anerley, the murderer made his escape. Inspector' – he turned to the officer in command of the local police – 'do me a favour. Put your men in charge of this carriage and let the train proceed. Norwood Junction is the next station, I believe, and there's a side track there. Have the carriage shunted and keep close guard over it until Mr Narkom and I arrive.'

'Right you are, sir. Anything else?'

'Yes. Have the stationmaster at the junction equip a hand car with a searchlight, and send it here as expeditiously as possible. If anybody or anything has left this train between this point and Honor Oak Park, Mr Narkom, this thin coating of snow will betray the fact beyond the question of a doubt.'

Twenty minutes later the hand car put in an appearance, manned by a couple of linesmen from the junction, and, word having been wired up the line to hold back all trains for a period of half an hour in the interests of Scotland Yard, Cleek and Narkom boarded the vehicle and went whizzing up the metals in the direction of Honor Oak Park, the shifting searchlight sweeping the path from left to right and glaring brilliantly on the surface of the fallen snow.

Four lines of tracks gleamed steel-bright against its spotless level – the two outer ones being those employed by the local trains going to and fro between London and the suburbs, the two inner ones belonging to the main line, but not one footstep indented the thin surface of that broad expanse of snow from one end of the journey to the other.

'The murderer, whoever he is, or wherever he went, never set foot upon so much as one inch of this ground, that's certain,' said Narkom, as he gave the order to reverse the car and return. 'You feel satisfied of that, do you not, my dear fellow?'

'Thoroughly, Mr Narkom – there can't be two opinions upon that point. But at the same time he *did* leave the train, otherwise we should have found him in it.'

'Granted. But the question is, *when* did he get in and *how* did he get out? We know from the evidence of the passengers that the train never stopped for one instant between London Bridge station and Anerley; that all compartments were alight up to the time it passed Honor Oak Park; that nobody aboard of it heard a sound of a pistol shot; that the assassin could not have crept along the footboard and got into some other compartment, for *all* were so densely crowded that half a dozen people were standing in each. My dear chap, are you sure – are you really *sure* that it isn't a case of suicide after all?'

Cleek gave his shoulders a lurch and smiled indulgently.

'My dear Mr Narkom,' he said, 'the position of the revolver in the dead man's hand ought, as I pointed out to you, to settle that question, even if there were no other discrepancies. In the natural order of things, a man who had just put a bullet into his own brain would, if he were sitting erect – as Lord Stavornell *was* – drop the revolver in the spasmodic opening and shutting of the hands in the final convulsion; but, if he retained any sort of a hold upon it, be sure his forefinger would be in the loop of the trigger. Then – if you didn't remark it – there was no scorch of powder upon the face—' He stopped and laid a sharp, quick-shutting hand on the shoulder of one of the two men who were operating the car. 'Turn back!' he exclaimed. 'Reverse the action and go back a dozen yards or so.'

The car slowed down, stopped, and then began to back, scudding along the rail until Cleek again called it to a halt. They were within gunshot of the station at Sydenham when this occurred; the glaring searchlight was still playing on the metals and the thin layer of snow between, and Cleek's face seemed all eyes as he bent over and studied the ground over which they were gliding. Of a sudden, however, he gave a little satisfied grunt, jumped down and picked up a shining metal object about two and a half inches long which lay in the space between the tracks of the main and the local lines. It was a guard's key for the locking and unlocking of compartment doors – one of the small, T-shaped kind that you can buy of almost any ironmonger for sixpence or a shilling any day. It was wet from contact with the snow, but quite unrusted – showing that it had not been lying there long – and it needed but a glance to reveal the fact that it was brand-new and of recent purchase.

He held it out on his palm as he climbed back upon the car and rejoined Narkom.

'Wherever he got on, Mr Narkom, here is where the murderer got off, you see, and either dropped or flung away this key when he had relocked the compartment after him,' he said. 'And yet, as you see, there is not a footstep – beyond those I have myself just made – to be discovered anywhere. From the position in which this key was lying, one thing is certain, however: our man got out on the opposite side from the platform toward which the train was hastening, and in the *middle of the right of way.*'

'What a mad idea! If there had been a main line express passing at the time, the fellow ran the risk of being cut to pieces. About this spot they would be going like the wind.'

'Yes,' said Cleek. 'Going like the wind . . . and the suction would be enormous between two speeding trains. A step outside and he'd have been under the wheels in a wink. Yes; it would have been certain death, instant death, if there had been a main line train passing at the time; and – that he was not sucked down and ground under the wheels, proves that *there wasn't!* Let us get on.'

'Any idea, old chap?'

'Yes – bushels of them. But they all may be exploded in another half-hour.'

'Which means?'

'That I shall leave the hand car at Sydenham, Mr Narkom, and 'phone up to London Bridge station – there are one or two points I wish to ask some questions about. Afterwards, I'll hire a motor from some local garage and join you at Norwood Junction in an hour's time. One question, however: Is my memory at fault, or was it not Lord Stavornell who was mixed up in that little affair with the French dancer, Mademoiselle Fifi de Lesparre, who was such a rage in town about a year ago?'

'Yes; that's the chap,' said Narkom in reply. 'And a rare bad lot he has been all his life, I can tell you. I dare say that Fifi herself was no better than she ought to have been – chucking over her country-bred husband as soon as she came into popularity and had men of the Stavornell class tagging after her – but whether she was or was not, Stavornell broke up that home, and if that French husband had done the right thing, he would have thrashed him within an inch of his life instead of acting like a fool in a play and challenging him. Stavornell laughed at the challenge, of course, and if all that is said of him is true, he was at the bottom of the shabby trick which finally forced the poor devil to get out of the

315

country. When his wife – Fifi – left him, the poor wretch nearly went off his head, and, as he hadn't fifty shillings in the world, he was in a dickens of a pickle when *somebody* induced a lot of milliners, dressmakers, and the like of whom it was said that Fifi owed bills, to put their accounts into the hands of a collecting agency and to proceed against him for settlement of his wife's accounts. That was why he got out of the country post-haste. The case made a great stir at the time, and the scandal of it was so great that, although the fact never got into the papers, Stavornell's wife left him, refusing to live another hour with such a man.'

'Oh, he had a wife, then?'

'Yes. One of the most beautiful women in the kingdom. They had been married only a year when the scandal of the Fifi affair arose. That was another of his dirty tricks – the forcing of that poor creature to marry him.'

'She did so against her will?'

'Yes. She was engaged to another fellow at the time – an army chap who was out in India. Her father, too, was an army man – a Colonel something or other – poor as the proverbial church mouse; addicted to hard drinking, card playing, horse racing, and about as selfish an old brute as they make 'em. The girl took a deep dislike to Lord Stavornell the minute she saw him – knew his reputation, and refused to receive him. That's the very reason he determined to marry her, humble her pride as it were, and repay her for her scorn of him. He got her father into his clutches – deliberately, of course – lent him money, took his IOUs for card debts, and all that sort of thing, until the old brute was up to his ears in debt, and with no prospect of paying it off. Of course, when he'd got him to that point, Stavornell demanded the money, but finally agreed to wipe the debt out entirely if the daughter married him. They went at her, poor creature, those two, with all the mercilessness of a couple of wolves. In the end she gave in; then Stavornell took out a special licence, and they were married. Of course, the man never cared for her; he led her a dog's life.'

'Poor creature!' said Cleek sympathetically. 'And what became of the other chap – the lover out in India?'

'Oh, they say he went on like a madman when he heard it. Swore he'd kill Stavornell, and all that, but quieted down after a time and accepted the inevitable with the best grace possible. Crawford is his name. He was a lieutenant at the time, but he's got his captaincy since, and I believe is on leave and in England at present – as madly and as hopelessly in love with the girl of his heart as ever.'

'Oho!' said Cleek, with a strong rising reflection. 'Then Fifi's husband isn't the only man with a grievance and – a cause? There's another eh?'

'Another? I expect there must be a dozen, if the truth were

known. There's only one creature in the world I ever heard of as having a good word to say for the man.'

'And who might that be?'

'The Hon. Mrs Brinkworth, widow of his younger brother. You'd think the man was an angel to hear *her* sing his praises. But I suppose even the devil's got a good spot in him somewhere, if one only knows where to look for it. Evidently the Hon. Mrs Brinkworth does. *Her* husband, too, was a wild sort. Left her up to her ears in debt without a penny to bless herself, and with a boy of five to rear and educate. Stavornell seems always to have liked her. At any rate, he came to the rescue, paid off debts, settled an annuity upon her, and arranged to have the boy sent to Eton as soon as he was old enough. I expect the boy is at the bottom of this good streak in him if all is told; for, having no children of his own – I say! By George, old chap! Why, that nipper – being the heir in the direct line – is Lord Stavornell himself, now that the uncle is dead! A lucky stroke for *him*, by Jupiter!'

'Yes,' agreed Cleek. 'Lucky for him; lucky for Lady Stavornell; lucky for Captain Crawford, and *unlucky* for the Hon. Mrs Brinkworth and Mademoiselle Fifi de Lesparre. So, of course – Sydenham at last. Join you at Norwood Junction as soon as possible, and – I say, Mr Narkom!'

'Yes, old chap?'

'Wire through to the low-level station at Crystal Palace,

will you? and enquire if anybody has mislaid an ironing board or lost an Indian canoe. See you later. So long!'

Then he stepped up on to the station platform and went in quest of a telephone booth.

It was after nine o'clock when he turned up at Norwood Junction as calm, serene and imperturbable as ever, and found Narkom awaiting him in a small private room, which the station clerk had placed at his disposal.

'My dear fellow, I never was so glad!' exclaimed the superintendent, jumping up excitedly as Cleek entered. 'What kept you so long? I've been on thorns. Got bushels to tell you. First off, as Stavornell's identity is established beyond doubt, no time has been lost in writing the news of the murder to his relatives. Both Lady Stavornell and Mrs Brinkworth have wired back that they are coming on. I expect them at any minute now. And – Cleek! Here's a piece of news for you. Fifi's husband is in England. The Hon. Mrs Brinkworth has wired me to that effect. Says she has means of knowing that he came over from France the other day; and that she, herself, saw him in London this morning when she was up there shopping.'

'Oho!' commented Cleek. Then: 'Find anything at the Crystal Palace low level, Mr Narkom?'

'Yes. My dear Cleek, I can't conceive what reason you can have for making such an enquiry, but—'

'Which was it? Canoe or ironing board?'

'Neither, as it happens. But they've got a lady's folding cutting table – you know the sort: one of those that women use for dressmaking operations and which fold up flat so they can be tucked away. Nobody knows who left it, but it's there awaiting an owner, and it was found—'

'Oh, I can guess that,' interposed Cleek nonchalantly. 'It was in a first-class compartment of the five-eighteen from London Bridge, which reached the low level at five forty-three. No, never mind questions for a few minutes, please. Let's go and have a look at the body. I want to satisfy myself regarding the point of what in the world Stavornell was doing on a suburban train at a time when he ought, properly, to be on his way home to his rooms at the Ritz preparing to dress for dinner; and I want to find out, if possible, what means that chap with the little dark moustache used to get him to go out of town, in his ordinary afternoon dress, and by that particular train.'

'Chap with the small dark moustache? Who do you mean by that?'

'Party that killed him. My 'phone to London Bridge station has cleared the way a bit. It seems that Lord Stavornell engaged that compartment in that particular train by telephone at three o'clock this afternoon. He arrived all alone, and was in no end of a temper because the carriage was dirty, had it swept out, and then the porter says that he found him laughing and talking with a dark-moustached little man – apparently of continental origin – dressed in a Norfolk suit and carrying a brown leather portmanteau. In that portmanteau was an air pistol for one thing: also a mallet or hammer, and that wet cloth we found, both of which were for the purpose of smashing the electric light globe without sound. And he went into that compartment with his victim!'

'Yes, but, man alive, how did he get *out*? Where did he go after that, and what became of the brown leather portmanteau?'

'I hope to be able to answer both questions before this night is over, Mr Narkom. Meantime, let us go and have a look at the body and settle one of the little points that bother me.'

The superintendent led the way to the siding where the shunted carriage stood, and Cleek was soon deep in his examination.

Aided by the better light, he now perceived something which, in the first hurried examination, had escaped him – or, if it had not (which is, perhaps, open to question), he had made no comment upon it. It was a spot about the size of an ordinary dinner plate on the square of crimson carpet which covered the floor of the compartment. It was slightly darker than the rest of the surface, and was at the foot of the corner seat directly facing the dead man.

'I think we can fairly decide, Mr Narkom, on the evidence of that,' said Cleek, pointing to it, 'that Lord Stavornell did have a companion in this compartment, and that it *was* the little dark man with the false moustache. Put your hand on the spot. Damp, you see – the effect of someone who had walked through the snow sitting down on this particular seat. We've got past the point of "guesswork" now. We've *established* the presence of the second party beyond all question. We also know that he was a person with whom Stavornell felt at ease and was intimate enough with to feel no necessity for putting himself out by entertaining with those little courtesies one is naturally obliged to show a guest.'

'How do you make that out?'

'This newspaper. He was reading at the time he was shot. You can see for yourself where the bullet went through – this hole, here, close to the top of the paper. When a man *invites* another man to occupy with him a compartment which he has engaged and then proceeds to read the news instead of troubling himself to treat his companion as a guest, it is pretty safe to say that they are acquaintances of long standing and upon such terms of intimacy that the social amenities may be dispensed with inoffensively.

'Now look! No powder on the face, no smell of it in the compartment; and yet the pistol found in his hand is an ordinary American-made twenty-eight calibre revolver. We have an amateur assassin to deal with Mr Narkom, not a hardened criminal, and the witlessness of the fellow is enough to bring the case to an end before this night is over. Why didn't he discharge that revolver today and have enough sense to bring a thimbleful of powder to burn in this compartment after the work was done? One knows in an instant that the weapon used was an air pistol. I don't suppose that there are three places in all London that stock air pistols, and I don't suppose that they sell as many as two in a whole year. But if one has been sold or repaired at any of the shops in the past six months – well, Dollops will know that in less than no time. I 'phoned him to make enquiries.'

As he spoke he bent over the dead man and commenced to search the clothing. He slid his hand into the inner pocket of the creaseless morning coat and drew out a pocket notebook and two or three letters. All were addressed in the handwriting of women, but only one seemed to possess any interest for Cleek. It was written on pink notepaper, enclosed in a pink envelope, and was postmarked 'Croydon, 9 December, 2.30 p.m.', and bore those outward marks which betokened its delivery not in course of post, but by express messenger. One instant after Cleek had looked at it he knew he need seek no further for the information he desired.

'Piggy,' it read. 'Stupid boy, the ball of the dress-fancy is not for tomorrow, but tonight; I have made sudden discoverment. Come quick – by the train that shall leave London Bridge at the time of twenty-eight minutes after the hour of five. You shall not fail of this, or it shall make much difficulties for me, as I come to meet it on arrival. Do not bother of the costume – I will have one ready for you. I have one large joke of the somebody else that is coming which will make you scream of the laughter. Burn this. – FIFI.' And, at the bottom of the sheet: 'Do burn this. I have hurt the hand and must use the writing of my maid; and I do not want you to treasure that.'

'There's the explanation, Mr Narkom,' said Cleek as he held the letter out. 'That's why he came by this particular train. There's the snare. That's how he was lured.'

Narkom opened his lips to make some comment upon this, but closed them suddenly and said nothing. For, at that moment, one of the constables put in an appearance with news that 'Two ladies and two gentlemen have arrived, sir, and are asking permission to view the body for purposes of identification. Here are the names, sir, on this slip of paper.'

'Lady Stavornell, Colonel Murchison, Hon. Mrs

Brinkworth, Captain James Crawford,' Narkom read aloud; then looked up enquiringly at Cleek.

'Yes,' he said. 'Let them come.'

Then he stood looking up at the shattered globe and rubbing his chin between his thumb and forefinger and wrinkling up his brows after the manner of a man who is trying to solve a problem in mental arithmetic. And Narkom – unwise in that direction for once – chose to interrupt his thoughts, for no greater reason than that he had thrice heard him mutter 'Suction – displacement – resistance.'

'Working out a problem, old chap?' he ventured. 'Can I help you? I used to be rather good at that sort of thing.'

'Were you?' said Cleek a trifle testily. 'Then tell me something: combating a suction power of about two pounds to the square inch, how much wind does it take to make a cutting table fly, with an unknown weight upon it, from the Sydenham switch to the Low Level station? When you've worked that out, you've got the murderer. And when you do get him – well, he won't be any man you ever saw or ever heard of in all the days of your life! But he will be light enough to hop like a bird, heavy enough to pull up a wire rope with about three hundred pounds on the end of it, and – there will be two holes of about an inch in diameter and a foot apart in one end of the table that flew.'

'My dear chap!' began Narkom in tones of blank

bewilderment, then stopped suddenly and screwed round on his heel. For a familiar voice had sung out suddenly a yard or two distant – 'Ah, keep yer 'air on! Don't get to thinkin' you're Niagara Falls, just because yer got water on the brain!' And there, struggling in the grip of a constable, who had laid strong hands upon him, stood Dollops, with a kit-bag in one hand and a half-devoured bath bun in the other.

'All right there, constable – let the boy pass. He's one of us!' rapped out Cleek; and in an instant the detaining hand fell, and Dollops's chest went out like a pouter pigeon's.

'Catch on to that, *Suburbs?*' said he, giving the constable a look of blighting scorn and swaggering by like a mighty conqueror. 'Nailed it at the second rap, guv'ner,' he added in an undertone to Cleek. 'Fell down on Gamage's, picked myself up on Loader, Tottenham Court Road. Fourteen, twelve, seven, a – manufactured Stockholm. Valve tightened – old customer – day before yesterday in the afternoon.'

'Good boy! good boy!' said Cleek, patting him approvingly. 'Keep your tongue between your teeth. Scuttle off and find out where there's a garage, and then wait outside the station till I come.'

'Right you are, sir,' responded Dollops, bolting the remainder of the bun; then he ducked down and slipped away; and Cleek, stepping back into the shadow where his features might not be too clearly seen until he was ready that they should be, stood and watched narrowly the small procession which was being piloted to the scene of the tragedy. A moment later the four persons already announced passed under Cleek's watchful eye, and stood in the dead man's presence.

A moment he stood there silent – watching, listening, making neither movement nor sound – then of a sudden he put forth his hand and tapped Narkom's arm.

'Detain this party – every member of it – by any means – on any pretext, for another forty-five minutes,' he whispered. 'In three quarters of an hour the murderer will be here on this spot with me!' Then he screwed round on his heel and, before Narkom could speak, was gone: soundlessly and completely gone – just as he used to go in his vanishing cracksman's days – leaving just that promise behind him.

It wanted but thirteen minutes of being midnight when the gathering about the siding where the shunted carriage containing the body of the murdered man still stood received something in the nature of a shock when, on glancing round as a sharp whistle shrilled a warning note, they saw an engine, attached to one solitary carriage, backing along the metals and bearing down upon them.

'I say, Mr Knockem or Narkhim or whatever your name is,' blurted out Colonel Murchison, as he hastily caught the Hon. Mrs Brinkworth by the arm and whisked her back from the metals, leaving his daughter to be looked after by Captain Crawford, 'look out for your blessed bobbies. Somebody's shunting another coach in on top of us; and if the ass doesn't look what he's doing . . . There! I told you!' – as the coach in question settled with a slight jar against that containing the body of Lord Stavornell. 'Of all the blundering, pig-headed fools! Might have killed some of us. What next, I wonder?'

What next, as a matter of fact, gave him cause for even greater wonder; for, as the two carriages met, the door of the last compartment in the one which had just arrived opened briskly, and out of it stepped: first, a couple of uniformed policemen; next, a ginger-haired youth with a kit-bag in one hand and a saveloy in the other; then the trim figure of the lady who had so long and popularly been known in the music-hall world as Mile Fifi de Lesparre, and last of all—

'Cleek!' blurted out Narkom, overcome with amazement, as he saw the serenely alighting figure. And 'Cleek?' went in a little rippling murmur throughout the entire gathering – civilians and local police alike.

'All right, Mr Narkom,' said Cleek himself, with a slight shrug of the shoulders. 'Even the best of us slip up sometimes; and since everybody knows now – well, we'll have to make the best of it. Gentlemen – ladies – you, too, my colleagues: my best respects. Now to business.' Then he stepped out of the shadow in which he had alighted into the full glow of the lanterns and the flare which had been lit close to the door of the dead man's carriage, conscious that every eye was fixed upon his face and that the members of the local force were silently and breathlessly 'spotting' him. But in that moment the weird birth-gift had been put into practice; and Narkom fetched a sort of sigh of relief as he saw that a sagging eyelid, a twisted lip, a queer blurred *something* about all the features, had set upon that face a living mask that hid effectually the face he knew too well.

'To business?' he repeated. 'Ah, yes, quite so, my dear Cleek. Shall I tell the ladies and gentlemen of your promise? Well, listen. Mr Cleek is more than a quarter of an hour beyond the time he set, but – he gave me his word that this riddle would be solved tonight – tonight, ladies and gentlemen – and that when I saw him here the murderer would be with him.'

'Oh, bless him! bless him!' burst forth Mrs Brinkworth impulsively. 'And he brings her – that wicked woman! Oh, I knew that she had something to do with it – I knew – I knew!'

'Your pardon, Mrs Brinkworth, but for once your woman's intuition is at fault,' said Cleek quietly. 'Mademoiselle Fifi is not here as a prisoner, but as a witness for the Crown. She has had nothing even in the remotest to do wtih the crime. Her name was used to trap Lord Stavornell to his death, but the lady is here to prove that she never heard of the note which was found on Lord Stavornell's body; to prove also that, although it is true she did expect to go to a fancy dress ball with his lordship, that fancy dress ball does not occur until next Friday, the sixteenth inst. – not the ninth; and that she never even heard of any alteration in the date.'

'Ah, non! non! non! nevaire – I do swear!' chimed in Fifi herself, almost hysterical with fright. 'I know nossing – nossing!'

'That is true,' said Cleek quietly. 'There is not any question of Mademoiselle Fifi's complete innocence of any connection with this murder.'

'Then her husband?' ventured Captain Crawford agitatedly.

'It so happens that I know for a certainty M. Philippe de Lesparre had no more to do with it than did his wife.'

'But, my dear sir,' interposed the colonel. 'The – er – foreign person at the station – the little slim man in the Norfolk suit – the fellow with the little dark moustache? What of him?'

'A great deal of him. But – well, that the little dark man is a little dark fiction; in other words, he does not and never did exist!'

'What's that?' fairly gasped Narkom. 'Never existed? But, my dear Cleek, you told me that the porter at London Bridge saw him, and—'

'I told you what the porter told me – what the porter thought he saw, and what we shall, no doubt, find out in time at least fifty other people thought they saw, and what was, doubtless, the "good joke" alluded to in the forged note. The only man against whom we need direct our attention, the only man who had any hand in this murder, is a big, burly, strong-armed one like Colonel Murchison here.'

'What's that?' roared out the Colonel furiously. 'By the Lord Harry, do you dare to assert that I – I, sir, killed the man?'

'No, I do not. And for the best of reasons. You never put foot aboard the five twenty-eight from the moment it started to the one in which it stopped. And at that final moment, Colonel' – he reached round, took something from his pocket, and then held it out on the palm of his hand – 'at that final moment, Colonel, you were passing the barrier at the Crystal Palace Low Level with a lady whose ticket from London Bridge had never been clipped and with this air pistol, which she had restored to you, in your coat pocket!'

'W-w-what crazy nonsense is this, sir? I never saw the blessed thing in all my life.'

'Oh, yes, Colonel. Loader, of Tottenham Court Road, repaired the valve for you the day before yesterday, and I found it in your room just— Quick! nab him, Petrie! Well played! After the king, the trump – after the confederate the assassin! And so—' He sprang suddenly, like a jumping cat; there was a click of steel, a shrill, despairing cry, then the rustle of something falling; and when Captain Crawford and Lady Stavornell turned and looked he was standing, with both hands on his hips, looking frowningly down on the spot where the Hon. Mrs Brinkworth lay, curled up in a limp, unconscious heap with a pair of handcuffs locked on her folded wrists.

'I said that when the murderer was found, Mr Narkom,' he said as the superintendent moved toward him, 'that it would be no man you ever saw or ever heard of in all your life. I knew it was a woman from the bungling, unmanlike way that pistol was laid in the dead hand; the only question I had to answer was which woman – Fifi, Lady Stavornell, or this wretched little hypocrite. Here's your "little dark man" – here's the assassin. She made Stavornell think that she, too, was going to the fancy ball, and that the surprise Fifi had planned was for her to meet him as she did and travel with him. When the train was under way she shot him. Why? Easily explained, my dear chap. His death made her little son heir to the estates; during his minority she would have the handling of the funds; with them she and her precious husband would have a gay life of it in their own selfish little way!'

'Her what? Lord, man, do you mean to say that she and the Colonel—'

'Were privately married seven weeks ago, Mr Narkom. The certificate of their union was tucked away in Colonel Murchison's private effects, where it was found this evening.'

'How was the escape from the compartment managed after the murder was accomplished?' said Cleek, answering Narkom's query, as they whizzed home through the darkness together by the last up train that night. 'Simplest thing in the world, sir. As you know, the five twenty-eight from London Bridge runs without stop to Anerley. Well, the five-eighteen from the same starting point runs to the Crystal Palace Low Level, taking the main line tracks as far as Sydenham, where it branches off at the switch and curves completely away in an opposite direction. That is to say, for a considerable distance they run parallel, but eventually diverge. Now, as the five-eighteen is a way train with several stops, the five twenty-eight, being a through one, overtakes her, and several times between Brockley and Sydenham they run side by side – at so steady a pace and on such a narrow gauge that the footboard running along the side of the one train is not more than two and a half feet separated from the other. Their pace is so regular, their progress so even, that one could with ease step from the footboard of the one to the footboard of the other but for the horrible suction which would inevitably draw the person attempting it down under the wheels. Well, something had to be devised to overcome the danger of that suction. But what? I asked myself; for I guessed from the first how the escape had occurred, and I knew that such a thing absolutely required the assistance of a confederate. That meant that that confederate would have to do on the five-eighteen exactly what they had trapped Stavornell into doing on the other train – that is, secure a private compartment, so that when the time came for the escape to be accomplished he could remove the electric bulbs from the roof of his compartment, open the door, and when the two came abreast the assassin could do the same on the other train, and presto! the dead man would be alone. But what to use to overcome the danger of that horrible suction?'

'Ah! I see now what you were driving at when you enquired about the ironing board or the Indian canoe. The necessary sections to construct a sort of bridge could be packed in either?'

'Yes. But they chose a simpler plan – the cutting table. A good move that. Its breadth minimised the peril of the suction; only, of course, it would have to be pulled up afterwards (to leave no clue), and the added space would call for enormous strength to overcome the power of that suction: and enormous strength meant a powerful man. The rest you can put together without being told, Mr Narkom. When that little vixen finished her man she put out the lights, opened the door (deliberately locking it after her to make the thing more baffling), crossed over on that table, was helped into the other compartment by Murchison, and then as expeditiously as possible slipped on the loose feminine outer garments she carried with her in the brown portmanteau; the table was hauled up and taken in (nothing but wire rope for that, sir), and the thing was done. Murchison, of course, purchased two tickets, so that they might pass the barrier at the Low Level unquestioned when they left; but he wasn't able to get the extra ticket clipped at London Bridge because there was no passenger for it. That's how I got on to the little game! For the rest, they planned well. Those two trains being always packed, nobody could see the escape from the one to the other, because people would be standing up in every compartment and the windows completely blocked. But if— Hullo! Victoria at last, thank goodness; "and so to bed," as Pepys says. The riddle's solved, Mr Narkom. Good night.'

FREEMAN WILLS CROFTS

Freeman Wills Crofts was born in Dublin, Ireland in 1879. He worked in Civil Engineering for the early part of his life, mostly on railways around Northern Ireland, but was forced to take an extended period of leave in 1918 due to an unknown illness. It was during this time, due in large part to boredom, that Crofts began to write. His first novel, *The Cask* (1920), instandy established him as a new master of detective fiction. Over the next thirty years, Crofts produced almost a book per year, in addition to a large number of short stories and plays. His best-known creation, introduced in his fifth book, *Inspector French's Greatest Case* (1924), was Inspector Joseph French, who often solved apparendy unsolvable cases thanks to the dense intricacies of railway timetables. Croft is now regarded as one of the greats of the so-called 'Golden Age if Detective Fiction', and Raymond Chandler described him as "the soundest builder of them all when he doesn't get too fancy."

ETHEL LINA WHITE

Ethel Lina White was born in Born in Abergavenny, Wales in 1876. She started writing as a child, contributing essays and poems to children's papers. For many years, she worked at the Ministry of Pensions in London, but she quit in her late forties in order to pursue writing. Her first three works, published between 1927 and 1930, were mainstream novels. Her first crime novel, published in 1931, was *Put Out the Light*. From this point onwards, White was a prolific author, and became one of the best-known crime writers in Britain and the US during the thirties and forties. Her novels *Some Must Watch* and *The Wheel Spins* were both made into popular films, as *The Spiral Staircase* and *The Lady Vanishes* respectively. Her 1942 novel *Midnight House* was adapted into *The Unseen* (1945), based on a screenplay co-authored by Raymond Chandler. White died in London in 1944, aged 68.

RONALD KNOX

Ronald Knox was born in Kibworth, England in 1888. He was educated at Eton College, before winning the first classics scholarship to Balliol College, Oxford, in 1905. Upon graduating, Knox became a fellow of Trinity College, Oxford and was ordained as an Anglican priest, only to leave in 1917 and convert to Catholicism. Knox detailed this spiritual journey in two privately printed books, *Apologia* (1917) and *A Spiritual Aeneid* (1918). While a Catholic chaplain at the University of Oxford – a post he held for thirteen years — Knox began to write detective stories, quickly becoming a master of the genre. In 1929, he codified the rules for detective stories into a 'decalogue' of ten commandments. Between 1925 and 1937, Knox penned six detective novels, and a number of much-anthologized short stories, including 'The Adventure of the First Class Carriage'. He was also was one of the founding members of the famous Detection Club. Aside from his detective fiction, Knox was a well-known theologian writer, penning more than thirty highly varied works on religious topics.

VICTOR L. WHITECHURCH

Victor Lorenzo Whitechurch was born in Chichester, England in 1868. He attended Chichester Theological College, and after various positions as curate became vicar at St. Michael's, Blewbury in 1904. In 1913, Whitechurch was appointed Chaplain to the Bishop of Oxford, and five years later became rural Dean of Aylesbury. Over the course of his life, he wrote many novels on a variety of themes, but is probably best-known for his stories featuring Thorpe Hazell, a vegetarian railway detective. These stories appeared in *Strand Magazine, Railway Magazine, Pearson's* and *Hamsworth's*, and were known for their meticulously researched depictions of police procedure. Whitechurch died in 1933, aged 65.

ERNEST BRAMAH

Ernest Bramah Smith was born was near Manchester in 1868. He was a poor student, and dropped out of the Manchester Grammar School when sixteen years old to go into the farming business. During his late teens, he began to contribute short stories and vignettes to the *Birmingham News*. A few years later, he moved to London's Grub Street – famous for its concentration of impoverished 'hack writers' – and eventually became editor of a number of journals.

Bramah found commercial and critical success with his first novel, *The Wallet of Kai Lung*, in 1900. The character of Kai Lang – a travelling storyteller in China – went on to feature in a number of his works, many of which featured fantasy elements such as dragons and gods, and utilised an idiosyncratic form of Mandarin English. Something of a recluse, Bramah also wrote political science fiction – in fact, his 1907 novel *The Secret of the League* was acknowledged by George Orwell as a forerunner to his famous novel *Nineteen Eighty-Four* – and even tried his hand at detective fiction. At the height of his fame, Bramah's mystery tales, featuring the blind detective Max Carrados, appeared alongside Sir Arthur Conan Doyle's *Sherlock Holmes* stories in the *Strand Magazine*, even occasionally outselling them. Bramah died in 1942, aged 74.

CRAIG RICE

Georgiana Ann Craig was born in Chicago in 1908. Her parents were highly neglectful of her, and Rice was raised by her aunt and uncle in Wisconsin. It is her uncle who has been credited with introducing the young Rice to mystery and speculative fiction by reading her the work of Edgar Allen Poe each evening.

During the late twenties and early thirties, Rice returned to Chicago and tried her hand at fiction-writing, music and acting, while earning a living writing for various local papers. She also worked as a radio writer and producer, and married three times. Her first hard-won success came in 1939, with the novel *Eight Faces at Three*, featuring a trio of protagonists – Jake Justus, Helene Brand and John Joseph Malone – who would go on to star in the majority of her fiction. Over the next decade Rice went on to produce between one and four mysteries a year, in a style that uniquely combined the hard-boiled detective tradition with surreal, screwball comedy. She had a devoted readership, and in 1946 became the first mystery writer to appear on the cover of *Time* magazine.

Rice's health deteriorated, however. In something of a mirroring of her often wild characters, she became a chronic alcoholic, and even attempted suicide more than once. Having produced more than twenty novels, she died in Chicago before her fiftieth birthday.

JOHN OXENHAM

John Oxenham was the pen name of William Arthur Dunkerley, born in Manchester, England in 1852. He spent much of his life in Ealing, West London, where he served as deacon and teacher at the Ealing Congregational Church. In the 1920s, became the mayor of Worthing, Sussex. He was a prolific writer, producing more than 40 novels, a number of books of verse, a large body of poetry, and short fiction. His collection *Bees in Amber: A Little Book of Thoughtful Verse* (1913) was a popular bestseller, and he was a major contributor to Jerome K. Jerome's *The Idler* magazine. Oxenham died in 1941, aged 88.

BARONESS EMMA ORCZY

Baroness Emma Magdolna Rozalia Maria Jozefa Borbala "Emmuska" Orczy de Orczi was born in Heves County, Hungary, in 1865. Her family moved between Budapest, Brussels and Paris, before settling in London in 1880, where Orczy attended West London School of Art and then Heatherley's School of Fine Art. It was here that she met her future husband, a young illustrator named Montague MacLean Barstow. The two of them married in 1894.

Orczy and Barstow were not well-off, and Orczy started to work with her husband as a translator and an illustrator to supplement his low wage. In 1899, the same year that they had their first and only child, Orczy produced her first novel, *The Emperor's Candlesticks*. However, real success came in 1903, when she and Barstow wrote a play based on one of her short stories, set during the French Revolution. *The Scarlet Pimpernel* was not an instant success, but following a rewritten last act and an opening in the West End, the play went on to run for four years in London, playing more than 2,000 performances. It broke many stage records, was translated and produced in various other countries, and underwent several revivals.

Orczy went on to write over a dozen sequels to *The Scarlet*

Pimpernel, as well as a good amount of popular mystery fiction and adventure romances, some of which feature early examples of female lead detectives. Her money worries vanished; in fact, Orczy became so well-off that she was able to buy an estate in Monte Carlo. During the First World War, she worked hard to recruit female volunteers for active service. She also lived through the Second World War, before dying in Henley-on-Thames of old age.

JOHNSTON MCCULLEY

Johnston McCulley was born in Ottawa, USA in 1883. He worked as a police reporter for *The Police Gazette*, and served as an Army public affairs officer during World War I, before going on to a career in pulp fiction and screenwriting. Over the course of his life, McCulley penned fifty novels, hundreds of stories, and a raft of screenplays for both film and television. He is perhaps most notable as the creator of the masked vigilante, Zorro — who first appeared in McCulley's 1919 story, 'The Curse of Capistrano'. Zorro continued to appear in his work for the next forty years. Amongst McCulley's other well-remembered creations are Black Star, The Spider, The Mongoose, and Thubway Tham — all popular characters of the pulp era.

THOMAS W. HANSHEW

Thomas W. Hanshew was born in Brooklyn, New York, USA in 1857. He started acting at a young age, appearing on stage from the age of 16, before turning to writing. Over the course of his life, he published more than 150 novels, often under the pen name 'Charlotte May Kingsley'. By far his best-known creation was the detective Hamilton Cleek, who possessed the "nature-bestowed power" to morph his face into whatever shape he desired, and was nicknamed "the man of the forty faces." Critics view Hanshew's short fiction as considerably superior to his novels, which are often ludicrously plotted.